ABOUT THE AUTHOR

Originally from Northern Ireland, Jacqueline Harrett has lived in Cardiff with her husband for over thirty years. Her two grown-up children also live in the capital city.

The DI Mandy Wilde series is set mainly in Cardiff with a dogged and potty-mouthed detective who is determined to solve the mystery at the heart of the story.

The novels have been described as 'crime fiction with a social conscience' (grumpyoldbooksblogspot.com).

A multi-genre author, Jacqui has published non-fiction; *Exciting Writing,* (Sage), *Tell me Another…* (UKLA); children's stories; and short stories in anthologies. She has co-authored a novel with Janet Laugharne, *What Lies Between Them,* (Dixi, 2022) and a novella, *Angelo's Journey: From Bardi to Pontypridd.* (Harland Press, 2024.)

Death by Intent is the fourth in the DI Mandy Wilde series. Life just carries on throwing up problems for Mandy, both at home and in work.

Published in Great Britain in 2025
By Diamond Crime

ISBN 978-1-915649-47-8

All characters appearing in this work are fictitious. Any resemblance to real persons, living or dead, is purely coincidental.

DIAMOND BOOKS

Diamond Crime is an imprint of Diamond Books Ltd.

Book Cover Design by Kathleen Harryman
https://www.kathleenharryman.co.uk

As always thanks to the team at Diamond Crime for their support, editorial advice and good humour.

To my family for their patience in listening to me talk characters, complications and plot. They don't glaze over very often.

To my beta readers, for their support and reassurance, as always, and for pointing out where things are not working.

Also, my thanks to the Criminal Fairies and Writers Enjoying Words for their interest and encouragement and spreading the word. A great bunch of writers.

I also want to thank Noelle who read, commented on 'With Grave Consequences' and then gave me the name Cassian for this novel. He's a minor character but important to the story.

Finally, to all those readers who have made contact through social media and at events. A special thank you to the wonderful readers who leave reviews. It's so important for visibility. Reviews are the best present a writer can ever receive.

Also by Jacqueline Harrett:
Books One, Two and Three of the DI Mandy Wilde Novels
The Nesting Place
The Whispering Trees
With Grave Consequences

Published by

DIAMOND
CRIME

For information about Diamond Crime authors
and their books, visit:
www.diamondbooks.co.uk

For Honor

Keep Reading. Keep Smiling

Death by Intent

A DI Mandy Wilde Novel

JACQUELINE HARRETT

CHAPTER ONE

Barbara Vixen was dead long before the fireworks announcing the New Year exploded across the Cardiff sky. It was the second of January before her putrefying body was found. The call had come from a postal worker. Receiving no reply he had peered through the window and spotted the body. Not the best start to the New Year.

Sub-zero temperatures left a sugar frosting of ice everywhere and the beginning of the year had started with a whimper as far as DI Mandy Wilde was concerned. The team was being shadowed for a month by her former fiancé, DCI Lucas Manning. It was a cause of constant irritation. She longed to get out of the office and away from scrutiny.

When news of the death first came into the police station it was Mandy's opportunity to show Lucas how she worked, and her skills as a detective inspector. She'd tried to protest about the observation exercise, some initiative created by someone higher up the ladder no doubt, citing a conflict of interest. Superintendent Withers wasn't listening to any of her protestations.

"Your relationship was a long time ago. Not current. Besides, you are both professionals, aren't you? Able to put little differences aside? Eh?"

He made it clear that Lucas was there to observe and not interfere, but she had noticed how Josh tended to ask the older man's opinion. Bloody brown-nosing. She said nothing but glared each time Josh referred to Lucas. The glares went unobserved by Josh who seemed oblivious to her displeasure. At least Olivia and Helen, the rest of her team, didn't seem to be inclined to become cheerleaders for Lucas.

The house where the body was found was in Llandaff, not far from the village, with limited parking nearby. Grey skies loomed above them, the cold snap giving way to more stormy conditions, as promised by the weather forecast. The frost was melting, and the small front garden was a muddy morass after many boots had trampled over it.

The pathologist, Rishi Mallik, was already there with his team. Mandy and Josh arrived minutes before DCI Manning, who had to park his ancient Volvo further away. Mandy assumed he'd be driving a flashy sports model, or maybe a BMW. At least they hadn't shared lifts. She'd been too quick for that, out of the station door with Josh in hot pursuit before he could say Hell's Bells. She knew Helen would be able to give Lucas the address, but he wasn't familiar with the new road layouts in Cardiff. The attempt at evasion had been noted and he was not happy.

"Perhaps next time we should travel together."

Phrased as a suggestion, it sounded more like an order. Mandy shrugged, hiding a smirk.

News had travelled. A few people were hanging about, including one face she recognised. Tod Blakeney, local reporter. How did he do it? He had a nose for trouble, always around when he could smell a story.

"Hey, Mandy." His voice carried across the mutterings of the crowd. "What's happened here? Any info?"

"Friend of yours?" asked Lucas.

Before she could open her mouth, Josh had answered. "Local reporter. He's got the hots for the boss." He grinned widely until he saw Mandy's face. The look she gave him would have melted steel.

As they got to the door of the cottage, Rishi emerged. He pulled his face mask down and took a deep breath.

"You will require more than a spot of Vick under your nose for this one, DI Wilde. She is not fresh." His eyes flicked to the tall figure behind her. "DCI Manning, I presume. We have an interesting one for you this morning." Formal and correct, as usual.

Mandy could see speculation on Rishi's face before he replaced the mask and re-entered the house. Josh turned a shade of avocado. Her stomach turned as well. It must be bad if Rishi needed to warn them. Donning overalls and masks they entered. The body was towards the back of the room. The remains of a woman; face down on the floor. She was dressed in trousers and thick sweater, in a shade of navy. Her feet were encased in sheepskin slippers, one of which had slipped showing the sole of a thick sock, also blue. A stream of dried vomit lay beside the body and a small side table had been overturned. Mandy spied an opened packet of painkillers, Tramadol, a glass and spectacles. Despite the masks, the smell of death was overwhelming. Rishi seemed unperturbed.

"So, what have we got, Rishi?"

"Female. In her sixties, at a guess. Well-nourished before the flies got at her. Tall, about five foot seven inches. Her clothing is of decent quality, and she is generally well-groomed from what I can make out. As you can see, she had vomited," he indicated the marks on the floor. "She has a mark on her forehead." He pointed to an area darker than the rest of the discoloured skin.

"An attack?"

Rishi shrugged. "There are no other signs and no indication of anyone breaking in. Everything else looks as one should expect."

"So, she could have knocked over the table herself." Mandy surveyed the scene. A patio door leading to the garden was locked, the key on the inside. No signs of forced entry. "Maybe she hit her head when she fell."

Rishi made no comment.

Despite the season there wasn't much in the way of Christmas decorations around the house. A wilting poinsettia sat on the floor. Two cards. Mandy bagged them after glancing inside. One said Charlie and family. It had a snow scene on the front. The second was religious themed with the stable scene. Inside the letter M. No other identification.

"How long has she been dead?" asked Mandy.

"Several days. At a guess, she died sometime around Christmas. I can be more accurate after the postmortem."

"And do we have an identity?"

Rishi pointed to the pile of post someone had stacked on a chair. Mandy checked the envelopes. B. Vixen. They would need to check but it seemed unlikely to be anyone else.

As if reading her mind, Rishi said, "We can confirm

identity with dental records, of course."

She nodded and turned around to speak to Josh, but he was nowhere to be seen. Lucas was right behind her with the answer to Josh's whereabouts.

"He's gone outside. Afraid to make an exhibition of himself, I reckon."

Mandy could hear the smile in Lucas's voice.

"Is it too early for cause of death? Any hunches, Rishi?"

Kind brown eyes met hers. "DI Wilde, I prefer to give an opinion when I am apprised of all the facts." He hesitated. "We will know more after I examine the body and the stomach contents."

The SOCOs, Scenes of Crime Officers, were busy checking the room and removing anything they found of interest. Mandy spotted a laptop and a mobile phone being bagged. Those would need to go to forensics. With luck, it would be easy to access the data. If not, the tech guys would work their magic.

"We'll let you get on, Rishi. The team can gather anything they think could be relevant and we'll see you later. Time for the PM?"

"I shall take her back to the mortuary within the hour. It has been a quiet start to the year. Did you want to attend?"

With a fleeting glance at the corpse on the floor, Mandy shook her head. "I'll pop over later. We've got work to do first. Thanks, Rishi."

It was a blessing to get out of the house and breathe some relatively clean air. Mandy could almost taste the rancid tang of death and longed for a warm drink to clear her palate. A police cordon hadn't stopped a few rubberneckers gathering. It didn't take long for news to get around. At least Tod seemed to have buggered off, which was a relief.

Mandy spoke to the uniformed officer at the door. "Who found her?"

"I did Ma'am. We had a call from the postal worker, Barry Reece. He tried to deliver a parcel. He peered through the window when there was no reply. He could see the lady on the floor so rang emergency services."

"Where is he? We'll need to speak to him."

"He had deliveries to make, Ma'am. We've got his contact details." He gave her a slip of paper with a mobile number. Mandy grunted. Chasing up witnesses who should have been detained at the scene was not a good start to the investigation. And where the hell was Josh?

As if on cue, DS Josh Jones appeared looking slightly less green than he had in the house.

"I've been talking to the neighbours to see if they saw or heard anything. We've got a name. Barbara Vixen. Sixty-seven. Lived alone. No-one has seen her since before Christmas. The neighbour to the right facing us," he pointed, "is deaf and doesn't hear much. The lady on the left was more forthcoming. Mrs Yvonne Hunter. She was away from Christmas Eve until after the New Year."

"That confirms the information we've got already. Anything else? What have you found out about the victim?"

Josh checked his notebook. "Bit of a recluse. Odd. Didn't connect with any of her neighbours." He paused.

"Bit of a God Squad candidate too by all accounts."

"Well, we aren't far from Llandaff Cathedral. Nice spot for a bit of worship if you're so inclined," said Mandy.

"Not there. Some place called The Church of the Forgotten Souls. Not really mainstream by the sounds of things. Run by a priest called Father Michael. He's been distributing leaflets in the area. The neighbour spotted him going in," he nodded towards the house where SOCOs were busy, "a number of times, she said."

Mandy rolled her eyes. "Never heard of it. Church of the Forgotten Souls. Sounds like some bloody weird cult thing. Well done, Josh. You can check it out unless you'd prefer to come to the PM?" She had to suppress a smile. As if anyone would choose to see a putrefied body being dissected. She didn't admit to passing up that opportunity herself. "Do you want to follow DS Jones, sir?" she asked, turning towards Lucas Manning.

"Oh, I think I'll shadow you instead, DI Wilde. Watch the leader at work. Isn't that why I'm here?" He smiled and Mandy wasn't sure if he was trying to wind her up or not. Bloody Lucas. It was going to be a long month with him dogging her every step. She wondered if he ever reflected on their broken engagement all those years ago. Probably never gave it a thought. He never mentioned his ex-wife either, even in casual conversation with the team. Now he was looking at her with that faint half smile. Judging her by his own standards.

"So, what's your theory, sir?" Put the ball back in his court. She was fed up with his games already.

"No speculation until we see what the body tells us. I deal in facts, not hunches." Mandy turned away so he couldn't see her roll her eyes again. "And less of the 'sir' business. I know you're just trying to annoy me so let's stop playing silly buggers and get on with our jobs, shall we?"

There was an edge to his voice. He was used to authority and having people do as he asked. Mandy said nothing, resentment seething under her nonchalant shrug of the shoulders. Lucas was bringing out the worst in her. She knew it but couldn't seem to help herself behaving like a petty teenager.

"Whatever."

CHAPTER TWO

The Church of the Forgotten Souls was tucked away in a side street in Canton. Formerly a shop, it had been converted into a meeting place. The large front window had been masked by a mural of trees, animals and a large cross, the paint restricting visibility. It was on a corner so had two doors, one at the front and one at the side which originally would have been to the living quarters above the shop. Josh tried the front door. It was locked. He made his way to the side door and lifted a hand to ring the doorbell. The door opened and he was almost knocked off his feet by a tall, bulky man with long thinning hair, dyed black, a ginger beard and prominent eyebrows. From the set of his nose it had been broken, maybe more than once.

"May I help?" He bestowed a glowing smile on Josh. "God is always with us and will help the righteous and the lost souls."

There was no answer to that, so Josh pulled out his warrant card and displayed it for the man to read. "I'm looking for Father Michael."

"And you have found him. Why are the police interested in speaking to me, I wonder?" He raised one of his eyebrows, the smile remaining fixed but with a wariness in his dark eyes that hadn't been there before.

"Perhaps if we could go inside?" Although the

street was empty, discussing the details of the case in the open air was not recommended. Besides, Josh reckoned it would be warmer inside. The January wind was tunnelling down the narrow street making his eyes water.

"But of course, Detective Sergeant Jones. You are most welcome, as are all who seek enlightenment. The Church of the Forgotten Souls is for many people in all walks of life." He indicated for Josh to enter, squeezing himself against the wall to enable him to do so.

As he passed, Josh thought he detected a faint smell of stale alcohol. The hallway was dingy, the walls painted a dull shade somewhere between green, grey and blue. Sludge. It could be one of those designer colours Josh saw in the magazines his wife Lisa liked to buy. Somehow, he doubted it.

There was an open door on the left. As they passed, he spotted a youth cleaning something. The spotty-faced lad looked up and then away. The priest said, "Straight ahead, Sarge." His tone was almost mocking which annoyed Josh. To the lad he said, "Tea, Cassian. Prayer room. Be quick about it. Sergeant?" Josh shook his head. The place didn't inspire him with the desire to stay there any longer than necessary.

To the right of the narrow corridor, a little further along, a door was already open. This must have been the original shop floor. The artwork Josh had seen from the outside was clearer inside and continued around the walls of the room. It had space for about thirty chairs, a mish mash of shapes and sizes, set in two circles, one inside the other. As well as the front door to the building another door led from the room.

A large cross, constructed crudely from planks stained and showing signs of wear, made Josh think they had once been floorboards. No sign of the traditional nativity scene often in churches at this time of the year. A plug-in air dispenser wafted floral scents into the room, but the underlying odour was damp. Parts of the wall displayed flakes of peeling paint. This was not a place that had money lavished on it.

"Do take a seat," Father Michael pointed to the chairs and pulled two from the circle so they could both sit down, facing each other. "Now why, I wonder, are the South Wales police interested in speaking to me?"

The smile never left his face although it didn't reach his eyes. Perhaps a defence mechanism, or the professional persona he liked to project to the public. It was difficult to judge.

Josh cleared his throat. 'I'm here to speak to you about a member of your congregation–"

"I call them my flock."

"–Mrs Barbara Vixen."

"Barbara. Goodness. That is a surprise. Has she been up to something naughty?" Again, that mocking tone.

Josh could feel his jaw tighten. Something about the man made him feel angry. It was as if everything was a private joke, and he was somehow above the law.

"Mrs Vixen was found dead this morning, sir."

At last, a reaction. The smile dropped. Father Michael crossed himself. "May God bless her soul and envelop her in his heavenly grace. How very tragic. What happened?"

"We're unsure about cause of death." Josh made a show of taking out his notebook before asking, "When did you last see Mrs Vixen?"

"Hmmm," the priest glanced towards the ceiling. "It would have been before Christmas. Yes, of course. I called just before Christmas Eve, very briefly. She'd missed our last gathering. I wanted to speak to her before the festivities and deliver a card."

"How did she seem?"

"A little distracted. We talked for a short time, and then I left."

"Do you have any idea what time that was? What did you talk about?" Josh made a note.

"It would have been around lunchtime. Or perhaps just after. Maybe one o'clock or thereabouts. We discussed the youth club. Barbara was helping out with that." He took a breath as if trying to remember the conversation. "We talked about all sorts of things. The news. How Christmas was no longer about God." He shrugged. "Nothing out of the ordinary."

"How was she? Did she complain about feeling unwell at all?'

The priest laughed. "When people get to a certain age, they become obsessed with their health.

Barbara always had some ache or pain. I tended to ignore her complaints. Uncharitable for a man of the cloth, I know."

Josh stopped writing his notes. "Anything in particular, the last time you spoke? Why had she not attended the gathering?"

"The start of a cold she thought. Headaches, a bit breathless. That sort of thing. Nothing much to worry about."

"Except she's dead now." Josh waited for a reaction.

"Indeed. A sobering thought. We never know when He will call us to His bosom."

Cassian entered at that point, almost shuffling. He carried a mug in both hands which he passed to Father Michael. He was dressed in dark tracksuit bottoms with dust and fluff around the legs, a dark hoodie and white trainers which looked new. A green beanie hat almost covered straggly strands of mouse-coloured hair.

Josh didn't respond to the comments. His family had been church goers. He had been brought up with religion so didn't roll his eyes like he knew Mandy would have done.

"What else can you tell me? What about her family? Was she intending to see anyone over the holiday?"

The priest stared at the cross, avoiding Josh's eyes. "Barbara didn't divulge a lot of information. She mentioned a brother, but I had the impression she didn't get on with him. I can't remember his name.

Families are often problematic. I'm not sure if she was divorced or widowed." He coughed. "As far as I'm aware she was intending to go somewhere on Christmas Day." He shrugged again. "We had a celebration here, of course. We provided a hot meal for those who wanted to share the day. Those people who are alone and seeking companionship. The forgotten souls of this city."

"That's the name of your–"

"Church. It may not be recognised as such by the pure ecclesiastical authority but nevertheless we are the family of God." He held his large hands together as if in prayer.

It made Josh feel uncomfortable. Something about the man. Mandy would have called it gut instinct, but Josh couldn't quite put a label on how he felt in this man's presence. There was a sort of magnetism about him that was compelling, but also frightening.

"Why did Mrs Vixen join the church? It's a bit," Josh struggled for the right word, "unconventional, isn't it?"

The priest raised his eyebrows. He shook his head.

"I think it was loneliness. The curse of the modern age. People are not connected in the same way. She'd moved and was finding it difficult to settle into retirement. A restless soul. With time on her hands perhaps she wanted to help others and belong to a warm community? Like our church." He spread his arms wide. "Who knows? God moves in different ways. It is not our place to question Him."

Josh was unimpressed. "Anything else you can tell us? Did you call or speak to Mrs Vixen again before Christmas?"

Father Michael shook his head. "No. Much to my chagrin. I have failed in my duty to the poor woman if she died alone. A heart attack, do you think?"

It was a leading question, and Josh wasn't going to answer. He closed his notebook satisfied he had gained sufficient information.

"The body was discovered today, sir. We're just attempting to establish a timeline and build a picture of Mrs Vixen from those who knew her." He took a card from his pocket. "If you have any further information, or if you think of anything which may be relevant, then please let us know."

"Of course. Most certainly DS Jones. We shall hold a prayer meeting for her tomorrow. Perhaps you'd like to attend?"

Josh made a sound which could have been interpreted as assent or dissent and stood up. "Thank you for your time, sir. We'll be in touch if we need to speak to you again."

The priest nodded. "Please let yourself out. I need to spend a few minutes in prayer for the soul of our dearly departed."

Relieved, Josh wasted no time in escaping the claustrophobic atmosphere of the place and was soon outside in the bracing air. He took a deep breath before heading towards his battered Corsa and the station to write up the interview.

CHAPTER THREE

Mandy stared at Lucas, her displeasure evident.

"Okay. Let's have a chat with the neighbours before we head to the mortuary. Let Rishi make a start on the postmortem." She glanced at the notes. "Mrs Yvonne Hunter on the left. Maybe we can find out a bit more about the deceased from her."

They rang the doorbell and a moment later heard a voice. "Who is it?"

"Video doorbell," Mandy whispered to Lucas before saying, "It's the police, madam. We'd like a few words, please." She held up her warrant card. They could hear the door being unbolted before a silver haired woman peered around the edge.

"Detective Inspector Wilde and Detective Chief Inspector Manning." They both displayed their credentials.

Mrs Hunter had a pair of spectacles hanging on a chain around her neck. She put them on and inspected the warrant cards before holding the door open.

"One can't be too careful these days," she said.

"Very wise, madam." Lucas gave her a winning smile.

"Although there are at least a dozen uniformed officers outside." The comment was low enough for Lucas to hear, but not Mrs Hunter. She was busy ushering them into a pleasant room furnished with a leather sofa and tub chair. It all looked neat and tidy with plants, photographs and ornaments on display.

In a similar way to Barbara Vixen's home, it had been converted to provide a more open space but the atmosphere here was warmer and the smell infinitely better. Plus, a string of cards adorned one wall and a small artificial Christmas tree with colour-changing lights was placed near a window. Mandy spotted a wedding photograph on a sideboard nestled between even more cards. Yvonne Hunter noted her interest.

"That was a long time ago. We would have been married forty years if John had lived to see it." She seemed lost in thought, her voice holding a hint of sadness. Then she gave herself a little shake. "I've just made some fresh Welsh cakes. Would you like a cup of tea and one of those?" she asked, as she indicated for them to sit down.

Mandy sat on the tub chair, firmer than she expected, almost rigid. She was about to refuse the refreshments, but Lucas said, "Thank you. That would be lovely. May I help you?"

"Oh no, dear. It's quite alright. Just make yourselves at home. I'll just be a minute." She hurried into the kitchen where they could hear the bubbling of the kettle and the rattle of plates.

Mandy gritted her teeth. She mouthed "What the –" at Lucas, pointing at her watch. He grinned back, unperturbed.

Mrs Hunter returned with a plate of Welsh cakes sprinkled with sugar, a big china teapot and some mugs to match. "Well, I'm guessing you'd prefer mugs to cups and saucers. Police work must be busy and make you thirsty." She perched on the sofa beside Lucas.

Mandy accepted a cup of tea but noticed Lucas was munching through his cake. Just like Josh, she thought, stomach first. Time to get on with things. A clunk from the kitchen heralded the entrance of a grey striped cat. It wandered in before settling in a basket holding magazines and newspapers. A fishy yawn and a stretch before the animal settled down to sleep. Mrs Hunter acknowledged the animal's presence with an indulgent eye.

"Sukey. She's very spoilt."

"What can you tell us about your neighbour? How long has she lived there?"

"Oh, let me see. Over a year. My friend, Liz, used to live there but she became very frail so moved to Pembrokeshire to be closer to her family. That would have been about August. No, September. Just before the children went back to school."

"About fifteen months, then. How well did you know her?" asked Lucas.

Mandy glowered at him. He was supposed to observe, not ask questions and not get in the way of her investigation.

"Was she a friend too?" Mandy was determined to take control again.

"Oh, Mrs Vixen was a very private person. She would pass the time of day, but I never warmed to her. We had very little to do with each other."

"When was the last time you saw her?"

Mrs Hunter took a sip of her tea, before replying. "It would have been before Christmas. I've been away, you see. I got home last night."

"Did you notice anything strange when you got home? Were there lights on next door for example?"

"I'm afraid I didn't notice anything. I've been with the grandchildren and, lovely as they are, I was exhausted and desperate for a cup of tea and an early night. When you get to my age you just want your own bed." She looked at them as if they could sympathise with her sentiments.

"We believe she belonged to a religious group?" Mandy waited to be enlightened.

Mrs Hunter pursed her lips. "The Church of the Forgotten Souls. As if Llandaff Cathedral wasn't good enough for her." They let that pass without comment. Mandy thought it could be a bit of snobbery. It told them more about Yvonne Hunter than her neighbour.

Lucas seemed too engrossed in the Welsh cake until he looked up and asked, "Did she have any visitors?"

Mandy simmered. She was just about to ask the same question.

"Not many that I'm aware of. The walls are thick in these old houses, you know, and I'm a little hard of hearing these days." She tilted her head a little. "That Father Michael visited a couple of times. There's something about that man." She gave a little shiver. "He doesn't seem like a man of God to me. Do you think there's something suspicious about her death? Has someone attacked her? Should I be worried about my safety?" She put a hand to her throat and swallowed.

"At the moment we aren't sure when or how Mrs Vixen died. We'd be obliged if you didn't speak to anyone..." Mandy thought about Tod hovering outside, "...about the matter. I'll leave you my card in case you remember anything or want to speak to me." Mandy passed over her business card. "Perhaps you could give us access to the videos from your doorbell. Just in case we spot something."

"Oh, I don't have the videos, my dear. You have to pay a subscription every month if you want that. Bit of a swizz if you ask me. Why do you need to see who's been around? Unless..."

She let the words hang in the air, looking to Mandy and then Lucas for some sort of assurance.

"We don't know what happened yet, but we do know Mrs Vixen has been dead more than a few days. There'll be quite a few police officers around over the next couple of days so don't worry." They stood, ready to leave.

"Thank you for the tea and delicious Welsh cakes," said Lucas when they reached the front door. It earned him a nod of approval from Mrs Hunter.

They could hear the door being bolted as they left the house.

"You've got sugar on your chin," said Mandy, smirking to herself as she walked down the path away from Lucas.

He seemed unconcerned, took out a

handkerchief and wiped his chin. "Where now? The other side?" He pointed to the house on the right of Barbara Vixen's home.

"Seems logical."

As they approached the house a uniformed officer stepped forward and spoke to them. "The lady who lives there has gone out. Bridge Club she said."

Mandy sighed. "We'll have to come back, I suppose, or send one of the team. Postmortem next. See what Rishi has to say. See you up there." She made for her car.

"Oh no you don't. I'm coming with you." Lucas caught up with her, his long strides making it easy.

"But your car's here."

"You can drop me back later or I'll cadge a lift with uniform. You don't shake me off that easily, DI Wilde."

No option. No excuses. Mandy clicked the key to open the door and said nothing until Lucas had put on his seatbelt, ready to leave. Then she turned on him.

"I thought you were supposed to observe. Twice in there you were asking questions. That's my job."

"Only trying to help. Instinct I suppose."

"Balls. With respect," she almost spat the words, "observation means looking not getting involved – sir."

Fuming, she crashed the car into gear and sped along Western Avenue towards Heath Park and the mortuary at the back of the hospital.

CHAPTER FOUR

It was surprisingly noisy as they approached the mortuary. Trolleys, pushed by porters, rattled along the corridors joining various parts of the building. The familiar clinical smells of the hospital building were superseded by formaldehyde and other unpleasant odours as they entered the room where the body lay. Mandy suspected Lucas didn't attend as many postmortems as she did during the course of a year, but he didn't blink or show any discomfort. In fact, his whole demeanour was calm and interested, as expected from a professional of his rank.

Rishi nodded at them. "You have missed the first act." A faint smile as if he'd made a joke. "I am just about to open the cranium."

"Headlines so far?"

"She has been dead for a little while. From the state of decay, I should estimate over a week, possibly more than ten days."

"Do we have a cause of death?"

Rishi peered at Mandy over his spectacles. "I have not finished the postmortem yet, DI Wilde. My report will be on your desk as soon as possible. Now, may I proceed?"

Mandy was a little taken aback. Rishi was always reluctant to make hypotheses without evidence but, when pressed, usually responded with a good-humoured remark. His tone was almost punitive, making her feel embarrassed in front of Lucas.

As if realising the effect of his words, Rishi lowered his voice. "So far, I have found no evidence of assault. Remember, time will have had a degenerative effect on the body – hence the bloating and discolouration. I have taken blood samples and stomach contents for analysis. I believe I know the cause of death but require confirmation. If anything is amiss, I shall ensure you are the first to know. Are you staying?"

"No, we'll get on. We need to make sure we have the correct identity for the body."

"Dental records should confirm her identity. Now," he pressed a button and the saw in his hand whirred into action.

With a nod they left him to his gruesome task. Outside the mortuary, Mandy sighed. "Rishi seems in a bit of a mood today. He's usually more forthcoming. The mother-in-law must be giving him extra grief."

"That could explain a lot. Mother-in-laws can have a negative effect."

Resisting the temptation to ask him anything further, Mandy wrapped her scarf tighter around her neck and marched towards the car park.

"Time to speak to the postie, I think. Let's make his day for him. He should have finished his rounds by now."

They made their way to the delivery office at Lansdowne Road only to discover it was shut. Mandy banged on the door to no avail.

"Damn it. Bloody hell."

"It's not a problem. You've got his address and number. Give him a call."

It was the obvious solution, and Mandy bit her tongue to stop a sarcastic comment. She'd already pulled out her mobile. She glared at Lucas. God, everything he did irritated her.

A woman's voice answered the call. Her tone was sharp. "He's gone to lie down. Been up since four, he has. Proper shook up finding a body like that. Not what you expect now, is it?"

Mandy could hear something like a mumbling voice in the background. "Ask him to give me a call or drop by the station, otherwise we'll pop along to see him at home later."

Silence greeted that remark, then a man's voice. "It's okay. I'll meet you in the herb garden by the cathedral in twenty minutes. I can't sleep anyway." He cut the call.

Lucas raised an eyebrow. He was standing close enough to hear part of the conversation. "He doesn't sound too keen to have us visit his home."

"Well, let's face it. Neighbours talk and they won't want coppers calling." She was whistling to herself as they headed towards the cathedral.

Llandaff Cathedral lay in a hollow down from a pleasant green area. An Anglican cathedral, it was one of the places visitors to the city liked to walk around. The centre of the village was little more than the High Street with its row of shops and a couple of pubs.

The herb garden was in what remained of the

Bishop's Palace of Llandaff at the top of the High Street. They entered it through the gatehouse.

A man was pacing up and down, smoking a cigarette. He lifted his head when he heard their footsteps on the path. Despite hours walking the streets delivering the mail his complexion was sallow, his expression dour.

"Mr Reece?"

They took out their warrant cards and introduced themselves. It was too cold to sit on one of the benches. They walked, their breaths forming mists as they spoke.

"I know you gave a statement to the officers at the scene, but I'd like you to tell me again what you saw and why you thought to ring the police."

He sniffed and took another pull on the cigarette before blowing the smoke sideways from his mouth. "I had a delivery. Small parcel but too big to go through the letterbox. I knocked but there was no reply. I know the woman, Mrs Vixen, is elderly so a bit slow to get to the door at times. I rang the doorbell and then looked through the window. She's got nets but there's a bit of a gap, see."

Considering he was probably pushing sixty describing Barbara Vixen as elderly was ironic. He stopped talking as though waiting for approval to carry on. When Mandy nodded, he continued.

"It looked a bit gloomy, but I could see something on the floor. It didn't look right so I called emergency services." He swallowed. "I didn't know what to do. I looked for a spare key, sometimes people put them under pots and stuff, but I couldn't find anything. Then the police came and an ambulance. I was late starting this morning so wanted to get on with my round. My wife doesn't like it if I'm home late. Dog needs walking and stuff like that."

"Did you see anything else? Or anyone leaving, hanging around?"

He shook his head. "I just deliver the post, like. Sometimes people say hello but most times I just shove the stuff through the letterboxes and get on."

"But you knew Mrs Vixen?"

"Had to knock once or twice. Not the friendliest of sorts. Not even a 'thank you'." He sniffed again.

"When was the last time you delivered anything there?"

He gazed into the distance. "Would have been between Christmas and New Year. Cards sent too late. Just shoved them through the letter box." He finished his smoke and stamped the butt on the ground.

Mandy stared at him until he lifted it and put it into the waste bin. "And you didn't notice anything unusual then? You didn't look through to see if she was at home?"

He frowned. "Why would I? I'm no peeping Tom. I do my job. That's all. What are you accusing me of?" His voice was raised. A couple who had just entered the herb garden paused at the signs of a disturbance, thought better of it, and left.

"I'm not accusing you of anything, Mr Reece. You did the right thing calling the police. I'm afraid

Mrs Vixen was dead when we found her. We're just trying to establish a timeline. Thank you for your help." She gave him her card. "If you remember anything else then please let us know."

He took the card, put it in his pocket and shuffled off.

"Got a bit of a chip on his shoulder, hasn't he?" Mandy said as they watched him exit.

"Hen-pecked, I'd guess. Judging from the way his wife spoke to you. Next?"

"Back to the station. I think I'll get Helen to do a bit of background on Mr Reece. Something doesn't feel right."

She set off at a trot, Lucas striding alongside.

CHAPTER FIVE

Everyone was busy when they got back. The never diminishing pile of paperwork kept them going. Reports and details from forensics would take time. Meanwhile they didn't have cause, or even time, of death. They would have to interview the other neighbour next. Mandy decided to call it a day.

"I'm heading off. Maybe Rishi will be more forthcoming tomorrow. Any luck on finding next of kin, Helen?"

"Her brother is the only relative as far as we know. Mr Charles Forbes. I've tried the contact number and uniform visited the house but he's abroad. He headed to the sun for Christmas by all accounts."

"The Charlie on the Christmas card. She was spending the day alone. Poor cow."

"Some people prefer to do that. Escape the hype. It's different with children. The excitement is infectious." Helen smiled. "And exhausting. Up at five on Christmas morning."

"I can understand the run to the sun. To be totally alone on the day must take something else." Mandy shrugged. "It could be death by natural causes, but Rishi's caginess makes me think there's something else. I'll be in early in the morning to make up for lost time." The latter remark was directed at Lucas. "I'm dropping Joy to the airport early. I'll head in after that."

"Your sister is still around then." It was half question, half statement. Lucas seemed interested.

"She's been," Mandy paused, unsure how to phrase things, "unwell. She's heading to Spain to allegedly look after our parents and Nan Betsi."

Before he could make further comment, Mandy made her getaway. Her cheeks burned as she thought about Lucas and his memories of Joy. The fallout for Mandy from some of her sister's pranks had been embarrassing. Best forgotten. Buried in the past, just like their engagement.

* * *

A delicious smell greeted her as she opened the door to her house in Brithdir Street. Joy's suitcase sat blocking the narrow hallway. It seemed, for once, her sister was ready before time. Mandy opened the door to the lounge. The Christmas tree twinkled in the corner. Through the glass door to the kitchen, she could see her twin at the hob. She went through and Joy lifted her head from the pot she was stirring.

"That smells divine," said Mandy. "What is it?"

Joy flashed a smile. "A one pot wonder. A sort of chicken soup but stuffed with vegetables. I've got crusty bread in the oven. Bit of a cheat. Those half-baked sourdough batons. I didn't want a heavy meal. We have to get up in the middle of the night to get to the airport."

"Sounds good to me. Where's Tabs?"

"Upstairs. She's got homework. I said it was better for her to do it now while I was busy. Once we've eaten, we can all sit down and watch a bit of telly or something."

"Good plan." Mandy gave her sister a thumbs up.

"I could get a taxi to the airport, you know." Joy carried on stirring but caught Mandy's eye.

"Cost a bloody fortune. Besides there's hardly any traffic about so early. I don't mind. I want to make sure you go."

They both laughed.

"What's so funny?" Tabitha appeared at the kitchen door. She looked pale and her eyes were red-rimmed. Another fallout from Joy's sporadic appearances in her daughter's life. Mandy experienced a surge of both sympathy and anger. It really wasn't fair on Tabitha. Joy yo-yoed in and out of her life like a favourite aunt while Mandy was left to do the mothering.

"Sisterly banter," said Mandy. "Now, let's eat. I could devour an elephant I'm so hungry."

A scratch at the window distracted them. Satan, next door's cat, wanted attention. They ignored him and with a disdainful meow he disappeared again.

After the meal they squashed together on the sofa and watched a film. Mandy could feel herself drifting off to sleep. At least with Joy gone she'd be able to get into her own bed again. The sofa was alright for a few nights, but it had been months. Tabitha was reluctant to go to bed, clinging to her mother like a toddler on her first day at nursery school. Joy had to promise to wake her and say goodbye before she would go to bed.

Mandy waited until she was sure Tabitha was out of earshot before she spoke.

"I shouldn't nag but you've got to get your act together. All this lack of stability isn't good for Tabs."

"She's got you, and I know if anything happened to me, you'd look after her. Wouldn't you, sis?"

"You don't need to ask. I love her to bits but this flitting in and out of her life like a blue-arsed fly isn't doing her any good."

"I don't need a lecture from you, sis. I know I'm not perfect and I'm grateful for your support these past few months. It's been hell for me, you know."

"It hasn't been a bloody picnic for any of us so cut the self-pity. Just promise me you'll think about the future when you get to Spain. Mam will fuss over you like you're a child but it's time you grew up. You've done your 'finding yourself' bit so time to be an adult."

Joy huffed and stood up. "I'm going to bed. We both need sleep, not arguments."

She flounced out of the room. Within minutes, Mandy could hear the squeak of the floorboards overhead as she wandered around before getting into bed. With a sigh, Mandy released the bed settee and set her alarm. Five hours sleep if she was lucky. Probably a sour face and sharp words from Joy when she woke. She knew Tabitha would be out of sorts for a couple of days. She'd have to remind her niece that she was going out to Spain for the Easter break.

Contrary to expectations, Joy was chirpy, bringing a slice of toast and cup of tea to Mandy before the alarm went off. Neither of them said much.

The drive to the airport, although it was still dark, was uneventful. The roads, as predicted, were quiet and the lights were green all the way through Ely on the road to Culverhouse Cross and beyond.

Mandy was reminiscing about her grandmother as they drove along Port Road past Barry.

"Maybe I'll come out and see everyone with Tabs at Easter. I used to love Nan Betsi's stories. All that stuff about her younger life and our grandfather Jeremiah across the seas. Jamaica, I think she said. I wonder what happened to him. Drowned at sea do you think?"

A snort of laughter exploded from Joy. "Oh God. You didn't believe all that crap, did you?"

"Why? I mean we've inherited this wiry hair and darker skin colour."

"She was making it all up. It was a way of keeping us entertained, I suppose. The truth is that our grandfather was an Irish sailor."

"What?"

"His name was Sean O'Reilly from Cork."

"Never. How the hell do you know that, Joy?"

"I found Mam's birth certificate one day when Betsi was sick. Mam said I was to stay with her, even though she was asleep." Joy giggled. "Do you remember the box she kept in the wardrobe under her shoes?"

"Yeah. The one she told us was private. I remember. She threatened me with a thrashing if I opened it."

"It was in there. Mam's birth certificate with her father's name. We're not part Jamaican or whatever you thought. We're part Irish."

Mandy sensed, rather than saw, the smile on her sister's face. "Well, the old devil. Nan Betsi stringing me along." Laughter filled the car. "I didn't think I was so gullible."

CHAPTER SIX

Mandy was tired before the day had started. The early start meant she was already experiencing an energy slump. And it wasn't even near lunchtime. At the morning briefing she set out the day's tasks.

"Helen, can you chase Rishi on the results of the PM, please? Tell him I'll pop along later. I don't know what was ailing him yesterday." She shook her head. "I'll take him some biscuits later and see if I can get to the root of the problem. And I'd like to know a bit more about our postie, Barry Reece. He was a bit shifty yesterday. I got the feeling he was hiding something."

She turned. "Olivia, could you check out the door-to-door team and see if there's anything further. Plus, background on Barbara Vixen. Anything that might help us to establish a timeline. We need to go and speak to the other neighbour. See when she last saw Mrs Vixen. We haven't established cause of death yet, but it will help the relatives if we can give them some idea of her last movements. Thanks."

She scanned the faces. "Any comments? Questions?"

"I'd like to look a bit into Father Michael's background," said Josh. "It struck me there was something not quite right. He just doesn't seem the type to be a man of God."

"It takes all sorts." Lucas interrupted, ignoring

Mandy's glower. "Take that Church On The Street in Burnley? Pastor Mick is an ex-drug dealer now helping others. Or The Scary Guy. There's this guy, covered in tattoos, who speaks to schoolkids about bullying. You can't judge someone by how you think they should look or fit into your stereotype."

"It wasn't just that." Josh coloured and was blustering as he responded to what sounded like a reprimand from the DCI. "I had a gut feeling he was hiding something, or at least not telling me everything. They're holding a prayer meeting for Mrs Vixen but there was the sense he was relieved she was dead. I can't put my finger on it, but something was amiss. Gives me the creeps."

Lucas half-smiled as Mandy leapt to Josh's defence.

"If you have a gut feeling about someone or something, I've found it's best not to ignore it. Nothing in the bloody book can teach you about instinct. It's that instinct that makes you a good detective, Josh. You carry on. I can interview Mrs What's her name, the neighbour, myself." Mandy checked her notes. "Myfanwy Peters."

"I'll come with you." Lucas was on his feet ready to go before Mandy could protest.

Damn. A boa constrictor couldn't feel more controlling than Lucas hanging closer to her than spandex. As soon as they got into the Juke, Mandy turned on him.

"How bloody dare you talk to my team like that? Have you any idea how long it's taken me to get Josh to realise he's a damned good detective. I know I put him down at times, but you're an outsider. He's used to me and knows how I operate. I don't mean half the sarky comments. You're a frigging DCI and should know better. Now I'll have to pick up the pieces. You're a total shit, Lucas. I don't care what you write in your report about me, but don't you dare pick on my team."

Exhausted by her outburst, Mandy leaned back in her seat, staring ahead and breathing deeply. Had she pushed it too far? She waited for the reprimand. She knew she shouldn't speak to a superior officer like that. Lucas could report her for being disrespectful and a disciplinary would follow. She could be demoted or worse.

Lucas sighed. "I'm sorry. You're right. I was out of line, and I'll talk to your DS when we get back. This little, shall we call it an outburst, will be unrecorded in my report. Except, of course, to say that DI Miranda Wilde is an extremely supportive leader, mindful of the needs of her team. Okay? Are we good? Shall we go and do the necessary?"

Mandy didn't trust herself to speak. Best to keep her mouth shut and get on with the task in hand. She nodded, grunted and started the engine, slamming the car into gear with more force than required which resulted in a grating noise. Lucas had enough sense not to comment.

All seemed peaceful enough as they approached the area. Barbara Vixen's house had crime scene tape across the front and a uniformed officer patrolling to stop nosy neighbours and journalists from trying to peer in.

"Want to work your charms on this one?" asked Mandy as they approached. "By all accounts she's heading towards ninety, maybe older, and deaf as a post."

"But she likes her Bridge Club."

He'd been taking notice of the evidence. Of course. He didn't get to be a DCI by sleepwalking through life. He was trained to observe and remember details. Mandy opened her phone where she'd made notes.

"Myfanwy Peters. Lived here over forty years. Widow. She's got one daughter who lives in Pentyrch. Grandson sometimes stays overnight. Might be worth speaking to him if he was around over the holiday period."

Lucas nodded. He lifted the brass knocker in the shape of a lion's head and rapped three times on the door. No reply. He glanced at Mandy and then tried again, applying some force. The sound reverberated around the little overhead porch where they were standing. Eventually, the door opened and a white-haired old women peered out at them.

"Mrs Peters. We're police. I'm Detective Inspector Wilde and this is Detective Chief Inspector Manning. We'd like to ask you about your neighbour, Mrs Vixen." Mandy showed her warrant card, as did Lucas, and they waited for her reply.

"I've been expecting you. 'Bout time. They told me yesterday you'd want to talk to me. Don't just stand there letting in the cold air. Come in."

Although Myfanwy Peters had a sharp air about her and a forbidding frown on her wrinkled face, she had a warm home. Photographs of various family members littered every surface. Unlike the house next door, this seemed to be in the original configuration with two small rooms and a tiny kitchen at the rear. She led them to the back room.

Mrs Peters was a smoker. It clung to her clothing and an overfilled ashtray sat on a table beside a high armchair. She sat down and waved her arm.

"Best sit down."

The armchair had a companion and Lucas sat. A dropleaf dining table and two wooden dining chairs leaned against the wall. Mandy pulled out one of these, drew it closer, and sat down. Mrs Peters waited, watching them with beady eyes while lighting up a cigarette.

"We are trying to establish when your neighbour died." Lucas took the lead and turned on the charm. "Were you friendly with Mrs Vixen? What can you tell us about her and her movements."

"Not a lot. She kept herself to herself. Not the friendly sort at all. Quiet, mind. Never heard a sound. Not even the television." She chuckled. "I'm almost deaf and the television is always on high volume. Must have blasted her ears out."

"Did she ever complain?"

"All the time, my dear. Little notes through the door mainly. Last one threatening me with legal action. I'm ninety-one. Do I give a damn?" She pulled on the cigarette, coughed and grinned at them displaying stained teeth.

"When was the last time you saw Mrs Vixen?"

Mrs Peters stared at the ceiling, her eyes narrowing as she tried to recall.

"Hmmm. Couple of weeks ago maybe? Before Christmas anyway. All the days are the same when you get to my age. Only day I remember is Bridge Club. My social activity for the week."

"What about visitors?" Lucas pressed on.

"Oh, I get enough visitors, dear. I've three children, eight grandchildren and my first great-grandchild on the way. I hope I live long enough to see it." She coughed before pulling again on the cigarette.

Mandy could see Lucas in profile and noticed the faint twitch of his cheek.

"That's lovely for you. I meant did Mrs Vixen have many visitors?" He smiled at her.

"Not that I know. I can't see much from here at the back of the house. I saw that tall chap a couple of times in the summer. The one with the bushy ginger beard. He helped me trim the hedge and wouldn't take any money. Not many like that these days."

"Would that be Father Michael?"

Scratching her chin Mrs Peters replied, "I don't know his name, but he gave me a leaflet. Something about a church. I threw it away. I go to the cathedral when Beth, my daughter, takes me. Only about once a month now. That walk down is a killer on my knees."

A large tomcat interrupted them, as he waltzed in from the kitchen. He leapt on Mrs Peters' knee and started purring.

"This is Sweep. He's looking for food. Barbara Vixen didn't like him either. He used her garden as a toilet." She chuckled again. "What was I supposed to do about that, eh?"

"I believe your grandson stays with you sometimes." Mandy asked, thinking it was time she took over, or at least contributed to the conversation.

"Now and again. If there's something on in the stadium and it's convenient for him. He's a good lad, is Nathan."

"Did he stay over anytime around the Christmas period?" Mandy thought the grandson could be more observant.

"No. Last time was at the end of November. I had a bit of a dizzy turn and Beth told him to stay the night. Lot of fuss about nothing."

There was no more to be gained so they left the old woman to feed her cat.

"Our Mrs Vixen didn't exactly make friends and influence people, did she?" said Lucas. "I don't think she was a very good neighbour."

"No. From what we've found so far, she was a bit of a cow. Still, you would have thought someone would notice her absence. Sad really. Dying alone and no one giving a damn."

"Including Father Michael. Maybe DS Jones is right, and he is a bit dodgy," said Lucas. "I'll have a quiet word with Josh when I get the chance. Boost his confidence a bit."

It was difficult to resist rolling her eyes. Lucas thought a word from him would give Josh a lift of confidence. Maybe he was right, but he was still bloody annoying.

"At the moment we don't know cause of death. You can't charge someone for not caring enough. It's not like a neglected child. But, even if she died from natural causes, it's a poor show." Mandy was annoyed. "Years ago, everyone knew their neighbours and looked out for them. These days nobody gives a shit."

CHAPTER SEVEN

Back at the station there had been some progress. "Rishi wants to see you," said Helen, as soon as they appeared. "He sounded a bit out of sorts. He said he needs to talk to you about something."

"No report on the PM?"

"Not yet." Helen glanced down at her notes. "I did the background on Mr Reece. He's had points on his license for speeding–"

"Who hasn't?"

"Otherwise, nothing until about six months ago."

"And? What then?"

"Complaints about him leaving parcels when the owner was out and about his attitude. Three complaints and all from the same person." Helen pursed her lips. "Mrs Barbara Vixen. He's been with the service for twenty-three years and even won an award for service to the community a few years back."

"No wonder he was on edge and the wife was so defensive," said Lucas. "A blemish-free career marred by Barbara Vixen."

"And then he finds her dead body." Josh shook his head. "A coincidence?"

Mandy appeared to be thinking. "At the moment it looks like that. He didn't enter the house. He called emergency services. We definitely need to speak to Rishi. Pronto. Come on, Josh." She started towards the door.

"I was doing the background on Father Michael and–"

"That can wait for now," she said over her shoulder.

Josh grabbed his coat and followed her with Lucas beating him to it. When they got to Mandy's Juke she sighed. "It's going to be a bit cramped in the back. You can toss for it."

She saw Josh glance at Lucas and, without another word, he opened the back door and got in. Lucas slid into the front, fastened his seatbelt and gave her a quick smile. She had hoped he'd stay in the office. No such luck. There hadn't been time to check things with Olivia, but she knew anything significant would have been mentioned before they left.

Rishi looked as though he hadn't slept well. His jaw sagged and he had dark shadows under his eyes. Mandy raised a questioning eyebrow which he ignored.

"Helen said you wanted to speak to me."

"Indeed, Inspector." He cast his eyes over Josh and Lucas. "I was not expecting the cavalry too. No matter. I have something I think you may find of interest." Another look towards the others. "I have completed my postmortem examination on the body of Mrs Vixen. It is my opinion she died from carbon monoxide poisoning."

They digested the information for a moment. Rishi continued. "After a period of time these things become more difficult to ascertain. I took a sample of the liver and asked for GPE analysis." Seeing the blank faces, he elaborated. "It stands for gas phase electrochemical which enables detection of carbon monoxide in small samples by..."

"And this test indicated carbon monoxide was present. I thought the skin turned red with carbon monoxide poisoning, but I suppose the body had decomposed too much for that to show." Mandy interrupted what she suspected was going to be a long lecture from Rishi.

"Didn't she have a carbon monoxide alarm?" asked Josh. "I thought everyone had those these days. The fire brigade will install them for elderly people. Our neighbour had one fitted by them. What could have caused it? She must have known something was wrong."

"The symptoms are varied. Sometimes the person experiences headaches, dizziness, chest pains. They may feel tired as though they have a viral infection. It can be cumulative in some cases. These things are rarely straightforward." Rishi peered at them.

"If I recall there was a packet of painkillers on the floor so she must have been feeling unwell," said Mandy. "We need to check with her GP. What about the head wound? Any significance?"

"That was consistent with the fall. It appears she collapsed and hit her head on the edge of the hearth around the wood burner."

"An unfortunate accident. From what we're hearing she wasn't exactly Mrs Popularity. I wondered if she'd been attacked. If it's a natural death I suppose we need to leave things to the coroner. Thanks, Rishi."

Mandy took a packet of chocolate ginger biscuits out of her pocket. "Thought you needed a bit of cheering up. Mother-in-law trouble again?"

Rishi's sigh was long and deep. "She has decided she no longer wishes to live alone. She wants to move in with us. My life is over."

"Nightmare for you." Mandy's tone was sincere. Rishi's mother-in-law made life very unpleasant for him.

"You have no idea how often I dream about having her on that table with my scalpel poised." He inclined his head to the postmortem table.

"I think a better solution would be to find her a place in sheltered housing." Mandy's suggestion was met by a rolling of his eyes.

"Or on an island far, far away. Yes, Inspector. You are right. That woman is a demon." He held his hands up in a gesture of despair. Mandy pressed the biscuits into his palms, wondering how anyone could eat anything with the unpleasant odours of the mortuary wafting through their senses.

"Just say no."

"I wish it was so easy. At least the dead do not cause me pain." He turned away from them and sighed again.

The mood was low as they walked back to the car. Josh whistled. "I thought my mother-in-law was a pain but compared to Rishi's she's a teddy bear."

Lucas stayed silent but appeared to be deep in thought. "Looks like natural causes, unless anything else turns up. We should chase forensics on the phone and laptop before writing a report."

"What did you want to tell me about our Father Michael?" asked Mandy.

Josh's voice held a touch of excitement. "He's not all he pretends to be. He's got previous. Known as M. Carmichael. No forename – just M. He set up a company allegedly dealing in property. It was a scam. Getting money from the gullible for some sort of investment. No one knows where the money went as he declared himself bankrupt before he was arrested. They couldn't prove anything as some of the records had mysteriously disappeared, so he got away with a suspended sentence."

"Seems as though your gut feeling was right, DS Jones. My apologies for my previous scepticism. Well done," said Lucas, earning an approving nod from Mandy. Apologising showed Lucas to be a man who wasn't afraid to admit his mistakes. She liked that.

Josh wasn't finished. "That was seven years ago. After things calmed down, he went abroad for a bit, somewhere in the States and then Mexico. Came back here two years ago with a degree in theology and set up The Church of the Forgotten Souls. They have a website with his story and all sorts of information."

"Bet it doesn't tell the whole story. We'll have a look at it when we get back to base. It all sounds like a cover for something else. And the smarmy bugger was possibly the last one to see Barbara Vixen alive."

CHAPTER EIGHT

The website for The Church of the Forgotten Souls was intriguing. Foremost was a picture of Father Michael in his academic robes, holding a certificate. Mandy sat in front of her computer, scrolling through.

"Bullshit. Anyone could have a photo like that." She snorted, unimpressed.

"Read the rest," said Josh. Lucas joined them so he could read the screen too.

"It's so cheesy," she said. "Makes me want to throw."

Mandy could feel Lucas's breath on the back of her neck and smell his spicy aftershave. It made her feel uncomfortable, so she read aloud in the hope he'd give her some space.

"Listen to this crap. 'Hi, I'm Michael. I've done some bad things in my life, and I've been punished for them. Men punished me but God saved me. He made me see the error of my ways. Through the love of God and his son, Our Lord Jesus Christ, I have seen there is a different path. A path where I can do some good in the world and help others.'"

Mandy stopped and put two fingers into her mouth, making a heaving sound. Josh grinned. She continued scrolling down the page. "How can he write this crap? 'Yes. I have seen the light and the way. Jesus wants us to put down our burdens and follow him. He will guide and look after us. If you feel that society has failed you, that other people have failed you and that God has failed you, I am here to bring you back into the bosom of the Lord. You are never forgotten by God and The Church of the Forgotten Souls is here for you. Whatever you have done, however worthless you feel, I can assure you that God loves you. Come and join your fellows at our prayer meetings or just drop by to talk to someone. God is always here. He always listens. God's love will give you hope in a troubled world.'"

She sat back in her chair. "What the hell? And people fall for that shit?" She shook her head in disbelief. "I'd still like to know why Barbara Vixen went there. From what we know so far, she was no pushover."

"People look for spiritual assistance for many reasons," said Lucas. "The Christmas period can be a very hard time. All the enforced joviality when many people are at their lowest can make even the most optimistic folk feel a little low. From what we know, Father Michael is guilty of nothing except extending the hand of friendship."

"Yet both neighbours we spoke to mentioned him. Plus, Josh had a gut feeling about him. I think there's more to this Father Michael and his bloody weird church."

Lucas shook his head. "Death was probably accidental, and The Church of the Forgotten Souls is not your problem. You need to sort out the paperwork and send the details to the coroner to decide."

Mandy turned away so Lucas couldn't see her

rolling her eyes yet again. Telling her what to do. The sodding paperwork, for God's sake.

"Cuppa anyone?" Olivia broke the tension.

Mandy was finding that biting her tongue to avoid saying something crude, rude or both, was proving to be nigh on impossible. There was something niggling her about Barbara Vixen's death. She wasn't ready to give up yet. She followed Olivia into the kitchen.

"Have we got anything?"

"Nothing from door to door. Nobody saw anything unusual, like. Couple of comments from people which seem to confirm the feeling she was a bit of a poody. You still think there's something up, boss?"

"Yeah, I think I'd like another look around. Alone."

She glanced over her shoulder. Lucas was engaged in discussion with Josh. It looked intense. She hoped he was being supportive after her little outburst earlier. Nobody got to talk down to her team without repercussions. She groaned inwardly at the thought of the paperwork. She wouldn't be able to get back to nose around Barbara Vixen's house until the end of the working day. It was frustrating. In normal circumstances she'd have given the nod to Josh and headed off. With Lucas and his affirmation that the case was closed bar the shouting, or rather the paperwork, she didn't dare step out of line.

"Has there been anything from forensics? Mobile data or anything on the laptop yet?"

Olivia checked and shook her head. "Suppose they're a bit busy down there now."

"Is your little friend on duty?" The implication was clear. One of the technicians had the hots for Olivia, not realising he was sniffing around the wrong tree. Olivia played along with it, flirting with him. He responded sometimes by speeding up matters. He kept her informed about developments as soon as any results were available.

"I'll go and have a little chat in a bit, alright?" She grinned. If anyone could speed up the IT guys it was Olivia, perhaps because she was a bit of a nerd herself. Mandy sometimes wondered if Olivia would end up working in cyber-crime. It would suit her talents.

They settled down to deal with the report and the backlog of files relating to other crimes which never seemed to become any smaller. She was itching to get back to Barbara Vixen's house and have a root around. Something was amiss, she was sure, but what and when would she have the chance to do anything without her shadow?

Relief came in a strange fashion. Superintendent Withers came in with a face like someone had given him a whisky that turned out to be rat piss.

"DCI Manning. There's been a message from your Super. Perhaps you'd like to step into my office?"

Lucas followed and they could see through the glass that a serious conversation was taking place between the two men.

"I'd like to be a fly on that wall," said Olivia, her

eyes sparkling with mischief.

"Wouldn't we all? I'm going to make my escape while he's occupied. Where's the evidence bag with Barbara Vixen's keys? I'm not convinced there isn't something fishy about all this."

Olivia lifted a bag. "Two sets in 'ere. Front and back keys."

"One set will do. Can't leave an empty bag, can I?"

Josh looked up. "Want me to come with you?"

"No, you're alright. Keep 'Mr Do Everything by the Book' at bay. I thought Withers was tight-arsed, but our spook DCI is even worse. I'm off before he appears again."

"What do I say if he asks where you are?"

Mandy winked at him. "Use your imagination. Maybe I've run off with Tod Blakeney." With a laugh, she left, making sure she didn't pass the Super's office on the way. Back to schooldays, and the delight of fooling the teachers.

CHAPTER NINE

It was already dark by the time Mandy reached the house. The police tape was still across the door as a deterrent to voyeurs and would-be burglars as they knew the patrol cars would still be vigilant. The neighbours had already drawn their curtains. A faint pencil line of light escaped from Yvonne Hunter's house, but the home of Myfanwy Peters was shrouded. A dog barked somewhere close by, but no one was about to see her enter.

She switched on the light as soon as she located it, ensuring she pulled on gloves first. The smell of death and decay still permeated the air. Mandy wrinkled up her nose in response and pulled a mask out of her pocket. It should afford some protection from that God awful stink.

The spot where Barbara Vixen had been found was close to the wood burner. Had it been leaking fumes unnoticed? No carbon monoxide monitor? She looked up at the ceiling and saw a smoke alarm but nothing else. Most people had replaced those with dual purpose alarms. It seemed Mrs Vixen hadn't done the same. A pad of writing paper sat on a dresser at the back of the room. The top page had been ripped out. Mandy put the pad into an evidence bag. Could be just a shopping list or a letter to her brother but worth looking over. She didn't want to hang about too long if there was a gas leak of some sort. She opened the patio door wide to allow air to circulate.

The kitchen was compact. A plate was still sitting on the drainer plus two fine-bone china cups and saucers. Old fashioned. How many people used teacups and saucers these days? Two cups and saucers indicated she'd been entertaining. Mandy opened the cupboards. Everything was tidy and Barbara Vixen was frugal in her tastes. Perhaps she was short of money and cutting down on maintenance of the house and things like the boiler. She made a mental note to check Barbara's bank balance. It would be worth finding out when the boiler and wood burner had last been serviced. The heating was still on timer and the house was warm, but not hot. The temperature gauge showed a mean 16 degrees.

Opening the fridge, Mandy checked the contents. A chicken crown dated 27th December and a tiny Christmas pudding, some pre-prepared vegetables and a small bottle of pink Prosecco. It convinced Mandy this was Barbara's planned Christmas meal. The one she never got to eat.

A creaking from upstairs stopped her in her tracks. Probably just pipes expanding and contracting. Another creak. Floorboards shifting underfoot. Someone else was in the house. For once she wished she'd brought Josh with her. A bit of moral support. She debated calling for backup, but it could take too long. Most burglars were opportunists, not necessarily violent. She decided to take a chance.

At the bottom of the stairs, Mandy shouted, "Police. Whoever you are, come out now with your hands in the air." She pulled out her baton ready to attack if necessary. Silence. The creaking had stopped but the hairs on the back of her neck warned her of danger.

The stairway was in darkness, and she crept up on tiptoes avoiding the centre of each step – in case there were any loose boards to give away her position. Taking slow and shallow breaths, Mandy made her way to the narrow landing. Two bedrooms and a bathroom. The door to the latter was wide open so the intruder must be in one of the other rooms.

Mandy pushed open the door to the first room, ran her hand down the wall to locate the switch and the room lit up. With her back to the wall, she entered and peered behind the door. Nothing. She approached the other door.

"Okay, I know you're in there. Come out slowly."

She half-expected to see a cat appear. No response. Damn. Whoever it was intended to make things more difficult. She turned the handle of the door and pushed it open, stepping into the room. The door seemed to swing back further than she expected and then came crashing into her. Caught unawares and off balance the force knocked her over. Her head hit the doorpost. She had a vague impression of a figure passing before darkness descended.

* * *

"Where's DI Wilde?" Lucas cast his eyes around the

room. Mandy's chair was empty, her computer switched off. "Well?" The sharpness in his voice made them wince. Josh was the first to speak.

"She's gone to have another look at the victim's house, sir."

"By herself? Of all the irresponsible–" Lucas stopped, breathed deeply. "Spare keys?"

"She took them, sir. But there's another set." Olivia fetched them, putting the keys into his hand without making eye contact. Josh stood up as if to join him, but Lucas held up a hand. He didn't want any witnesses to the dressing down he was going to deliver. Miranda had always been headstrong and a bit unpredictable, but she was an inspector now, for God's sake. She should know how to play the game and not go off doing her own thing. Damn the woman.

When he got to Barbara Vixen's house the light was on and the front door ajar. He went inside and called her name but there was no reply. Just a deathly silence.

* * *

"Miranda. Miranda. Can you hear me?" The voice came from far away. Mandy tried to move but a wave of nausea overtook her, and she turned her head before vomiting. Opening her eyes was too difficult so she kept them shut and tried to sleep.

"Miranda. Don't go to sleep. Come on. An ambulance is on the way. Stay awake."

Despite her grogginess Mandy registered the voice. Bloody DCI bloody Manning. What was he doing here? He sounded a bit concerned. She half opened one eye, trying to remember what had happened.

"Don't bloody shout at me. My head hurts. Piss off."

The paramedics arrived and the next thing she remembered was the bright lights in the ambulance. They seemed to be going over every pothole in the road. Then the vehicle stopped moving.

"Turn the light off. Hurts." Her tongue was thick, and the words sounded slurred to her own ears, but the paramedic dimmed the lights a little.

"We're waiting in a queue for admittance," he said.

The following hours passed in a daze. The paramedic, she couldn't remember his name, kept talking to her and gradually she became more coherent and alert. She was wheeled into the hospital A&E department; despite her protestations she was fine. Just a bit of a headache. A doctor, who looked about twelve, pale blue eyes under-shadowed by purple bruised skin, asked her to follow his hands and shone a bright light into her eyes.

"How long were you unconscious?" he asked. Mandy shrugged. How the hell was she supposed to know that? Did he think she'd looked at a clock before passing out?

"You need to have an MRI and I think we'll keep you in overnight for observation."

"Can't stay in. I look after my niece."

"Can you make other arrangements? Is there someone else who can take over that responsibility? I'm not prepared to discharge you. Mild concussion I suspect, but we need to check there's nothing more serious."

Reluctantly, Mandy rang Kelly's mum. She agreed Tabitha could stay with them until Mandy was out of hospital.

"Tell her I'm fine. Doc is being over-cautious. I'll be home tomorrow." She crossed her fingers and lay back on the trolley wishing her head didn't hurt so much.

CHAPTER TEN

A night of disturbed sleep and Mandy was desperate to leave the confines of the hospital. She was up and dressed by the time the doctor was doing the rounds. A female doctor with almond shaped eyes and strained expression, who introduced herself as Cindy. She examined Mandy and read her notes.

"How's the head this morning?"

Ignoring the throbbing in her temple, Mandy pasted on her brightest smile, hoping it would fool the doctor.

"I feel fine. Can I go home now?"

Mandy tried not to wince as she moved her head following the doctor's instructions.

"There's been no brain damage that we can see on the scan. However, these things can be serious," Cindy touched the front of Mandy's temple, then, with a faint smile, said, "Plus, you've got a bit of a shiner there. You're a police officer. I suppose it's an occupational hazard. I'd advise you to have a couple of days off work."

"Yes, doctor. Thank you. I can go?"

"No driving until the dizziness settles."

"What dizziness?" Mandy assumed what she hoped was an innocent smile, opening her eyes wide to meet Cindy's speculative look.

The doctor raised an eyebrow, unconvinced. "Just do as I say. If the headache returns or if you have any other symptoms, then you need to return to A&E. You need rest and no stress. Your friend can take you home when you're ready. He's waiting outside."

The smile slid from Mandy's face. Friend? He? Josh? God, she hoped it wasn't Tod. It would be just like him to turn up in the hope of getting a story. She gritted her teeth. It would be better to get a taxi home.

"Are you ready, Miranda? Your transport awaits." Lucas turned heads from the nurses as he entered the ward.

They said little on the way back to Brithdir Street. It wasn't a long journey, and Lucas must have already found out where she lived as he didn't ask for directions and parked almost at her door. The students were still on holiday, so it wasn't the usual juggling game to find a space.

"Do you want a tea or coffee?" she asked him as he followed her into her home. It was uncomfortable to have him there, surveying the room and seeing her at her most vulnerable.

"I'll make it. You sit down. I'm sure I can find the necessary."

Why didn't he just go? "I need a shower. I didn't have any stuff with me at the hospital. I've still got sick in my hair."

"I noticed." He grinned at her, and Mandy blushed.

"I stink."

"You aren't exactly fragrant. I'll make tea and see what I can forage while you shower. I'm not going anywhere yet. Where's your niece?"

"At her friend's house. She'll be home later. I'll be fine. You don't have to hang about, Lucas. It's not part of your shadowing brief."

He looked resigned, almost disappointed by her remark. "I know. Relax a bit, will you? I'm an old friend and I want to help. I'll make you a cuppa and see what else is in the cupboard and fridge. Then, when you've eaten, and I know you're alright I'll clear off. You need some sleep. You look like a zombie."

Mandy opened her mouth to say something but changed her mind. "I won't be long."

The warmth of the shower was bliss. She winced as she washed her hair. There was only a faint abrasion on the back of her head where she'd collided with the door post. A glance in the mirror gave a more comprehensive picture. The bridge of her nose was blue and purple, the colour spreading to under both eyes and there was a bruise on her forehead. She dumped her clothes in the linen basket and pulled on clean joggers and sweatshirt. She knew her hair took ages to dry so she just rubbed a towel over it to remove excess moisture. She didn't want Lucas poking about any longer than necessary. No doubt he'd already examined her bookshelves as well as the contents of her kitchen cupboards.

He was sitting on the sofa with a cup of tea when she went downstairs. Waiting for her was her favourite mug, a pot of tea and a plate of toast and honey. For some reason the display of kindness made her want to cry.

She sat on a chair, grunted a thank you and

nibbled at the toast. It was good. Breakfast in hospital hadn't appealed and her stomach was growling.

"Is good." Her words were muffled through the toast, but Lucas nodded.

"You've a lovely home. Comfortable. Relaxing. Is that your niece?" He pointed at a photograph on the shelf above the television. Tabitha on her first day at high school.

"Yes. She's a gem." Mandy's voice glowed with pride. "Sweet child. Still a bit naïve but sensible too." She pointed at another photo, unframed, leaning up against the clock. "That's her in the middle. She played Maria in West Side Story just before Christmas. The teacher gave each member of the group a copy of the photograph as a souvenir."

A yawn caught Mandy unawares. Lucas got to his feet. "Time for you to go and have a nap. Superintendent Withers says you are not to come into work tomorrow either."

"But–"

"Orders. I've left my card on the table with my personal number on the bottom in case there's anything you need. And don't worry. I agree. There's something more to Barbara Vixen's death than we thought. We're looking into things as well as trying to find whoever did this to you." Lucas raised a hand towards her and for a moment she thought he was going to touch her face. She flinched. He paused, turned and picked up his coat before heading to the hallway.

"Rest. That's an order too."

When Tabitha arrived home half an hour later Mandy was fast asleep on the sofa, muttering to herself.

CHAPTER ELEVEN

Mandy was surprised to see Helen at lunchtime the next day. She was itching to know what was going on at the station and desperate to return to work.

Helen brought a huge bunch of flowers and a packet of macaroons with her.

"Not healthy I know but I guessed you needed something naughty to cheer you up a bit. How are you feeling?"

"Okay. The dizziness has gone. I think it was lack of food if I'm honest. I hadn't eaten all day then – whack. I've still got a bloody headache but nothing a couple of painkillers can't cope with. At least it's given me time to clear the Christmas clutter before twelfth night. Now, tell me what's been happening."

Helen laughed. "I told them I'd get a grilling. Let me put these flowers in water and you can make a cuppa before I fill you in."

Once they were settled on the sofa Helen outlined what had taken place since Mandy had been knocked out.

"DCI Manning came back and asked where you'd gone. He went ballistic when he heard you'd headed off on your own. He ranted at us." Helen lowered her voice, imitating the deep tone of Lucas's voice. "'How could she be so stupid? Crazy woman.' And so on. Withers didn't look too happy either. Poor Josh got a bit of a tongue lashing after."

"Oh no. Not another one." Mandy shook her head. She'd have to try and placate everyone when she got back. Maybe she could try the sympathy card.

Helen was in full flow, her face alight. "DCI Manning took the keys and zipped out muttering under his breath. Afterwards we heard you'd been taken to hospital. All we knew was that there had been an incident and you were injured. We didn't know if it was serious, only that you were in hospital with a head injury. Josh was grey when the news came in and I've never seen Olivia look upset before."

Mandy groaned. "At least they are taking Barbara Vixen's death as more than natural causes now."

"Forensics have been all over the place, dusting for fingerprints. They found your evidence bag Withers seems to be happy to let him do it too, which is a bit odd. I heard this morning they've got a match on the system."

Mandy's eyes lit up. "Anyone I know?"

"Father Michael's prints. No surprise. He told us he visited. His fingerprints were on the mantlepiece, fridge and front door. Nothing upstairs."

"Hmmmm."

"Can you remember something about the person who attacked you? Has anything come back to you?"

"Not much. A heavy smell. Like an animal smell. Perhaps a dog. Separate from the death stink downstairs. And there was something else." Mandy closed her eyes. "A sniffing sound. It was all so quick.

He dashed past me as I sank. I wasn't able to do anything."

"Well, at least if anyone asks you what happened to your face you can truthfully say you walked into a door."

They laughed together at the bad joke.

* * *

Josh wasn't laughing. DCI Manning was supposed to be observing but he had, in effect, taken the reins and determined to find out who had been in Mrs Vixen's house and attacked the boss. And the Super was letting him do it. Why? Manning barked orders at Josh. It wasn't fair. He wasn't DI Wilde's minder and if the boss wanted to do something hell and high water wouldn't stop her. Somehow, DCI Manning had placed the blame on the boss's attack firmly on Josh's shoulders.

"It's a pity you didn't go with DI Wilde when she headed out. If I hadn't been tied up with other matters, I'd have been there too. A few minutes earlier and we'd have caught him. Let's hope forensics come up with something useful."

"I'll press them for quick results, sir. I've a friend in the lab," said Olivia, glancing at Josh.

Lucas hadn't noticed. "CCTV for the area. The door into the garden was open so he must have got in and left by the same means. We need to speak to this Father Michael when we've gathered a bit more information. In my opinion all this 'I've found God' is a cover. Just as well you did a background check, Josh. Maybe he was trying to extort money from Mrs Vixen. It wouldn't be the first time he's been involved in that sort of little scam."

With a hint of impatience he asked Olivia, "Have we got Barbara Vixen's bank records and phone records yet? Check her phone for messages from Father Michael or anything that looks out of sync. His number or the church number is on that website. Any social media? Background? We need to know everything about her. It may have been a random burglar but why did they go upstairs when there was a television and various bits of silverware downstairs? Something smells. DI Wilde was right. Barbara Vixen's death may not have been accidental after all."

* * *

The Church of the Forgotten Souls was just as dreary and uninspiring as the last time Josh was there. Perhaps the services were more dynamic. At least the communal room provided warmth and some companionship for the lost and lonely. A youth took them through to the prayer room Josh had been in last time. Father Michael welcomed them both. Josh took more note of his surroundings this time. They had entered through one door, but the other was open giving an enticing glimpse of an office and what looked like a new computer, printer and dual monitors. Expensive equipment and a contrast to the shabby surroundings. A keypad operated lock was in place, so it seemed no risks of anyone absconding with the goods.

Lucas was on the warpath. He exuded confidence and determined to unnerve Father Michael. After introducing himself he got straight to the point of the visit. No niceties. No preamble.

"One of my colleagues was attacked at Mrs Vixen's house last night."

"How very unfortunate. No serious injuries, I hope." The platitudes seemed false, and the sardonic smile stayed fixed.

"We've had forensics in to search the house. We now believe Mrs Vixen's death may not be accidental and could be linked to the break-in."

Father Michael looked from Lucas to Josh and back again. "And? That is dreadful but I fail to see why you are telling me all this."

Josh was astonished at the arrogance of the man.

"Your fingerprints have been found in various places in the house. We know they are yours as they came up on the database, Mr M. Carmichael. It seems you have a few skeletons in your cupboard or at least a criminal record. We'd like to know where you were between five and six o'clock last night."

A definite smirk now as Father Michael replied.

"I made no secret of the fact I visited Mrs Vixen in her home before Christmas. Last night I was here. We had an impromptu prayer meeting. One of our congregation, Mr Tanner, came in about five. He was in some distress. His mother is very ill and had just been rushed to hospital. I gathered together those who were in the communal room, and we prayed for her soul. After that I took Mr Tanner to the hospital, and we sat with his mother until about eight o'clock. You can check. So," he opened his hands, palms up, "I couldn't be your intruder. Now, if there's nothing else." He stood.

Lucas wasn't finished. "We will certainly check. And I'd like a list of the members of your congregation. How many of them knew Mrs Vixen or had any dealings with her?"

"Mrs Vixen would be known to most members, especially the youth group. She made refreshments for them and helped them with computer skills." The smirk had gone. "Unless you have a warrant, I don't think I want to divulge those names and addresses. I need to think about protecting my flock."

"Your flock shouldn't have any reason to hide anything but maybe you have, Mr Carmichael. We'll be in touch." Lucas strode out with Josh following. As they left the building they almost collided with Cassian, who was standing outside.

"Hello, Cassian. Doing your bit for the church, are you? Bet you knew Mrs Vixen, didn't you?" said Josh.

Cassian's eyes opened wide, his mouth even wider and then he turned and ran down the road and into the nearest alleyway, out of sight. Josh and Lucas stood and watched.

"What the–" Josh shook his head.

"Someone we need to speak to it seems," said

Lucas.

CHAPTER TWELVE

Olivia was in the control room with other officers, trawling through CCTV footage from the areas close to Mrs Vixen's house on the night of Mandy's attack. It was quiet and dull for the most part. A few dog walkers, people going in and out of the pubs and the usual traffic meandering through the main area.

Lucas hadn't heard a car or motorcycle as he'd approached Mrs Vixen's house although they might have been well gone by then. He told Olivia to look for either a bicycle, electric scooter, or someone on foot. If that didn't yield any leads they could go back and check again. It was a slow process.

Olivia squinted through her specs as a delivery guy on a bike showed on one screen. She took note of the time and the logo on the bag. It wasn't likely to be him, but he may have heard or seen something. She got excited when she spotted a man running towards the village and followed him on a different camera. As he reached the bottom of High Street a woman emerged from a doorway and threw her arms around him. They were engaged in conversation for a few minutes before going into one of the pubs. He didn't look a likely suspect either, but Olivia made another note. They could check with the pub landlord and their CCTV if necessary. He could be a regular.

Switching around the screens she noticed a

hooded figure dressed all in black, except for white trainers, slope along the main road. He seemed to be wary, looking all around and not running but not wasting any time either. He headed towards Canton, and she lost him when he went down an alley way after crossing Western Avenue.

It was painstaking work trawling through everything. They looked further afield. The figure appeared again, a bit less wary but still hooded, heading down Penhill. The white trainers made it easy to identify him as the same person. She might be wrong, but Olivia had the tingly feeling she'd spotted the intruder. Following him from one camera to another she held her breath as he reached his destination, pulled down his hood and entered a building. The Church of the Forgotten Souls. That couldn't be a coincidence.

"Can I get some prints of these?" She made a note of the screen times and passed them over. Feeling pleased with herself, she returned to the office to show DCI Manning.

Josh was the first one to examine the printouts. "That's the lad who did a runner when he saw us. And he was there when I first went to the place. A definite person of interest. Cassian Jones."

Lucas appeared, listened to Olivia's explanation of how she'd tracked the lad and nodded. "Let's go and pick him up. Is he known to us?"

"I did a facial recognition, and it's come up, sir. He got a caution warning for possession of a small amount of weed, I mean cannabis, about a month ago."

"And you've got an address?"

"Yes, sir." Olivia rattled off the address.

"Right, Josh. Let's get him. Something is going on there."

No one was at home when they called at the address given for Cassian Jones. A neighbour peeped from behind nets, no doubt curious about the two strangers.

"He's probably at school," said Josh.

"Do you think? He wasn't at school earlier when we saw him outside the church." Lucas appeared to be thinking. "He likes the wacky baccy. Where would kids go to score around here?"

They looked around but there didn't seem to be anything obvious. The area was quiet. The street was made up of terraced houses with fronts on to the pavement, no shops where groups might meet, or cafe that he could see. He hadn't noticed any cars loitering which could point to a dealer.

"Maybe we should think more about where they'd go to smoke," said Josh. "There are a couple of places where we've had complaints about. Parks mainly with gangs of louts. From what I saw of Cassian, he's more likely to keep himself to himself. He's the sort to get picked on. Maybe that's why he's involved with the church thing. A sort of protection. I don't know."

Lucas was thinking. "Years ago, when I was working in the city, there was an area behind the cathedral where some smokers used to hang out. It's not far from here. Let's check it out."

They parked in the car park off Llandaff High Street and walked down the side of the cathedral.

"Do you believe in ghosts, Josh?"

Josh looked at him, obviously unsure what to make of the question.

"I don't know, sir. I've never seen one if that's what you mean. And I went on a ghost tour around St Fagan's once but didn't see anything." He looked perplexed as if he thought it was a trick question.

"They call this road, Cathedral Close, the Road of the Dead," said Lucas. "It's supposed to be haunted."

"Really? I suppose they bring the hearses down here for funerals. It's closest to the Lady Chapel. I did a tour of the building once. I like old churches and stuff. Are you a believer, sir?"

"You can drop the *sir* when we aren't in the office. Lucas will do." He looked up at the gargoyles on the building and quoted, 'there are more things in heaven and earth,'".

Josh cleared his throat but said nothing.

At the bottom of the hill, they turned left, making their way along the path behind the cathedral, their footsteps crunching on the gravel. In a couple of months, primroses and crocuses would be flowering in this graveyard but now it just looked dismal and neglected. A crow called out as they crossed over a bridge. After that the pathway became muddy in places. Brambles tugged at their trousers. It wasn't far to a clearing where a tree with roots above ground and a wall around its base became evident.

"The dope heads used to call this the magic tree," said Lucas. "Doesn't look as if it's popular today." The area was empty. A few discarded cigarette stubs, a couple of crisp bags and pop bottles littered the ground.

"You'd think they'd have more respect." Lucas shook his head and pointed to a spray of white roses set on the wall. "It's obviously a place of sentimental significance for some people. No Cassian." He sighed. "I don't want to go back to the Forgotten Souls yet. We know where Cassian lives. We can pick him up in the morning. If he's the one we want, I'm sure DI Wilde will be interested."

"She'd have him by the short and curlies if she knew," said Josh. Then realising his faux pas added, "in a manner of speaking that is. The boss wouldn't, well, she's a bit off the wall at times but she's–" Recognising he'd said more than he intended, Josh coloured and shut up.

Lucas grinned. "You're speaking metaphorically but knowing Miranda, DI Wilde, she'd certainly want to scare the wits out of him."

"She scares the wits out of me sometimes," said Josh. They both laughed.

"So, what's she like as a boss? Off the record. I promise what you say won't go into my report, but I'd like to know."

Lucas watched as Josh struggled with what to say. Although he had seen for himself how Miranda operated with her team, he wanted some sort of confirmation from those closest to her.

At last, Josh managed to reply. "She's fair and we know she's got our backs whatever happens. She'd rather take the blame than get any of her team into trouble."

"But she's a risk taker?"

Josh nodded. "She goes a lot by gut instinct."

"Rather than the book?"

Josh's expression told him the answer. Miranda Wilde had always acted on instinct. He didn't often agree with her methods, but she seemed to achieve good results, and her team were solid, decent cops. It wasn't always the case. Corruption in the force was growing in certain areas but, despite her dodgy family background, it seemed DI Wilde was one of the good ones. He experienced a sense of relief. He wanted to believe in her ability to do a good job. An honest job. The tension he'd sensed in his gut since arriving in Cardiff a few days ago began to melt.

"She gets results, doesn't she? Like a bloodhound."

"Oh, she won't give up, sir, I er mean, Lucas," said Josh. "She's determined to get to the truth, whatever it takes."

CHAPTER THIRTEEN

"Let's hope he appears sooner rather than later. It's too cold to be sitting around here for long."

Early next morning, Lucas and Josh were in an unmarked car within sight of the house where Cassian Jones lived with his mother. There was an older brother, but he'd moved to London and the father was allegedly working up north somewhere according to records. Mrs Jones left the house at 8.00am and Cassian wasn't long behind. He had a bag on his back and dressed in school uniform.

"Well, he's not skiving off today. Should we pick him up now or in school?" asked Josh.

"Let's corner him now. I'll get out and follow close behind. You go ahead of him, stop and call him. He's most likely to turn back and I'll get him then." Lucas got out of the car and followed at a distance. Cassian was on his phone, oblivious to anything.

Josh drove a little way past, pulled over and got out of the car. He waited until the lad was almost parallel to him before he spoke.

"Hey, Cassian."

Cassian looked up from his phone. When he registered who was speaking, he gasped and turned, straight into Lucas.

"We'd like a word with you. Down the station."

"I'm going to school. I'll get into trouble if I miss again."

"You've got bigger problems than a ticking off from a teacher, believe me, lad. In the car." Lucas glowered at him.

"You can't make me." A look of defiance, lips tight together, crossed his face.

Josh sighed. "It will be better if you come voluntarily. I don't want to have to arrest you. Just a quiet word."

"I 'aven't done nuthin'."

"We'll see about that. Now, what's it to be? Do I have to put the cuffs on?" Josh had no intention of using handcuffs, but it seemed to help the lad make up his mind.

His shoulders dropped and he said, "Okay, okay. Don't hassle me, man. I'll get in the car."

* * *

The morning was sharp and crisp with an edge to the air that caught the back of Mandy's throat like a rough cough. Her head was still cloudy at times, but enforced idleness didn't sit well with her. Plus, it looked as if they had a murder on their hands. And they'd managed to catch the person they were sure was the intruder. They'd struck lucky. No doubt the lad thought he'd be undisturbed. Mandy was just in the wrong place at the wrong time.

Carbon monoxide poisoning had been confirmed as the cause of Mrs Vixen's death, but they had no evidence that it was anything other than accidental. All the break-in had confirmed was some link with The Church of the Forgotten Souls.

A social worker had acted as a responsible adult in the first interview with Cassian Jones. The lad's mother had been informed and she was on her way. Cassian declined legal representation and seemed determined to say nothing. Mandy would have liked to push a bit further with the lad. The sullen 'no comment' interview needled her. She'd insisted on being the first one to talk to him. In reality, she'd have preferred an informal talk outside the station so she could put the fear of God in him without the need to record it. If only he'd spoken to Josh instead of doing a runner the first time.

It would be a bloody miracle if they managed to get anywhere with Lucas sticking to her like chewing gum on the sole of her shoe. Everything had to fit the tick box. Mandy thought about tactics. Being sullen and uncooperative hadn't worked. Maybe she should try sweetness and light? She sighed. Not a hope. He was wise to her moves, walking around as though he had a totem pole up his arse.

She thought of Cassian. Vulnerable and gauche. Would he open up more to a man? To Lucas, perhaps? What had he been looking for in Barbara Vixen's house when she'd interrupted? Mandy touched the slight bump on her temple. It still hurt. The bruising under her eyes was disguised with make-up. He should be charged with assault but threatening him made him clam up even more. Maybe good cop/bad cop would work. Worth a try.

She coughed. "Hey. Fancy a bit of interviewing

with me?"

Lucas glanced up from the document he was reading, raised an eyebrow. Mandy tried a friendly smile. "Cassian Jones is afraid of me."

A laugh. "He's not the only one. You might like to tone down that scowl a bit with the lad."

The smile disappeared. "Whatever. I thought you might want to make yourself useful for a change."

There was silence for a moment while Lucas stared at her. Mandy could feel herself tensing again. Then, with a shrug he said, "Let's do it. See if I can get him to relax a bit. Anything's better than 'no comment'.".

"Hey, boss. Cassian's mother has just turned up, demanding to see him." Josh grinned. "She's not exactly happy."

"Perfect. Time to get back in there. Josh you can sit this one out. DCI Manning is going to work his charm on our reluctant teenager."

* * *

Cassian looked up when they entered the interview room. His mother was escorted in by a uniformed officer and dashed to her son's side.

"I dunno what Cass is supposed to have done but he's a good boy really. Never misses a day at school and singing in that choir at the church to raise money for charity and stuff."

Mandy opened her mouth and closed it again. Lucas told her she should think before speaking.

Well, let him see what he could do to get that little bugger to talk.

They made introductions, Lucas bestowing a smile on the truculent mother and the even more truculent son. He made no mention of the assault.

"We are just trying to establish why Cassian was in Mrs Barbara Vixen's house. How did he get in and what was he doing there?" Lucas paused. "We know it was him. We followed him on CCTV leaving the area."

Mrs Jones sniffed. "Well, he knows where the key's kept, don't he? Did a bit of work in the garden for her and helped her tidy up after church services and stuff."

"Mam. I said, 'no comment'."

"You're not in a tv drama, Cass. It's best to tell the truth. The police won't take too kindly to that crap. Talk up. Tell them what's what, like."

Cass groaned, looked away.

Mandy's lips twitched. Mrs Jones was providing them with more clout than expected.

"What's he supposed to have done then? Why's he here?" She glared at them.

"Entering a property, the home of Mrs Barbara Vixen, without the owner's permission–"

"She's dead. He could hardly get permission now, could he?"

"–And assaulting a police officer in the course of their duty."

"You what?" She was looking less belligerent now with her anger directed towards her son. She cuffed him on the head. "What you been up to? You promised me you'd stay out of trouble."

"Sorry, Mam."

Mrs Jones tutted. Sensing he had the upper hand, Lucas pressed on. "So, we'd like to know why Cassian was in the house at that time. If we get the answers we want, the assault charges may be dropped."

Mandy kicked Lucas under the table. Bloody cheek. He hadn't been knocked out. Lucas ignored her. Cass looked at him then his mother.

"No comment."

Mrs Jones raised her hand again. Cass flinched, ducking away from her.

"Perhaps we'd better ask the duty solicitor to give you some advice before we press charges." Lucas stood and Mandy followed suit.

Outside the room she gave vent to her feelings. "What the hell do you mean 'we'll drop the assault charges' without consulting me? You're not the one who was knocked out. I could have a brain injury or a fractured skull."

Lucas raised an eyebrow. "Miranda, the softest part of you is your skull and that's rock solid. We need to leave his mother to do the hard work. Let's have a look and see what's going on."

They went into the adjoining room where they could see Cass and his mother through the one-way mirror. Although they couldn't hear what was going on they could see the drama unfolding. She was berating him at length, and occasionally cuffing him. He sat, cowering, his arms above his head to protect himself while she ranted. At last, it seemed some sort of agreement was reached, and they had heads together, talking more quietly.

"Time for us to go back in again, I think."

Lucas led the way again, placing the folder he was carrying on the table and indicating for Mandy to switch on the recorder.

"I should make it clear you are not under arrest at this point. You are entitled to have legal representation if you wish." He spoke to Mrs Jones, even though the words were for her son.

Cass picked at a spot on his chin. His mother nudged him.

"What you wanna know?" he said.

Mandy relaxed a bit. She might drop the assault charges if he came up with something to help them solve the case.

"What were you doing in Mrs Vixen's house on Tuesday evening?"

Cass kept picking his spot, his eyes fixed on the table. There was silence for a moment.

"Looking for sumthin'."

"What?"

"Stuff."

Mandy sighed audibly and Cass glanced at her before averting his eyes again.

"That's not good enough, Cassian. What stuff?" Although Lucas kept his voice steady and monotone a twitch in his cheek gave an indication of his frustration.

"Cass." Mrs Jones's voice held a warning note.

She raised her arm and Cass flinched.

"Photos."

It was like trying to squeeze toothpaste out of an empty tube.

"What photos?"

The lad shrugged. "Just photos."

With commendable patience, Lucas repeated. "What photos? Places? People? What exactly?"

"Dunno."

Lucas turned to Mandy. "I think we're wasting our time here, DI Wilde." He picked up the folder and moved his chair back. It scraped on the floor.

"I really dunno. Honest." There was an edge of panic in Cassian's voice. He looked at them and Mandy could see the gleam of tears in his eyes.

"Did someone send you to look for these photos, Cass?" Mandy kept her voice low, unthreatening.

A nod.

"Who?"

"No comment."

For fuck's sake. Mandy bit her lip to stop herself from swearing out loud. Lucas took the reins again.

"Someone you're afraid of, I think. Someone with influence," Lucas paused, "like Father Michael for example."

A definite look of panic now as Cass turned red and started to breathe rapidly. "I never said that. I never said nuthin'."

"Just a guess. You're right. You didn't say anything. You didn't give us a name. Don't worry. It was a lucky guess."

At last, they seemed to be making some progress. Lucas relaxed a little, but Cassian was almost out of his seat, flustered and obviously unnerved by how the interview had progressed. He was almost stuttering in panic.

"You won't ask him, will ya? He'll kill me. You don't understand."

He glanced at his mother and then back at them, raw fear evident in his eyes. Mrs Jones put a hand on his arm, not to hurt him this time, as a soothing gesture.

"You don't understand." He slumped in the chair.

"Did you find any photographs?" Lucas asked, voice calm and soothing.

"No," he swallowed. "He'll want me to go back."

"What did you tell him? Does he know you nearly killed a police officer?"

Lucas was all seriousness now. They had a lead, but more information might be possible if Cass could overcome his fear.

Cassian shook his head and mumbled "sorry" to Mandy. Despite the throbbing bump on her forehead, she felt a little less angry with him. Father Michael was an imposing figure. She could imagine him taking his anger and frustration out on this weedy and nervy youth. It didn't look as though they would get any more information from him today. As if reading her mind, Lucas stood.

"That's all for now but we *will* want to speak to

you again. We'll decide if we proceed with the charges against you. Keep your nose clean."

"You won't tell him what I said, will ya?" Cass grabbed Mandy's arm across the table, an act of desperation. Whatever hold Father Michael had on the lad, it was strong.

CHAPTER FOURTEEN

"It seems Josh's gut instinct about the not so lovely Father Michael was right." Back in the incident room, Mandy briefed the team. "Let's recap what we know and where we go from here. He's a wily bugger. If he knows we're on to him then I wouldn't be surprised if he upped and did a runner back to America. He's still got friends there, I'm sure."

"Good riddance," said Josh.

"Except we have a possible murder on our hands." Lucas was standing at the back, arms folded, a grim expression on his face. Noting the 'we' but not commenting on his inclusion in the team, she started writing on the board.

Barbara Vixen's body found by Barry Reece. Death by carbon monoxide poisoning.

"Do we think this was an accident or something else? What else? How could it have happened?"

"I did a bit of research on carbon monoxide poisoning. It could be caused by a blocked flue on the boiler or the wood burner. If there wasn't enough ventilation it could have accumulated over days," said Helen. "Perhaps we need to speak to her GP and see if she had complained about anything in the weeks before Christmas."

Mandy made a note and asked Helen to contact them.

"Who was the last person to see her alive? And

what other connections? Anything found by forensics?"

Olivia shook her head. "Nothing much. She used the laptop for a bit of online shopping and a few emails. All standard stuff. Marks, Tesco, Boots. Phone showed her last call was to her brother's number late on Christmas Eve. He didn't answer."

"So, we know she was still alive at that time. Good. It helps with the timeline. What else do we know about the victim?"

"She wasn't popular. She belonged to The Church of the Forgotten Souls. Quite involved with it as well it seems. Helped with youth club. Known to many members of the congregation." Josh was reading from his notebook.

"Okay. Who would gain from her death? Who hated her enough to want to see her dead?"

"Her brother, Charlie Forbes, stands to inherit the house and whatever she left unless there's a will to the contrary. Forensics haven't alerted us to anything like that yet." Helen again. "The brother's flying back from Spain as we speak, and we've asked him to come straight to the station. We've sent an officer to bring him here."

Under the heading, Suspects/Motive, Mandy wrote, Charlie Forbes (brother) – money. Inheritance?

"What about the postie who found her? Barry Reece could have held a grudge. A blemish-free career and then some old woman starts making accusations." Helen's suggestion made Mandy think again about his reluctance to speak to them.

She wrote his name on the board too and the word grudge with a question mark. She didn't really think he was connected. He'd just been unfortunate in finding the body. However, it wouldn't do any harm to have another word with him.

"Father Michael." Josh's voice was firm. "For my money he's top of the list. I reckon he could have been the last person to see her alive."

She added his name to the list. He was definitely her favourite too.

"Motive?"

"Maybe she's left money to the church in her will. And we don't know, do we, why the photographs Cassian Jones was looking for were important?" The suggestion from Olivia added to their deliberations.

"Motive unknown – possibly money," said Mandy.

She made another heading. Actions.

"Anything else on the phone records? Or bank records?"

"Couple of things just came through. Her last call was to her brother but there are several numbers she called on a regular basis. I haven't had no time to sort through yet," said Olivia, "Or the texts."

"I can help Olivia with the phone records. She's better at the money stuff and seeing patterns."

"Good. Thanks, Helen. We still haven't established when she died but it's my opinion it was either late on Christmas Eve or early Christmas morning. The food in the fridge looked like the makings of her festive meal. Now, the thing about poisoning is that the killer doesn't need to be there at the time. I think we should find out when her boiler was last serviced, and the wood burner, and why she didn't have a carbon monoxide monitor. Doesn't the fire service fit them free for pensioners?"

No one replied so she turned towards Josh. "While Helen and Olivia are working on the phone and bank records, we can pay another visit to the neighbours. Now we know it's possibly a suspicious death, we need to do a bit more digging. Oh, and Helen, call the GP first."

Despite her throbbing headache, Mandy was quite elated. Things were complicated and messy but at least they had something to do. Beat inertia any day. She grabbed her coat. "Are you coming, DCI Manning?" she asked, on her way out of the door.

"Where else would I be going?"

* * *

Yvonne Hunter seemed surprised to see three police officers on her doorstep. "Oh, I wasn't expecting anyone."

She invited them in. The room seemed stifling as the heating was on and a short blast of unexpected winter sunshine through the window added extra warmth. Four people seemed to overfill the space. Mrs Hunter was flustered. "My goodness, let me bring over another chair."

"Don't worry," said Mandy, lowering herself into

a beanbag, possibly meant for grandchildren or for Mrs Hunter to put her feet up. Declining the offer of tea, Mandy got straight to the point.

"Can you remember the last time you saw Mrs Vixen? You were away for Christmas, is that correct?"

"Yes. The afternoon of Christmas Eve until I got back late on the evening before the body was found. I can tell you now, detectives, I haven't been sleeping well since. I heard it was all a bit grim. Eaten by vermin and it was a violent death by all accounts." She waited, half-expecting a response no doubt; a bit of gossip to pass on in the local shops.

Mandy half-closed her eyes. It didn't take long for rumours and urban myths to spread. Next thing they'd be saying it was a ghost seeking revenge or other shit like that. These old houses were often reputed to be haunted. It wouldn't be easy to sell the cottage next door when all these odd stories became part of the local lore. It was best to ignore it and move on with the interview.

"And you remembered seeing Father Michael going into the house around Christmas Eve? Perhaps the day before?" Josh was checking on his notes.

"He was there quite a lot. He's not your usual man of the cloth, is he?" she said, shuddering a little. "I wouldn't want to get on the wrong side of him."

"Why's that?"

"Well," She clutched at her throat, "he's so big and forceful looking. And, I've heard him next door shouting at Mrs Vixen."

"Just before Christmas? The day you saw him?"

This was becoming very interesting.

"Oh no, a couple of weeks before then. I couldn't hear what was being said but I heard Barbara shouting as well. He left and slammed the door. I did go and ask her if she was alright afterwards, but she more or less told me to mind my own business."

"And her brother? We believe he's her only family. Did you see him visit anytime?"

"I can't say I noticed him on a regular basis. I'm assuming it was her brother who took her to the cafe in the village just before Christmas. I saw them there. Nobody else visited other than that priest or whatever he calls himself." She sniffed and pulled her cardigan around herself. Mandy thought she looked a little jaded. Post-Christmas blues perhaps.

"What about workmen? Did she have anyone do any jobs about the house? Painting, garden, electrician, gas engineer?"

"Alan serviced her boiler, but I don't recall seeing any other workmen. They tend to have loud radios on and always shout at each other, don't they?"

"Alan?"

"I recommended Alan to her when she moved in. He's very honest and reliable." She leaned forward a little as if to share a confidence. "He told me afterwards he wouldn't go near her again for double the fee. When he told her the boiler needed to be replaced, she threw him out. 'A nasty piece of work' is what he said. She had quite a temper."

"We'll need his contact details, please."

Yvonne got to her feet and went over to a

sideboard in the corner. She rummaged about in a drawer before bringing out a pile of business cards. She shifted through for a moment before separating one from the pile and giving it to Mandy. It had the name, Alan Jordan, Perfect Plumbing and Heating. Corgi registered and a mobile number. Mandy passed it to Josh.

"Did a lad called Cassian do any work for her?"

"Cassian Jones? Yes, I think so. He did some work for me too. Digging flowerbeds and the odd cleaning job. He told me he sings in the choir at that church so he would have known her. He's not in any trouble, is he?"

Ignoring the question Mandy continued.

"Did anyone hold a grudge against Mrs Vixen?"

Yvonne Hunter narrowed her eyes and hesitated before she asked, "Why are you interested, Inspector? I thought, despite all the talk, she'd just had a heart attack or something. You don't think, I mean, it wasn't…" She put a hand on her heart and took a few short breaths.

How to answer? Mandy glanced at Lucas. She didn't want to say too much but it wasn't easy to allay the woman's fears when they suspected foul play.

"We're just trying to check things and piece together a timeline and a profile of the deceased to give her brother some background information. It will help us in our report to the coroner. Mr Forbes, her brother, is returning from abroad today. You've been most helpful. Thank you."

As they stood to leave, Mrs Hunter said, "She did

have a cleaning lady for a while, another of my recommendations, but she gave her the sack. She accused the poor woman of theft in the shop. It caused quite a to do as you can imagine."

"And this woman's name?"

"Mary O'Rourke. She's got a job in the cafe now. Such a lovely woman. She's got a daughter who is autistic, so she needs the work. Typical bully, Barbara Vixen. Always was. It was awful. Poor Mary was in tears."

She saw them to the door. They could hear the chain being pulled across after the door closed.

"Well, that was useful. A couple of names to follow up and confirmation that Cass did some work for Mrs Vixen."

"Shall I go and look for Mary O'Rourke?" asked Josh. His stomach rumbled and Mandy laughed.

"Josh knows all the cafes in Cardiff, I think," she said to Lucas. "The reason he wants to go in search of the cleaning lady is because he's hoping for something to eat."

"Sounds a good idea to me. Come on. My shout," said Lucas, leading the way.

CHAPTER FIFTEEN

It was busy in the cafe. The aroma of coffee mixed with cheese and toasted teacake was warm and welcoming. A group of women by the window were shrieking with laughter and the noise went like a drill through Mandy's skull. She was drained already, and the day stretched ahead.

They found a corner and sat down before exploring the menu. Lucas took their orders and went to pay. Mandy scoured the staff for anyone that fitted the description Mrs Hunter had given them. Two waitresses were in their teens, probably students, and the woman behind the till was the owner. Regulars greeted her by her name, Debbie.

It seemed Lucas was determined to be affable, and Josh laughed at some of the stories he told about his rookie days and some of the intellectually challenged criminals he'd nicked. Mandy half-listened as she nibbled on a chicken and salad roll, scanning the room for anyone who could be the Mary they were looking for. Her vigilance was rewarded after about twenty minutes when a harassed looking woman, in her forties, came out from behind the staff door and went to speak to Debbie. Mandy strained to listen above the background noise.

"I'll be off now, Debbie. All sorted out the back and I've cleaned the toilets as well. See you tomorrow."

"Thanks, Mary. I hope Emily's in a good mood when she gets in from school."

Mary held up her hand displaying crossed fingers. She hefted her bag onto her shoulder and headed towards the door.

"Target." Mandy almost hissed at Josh and Lucas. "Leave this one to me. Finish your lunch."

She was out of the cafe fast on Mary's heels. "Mrs O'Rourke," she said, and the woman swung around to look at her. Her face was as creased as an old newspaper, late nights and hard work evident in her sallow skin.

"Yes. Who's asking?"

Mandy showed her warrant card and the woman paled. "Oh God. Has something happened to Emily?"

"It's got nothing to do with your daughter. You'll have heard about the death of Mrs Barbara Vixen. We're speaking to people who knew her well, just to get a profile for our report to the coroner."

"I don't think I fall into that category. Knowing her well. I worked for her for four months and then she bawled me out in the middle of the shop. Called me a thief. And do you know why? I picked up two windfalls from her apple tree on my way out after cleaning her house. I'd done an extra twenty minutes which the bitch didn't pay me for and then she wants to call me a thief over two bloody bruised apples. I hope she rots in hell." The woman's face had become animated, and she was red and panting after her outburst.

"When was that?"

"September. End of the month. I couldn't believe it. Dozens of them there on the ground rotting because she couldn't be bothered to pick them up. She saw me doing it and waved to me. Then the next day she's there all puffing and blowing calling me a thieving paddy as well. It would be laughable if it wasn't so pathetic. I'm about as Irish as Welsh lamb. Born and brought up in the Midlands. Just as well my Sean didn't hear her."

"Your husband?"

"Yes. He works away. Four months away, two home and then four away. Another couple of years and we'll have saved enough for the deposit on a little house. Rental prices are brutal, and I have to work around Emily. I didn't need that bitch sticking her knife in. Can't say I'm sorry to see her gone. The world's a better place without her sort."

The more she found out about Barbara Vixen the more Mandy thought she sounded a thoroughly unpleasant person. Mrs O'Rourke may have had a grudge against the victim, but was it enough to kill her?

"Have you seen or spoken to Mrs Vixen since that day? Have you been over there recently?"

Mary O'Rourke sniffed. "I've seen her. At a distance. I'd cross the road rather than darken her path again. If I believed in curses, I'd have set one on her. I know you shouldn't speak ill of the dead, but she deserved whatever she got. May God forgive me for such uncharitable thoughts." She crossed herself, glanced at her watch and said, "I've got to dash and pick up Emily. Fingers crossed she had a good day. I'm too dog tired for tantrums today."

Before she left, Mandy took a note of her address and employers. She had three jobs, all juggled within a tight timeframe.

Lucas and Josh were emerging from the cafe as the woman drifted out of sight.

"Well?" Lucas was the first to speak.

"We can add her to our list of suspects, but I don't think she was involved in Mrs Vixen's death. She was dismissed for lifting two windfalls, from many, lying under the apple tree. Barbara Vixen watched her do it but waited until the next day before sacking her in front of half the village." Mandy paused. "Why not say something at the time? If it was me, I'd give her a bag and tell her to take some more."

"Some people are not as generous of spirit as you are, Miranda."

Mandy squinted at Lucas. Was he taking the piss?

CHAPTER SIXTEEN

"From what we're hearing about this woman she hasn't exactly ingratiated herself into the local community, has she?" said Josh.

"Hell no. The opposite. The only place she seems to have created any sort of a more positive impression is that bloody weird church. We'll need to follow up on that shouting match Mrs Hunter told us about. Let's see if our plumber has anything interesting to say. He'd know about the dangers of carbon monoxide poisoning."

Alan Jordan answered his mobile on the third ring.

"Hi. Perfect Plumbing at your service." Mandy pulled a face. From her experience there was no such thing as a perfect plumber, but he sounded friendly enough. His tone wasn't quite so chirpy when he found out the police wanted to talk to him.

"I'm in Rhiwbina at the moment but I've a job in Caerphilly after. It's just changing a leaking tap so I shouldn't be too long. Want to give me a ring later?"

"Would you prefer to come to the station, or we can call at your home if you wish, sir?"

A heartful sigh was the answer. Mandy waited.

"Okay. I can take a ten-minute break between jobs. What if I meet you before I head over the mountain? There's a pub on the way. We could meet in the car park." He told them the name of the suggested meeting place.

"I know it. Okay. We'll see you there in thirty minutes." Turning to the others, Mandy said, "I don't think our perfect plumber is too excited to talk to us."

"There's a surprise," said Josh, grinning.

Even though they were early for the rendezvous, Alan Jordan was already there, waiting for them. The car park was half empty and two seagulls stood, sentinels, on the roof of a grey Volvo parked in one corner. They flew off screeching when Mandy, Josh and Lucas got out of the car.

Alan Jordan was easy to identify with Perfect Plumbing emblazoned on the side of his green van. He was inside the van on his phone when they approached. Mandy waved her warrant card at him through the window, and he gave her the thumbs up while still speaking to the customer.

"Another leaking loo," he said in explanation when he got out of the car. He was as tall as Mandy and broad with it. Perfect on the rugby pitch if he played although a growing paunch suggested otherwise. He seemed pleasant enough, understanding the situation in a flash.

"You said it was about Mrs Vixen. I heard she'd clocked it. I was over in that area yesterday. I also heard she hadn't been found for a few days either. Bet that was a nasty one."

There was no reply to that comment without giving more information than intended, something she was determined not to do. A cold wind made Mandy's eyes water and her ears were beginning to sting. Lucas seemed unaffected by the weather, but Josh pulled his collar up over his neck. Another car drew into the car park and the owner gave them a curious look as he headed indoors.

"Did you want to go inside to talk?" She half-hoped he'd agree but Alan Jordan shook his head.

"No time, love. Time's money when you're self-employed. No work means no pay. I don't know what I can tell you. I service Mrs Hunter's boiler on a regular basis. The neighbour, you know?"

Mandy nodded. "She gave us your contact details."

"Well, Mrs Vixen wanted me to look at her boiler as it was playing up a bit. I did what I could, but it was on its last legs. She didn't like it when I told her that mind. Ranted on about workmen and making excuses and extra work for themselves. I don't need that crap. I'm honest. I don't do a job unless it needs doing and that boiler needed to be replaced."

"What about the wood burner?" asked Josh.

"Not my concern, mate. I don't believe those things are eco-friendly like they say. How can they be? All that smoke and dust when you clean it out. Don't think she used it. No logs or anything about that I could see. Told her those things could be dangerous."

"Did she have a carbon monoxide monitor?" They knew there was no evidence of one, but Mandy was interested in his reaction to the question.

"Nope. That was another thing I suggested she should get but she more or less threw me out. I wouldn't go back there again anyway. Like I said, I'm honest and I try to be fair with my prices, especially with the older folks. God knows we've all had it hard, but some people. Well, the things I see," he shook his head, "you wouldn't believe the half of it."

"Oh, I think we would." Mandy smiled. "When did you last see Mrs Vixen?"

"Let me see. Must have been October. That cold snap we had. Some storm which turned out to be a bit of wind." He laughed. "Naming all these storms. Don't understand the logic of it myself."

"What might cause a build-up of carbon monoxide in a house? Your opinion, as a plumber that is."

"Lack of proper ventilation. A blocked flue or something like that. Carbon monoxide is colourless and odourless so very dangerous. That's why we always recommend proper servicing and a monitor." He glanced at his phone, checked the time.

"But Mrs Vixen didn't take your advice."

"I did what I could, but that boiler needed an upgrade. It should have been in a museum."

Josh was moving from foot to foot as the cold became more intense. There didn't seem to be much more they could glean from Alan Jordan. He turned to get into his van.

"I gather you didn't like her much?"

His laugh was a mirthless bark. "She was a vicious bitch. That cleaning woman was there, and she treated her worse than a dog. Once was enough. I wouldn't have gone back in to work for her for a grand an hour."

"One last thing. Where were you over the Christmas period?"

"I was away with my wife and kids from before Christmas Eve until after Boxing Day. We went to Bluestone. Cost a bomb." He looked Mandy in the eye. "You think I did her in? She wasn't worth it, believe me, love. Though I wouldn't be surprised if someone had. I expect there was a queue of people who would have liked to punch her lights out. A nasty piece of work."

"No love lost there," said Lucas when Alan Jordan had left. He'd given her a business card with a wink and a reminder if she needed a plumber anytime, he'd do special rates for her.

"Check that alibi, Josh. He seems genuine but you never know."

Helen rang to say Charlie Forbes was back in the country and ready to speak to them. They had also got a copy of the will. Everything was left to her brother.

"Helen, did you check with Mrs Vixen's doctor?"

There was a murmur on the other end of the phone. It was next on Helen's to do list.

"See if she'd visited the surgery recently. Any symptoms which could point towards her gradual poisoning? Don't take that crap about patient confidentiality. The woman's dead and this is a possible murder inquiry now."

CHAPTER SEVENTEEN

Although the weekend beckoned, Mandy knew, with an investigation developing into a possible homicide, there would be precious little relaxation for her. Even hours spent out of the station would involve going over what had happened, how it had happened and why. It seemed everyone she spoke to held a grudge against the woman. Enough to want to kill her? It was a pretty extreme form of revenge, if that is what it turned out to be.

Charlie Forbes was waiting in the foyer for them. He looked tired, dishevelled and wan beneath the holiday tan. His trousers were creased, and his Barbour jacket would have looked more at home on a farm. His breath was stale. Plus, his spiked hair reeked of some sort of cheap oil, possibly suntan lotion used to stop his scalp burning.

"I'm sorry for your loss," said Mandy. "I'm DI Wilde, Mandy, and the Senior Investigating Officer in this case."

Charlie Forbes looked confused. "I thought it was natural causes? She wasn't too good when I last saw her."

"Perhaps we should carry on this conversation elsewhere." Mandy led the way through and upstairs to a room used for more informal meetings. It was a bit dismal, not dissimilar to a hospital waiting room, but less austere than an interview room. Someone must have used it recently as the faint odour of tuna seemed to cling to the plastic covered seating. She asked for some water and a hot drink for Mr Forbes. When they were settled, she started her questions. Josh sat in a corner, unobtrusive, to make notes. Lucas thought his presence would be overkill so absented himself, to her relief.

"When did you last see your sister?"

"Just before Christmas. We asked her if she wanted to come to Lanzarote with us. My wife's idea. The peacemaker. Anyway, she said no. Typical of my sister."

"What do you mean by that, sir?"

"Barbara always thought she was better than everyone else. God knows why. Our mother was overly strict with her. Kept worrying that she'd get 'in the family way' and bring shame on our 'good name'. She made life difficult for Barbara. Turned her into a bit of a tough nut." He looked at the ceiling. "I was the baby, I suppose. It could be why we didn't get on. It was okay when we were little but teenage years… well, we went our separate ways. She's never been interested in me or my family. We tried." He rubbed a hand over his forehead and eyes.

"When you say she wasn't interested in you, or your family, did you have an argument over anything?"

He sighed. "Barbara was a difficult woman. She took a dislike to Jean, my wife. Despite that, Jean was forever trying to build bridges. Her family are very close, and she couldn't understand why my sister didn't want to know." He exhaled and shook his head. "Bottom line, my sister was a bully. She was a bully in school and in work. She drove one poor woman out of her job and to the edge of a breakdown years ago. She was forced to modify her approach after that, but there was a dark side to Barbara that I've never understood."

"Do you know she left everything to you and your family? We have a copy of her will. She owned the house outright and we are still looking at her bank details, but it should be a tidy sum." Mandy watched his face to see his reactions.

Charlie was unimpressed. "Frankly I don't give a shit who she left her money to. I don't want it. I'll do a deed of variation and pass it to my children."

His manner seemed genuine. His voice forceful. They'd need to check his financial background to make sure this assertion wasn't a cover up. She wondered what else Charlie Forbes didn't know.

"Your sister was a churchgoer, I believe."

He snorted. "That peculiar church. God knows what that was about. She found God in her later years? Do me a favour."

"Do you think your sister joined the church to help others? She volunteered with the youth club by all accounts." Mandy waited for a reaction.

"That's crap too. She only ever believed in herself and belittling others so she could feel good."

"The priest thought she was lonely and looking for a community to provide some companionship after retiring."

"We were her only family, but she rejected us. If some weird church gave her something we couldn't then that's quite sad. My sister was not an easy woman. I'm sorry she failed to make close friendships." Charlie looked Mandy in the eye. "I know you aren't supposed to be candid about the faults of the dead, but I won't be grieving. Our early childhood years were okay, the rest was toxic."

It struck Mandy again how Barbara Vixen was alone through her own actions. It was as if she spurned everyone who entered her path.

"You haven't asked how she died."

"I assumed a heart attack or stroke. As I said she didn't look great the last time I saw her. She was a bit strained and not as bossy as usual. I suppose I should have asked and risked having my head bitten off."

Mandy shook her head. "It was carbon monoxide poisoning."

He sat back in his chair, momentarily taken aback. "Really?"

"Was she complaining about being unwell?"

He thought for a moment, almost muttering to himself. "Carbon monoxide poisoning. That explains it."

They waited for an explanation following that remark. He was staring at the ceiling, eyes half closed. His phone buzzed but he ignored it.

"She was moaning on about a headache. I didn't take any notice. My sister was always complaining about something. Like the little boy who called wolf. Come to think about it I had a headache too when I was there. I was a bit nauseous and thought I'd picked up a bug. By the next day I was fine. I just assumed it was one of those viral things." He rubbed a hand over his forehead.

"It was a bit more than that, sir," said Mandy, with some sympathy. Perhaps he felt guilty for disbelieving his sister now he knew the facts.

Charlie Forbes had little more to tell them. He asked about the body and making funeral arrangements. He seemed taken aback when he was told his sister's body would not be released until all the relevant information was available for the coroner.

"I suppose I should see her. Don't you want me to identify the body?" He shuddered a little and was relieved when Mandy told him they had already identified his sister with dental records.

"How long? How long was she dead before they found her?"

"We think about ten days or so." Mandy thought of the corpse, putrefied and toxic smelling. Not the sort of information she wanted to share with the brother. He swallowed and nodded. Despite his condemnation of his sister, it seemed he was affected by the manner of her death.

When he'd left, Mandy went to speak to the team.

"Mr Forbes wasn't able to add much, except his sister complaining about a headache. Helen. Any luck with the GP?"

Helen shook her head. "She's been on leave.

The receptionist wasn't much help."

"Well, I think we need to speak to Mrs Vixen's doctor as soon as possible and see if she'd been complaining about any symptoms which could relate to carbon monoxide poisoning. And if so, for how long. I want another look at the house," she raised her hand as she could see Lucas about to say something. "I won't go alone, never fear. Forensics haven't found any photographs so perhaps we're looking at this the wrong way. Maybe these photographs are on her phone or saved to the internet or something."

"A sixty-seven-year-old woman? Really?" Olivia's voice held disbelief.

"Some older people are more tech savvy than they are given credit for so it's worth having another look in case there are hidden files or something. I'd like someone to look into her personal history. Her brother said she had bullied people all her life and driven one woman to a nervous breakdown. Let's check that out too."

"Now?" Josh looked at the clock. It was edging towards eight and they'd had a long day.

"I think we'll call it a day for now. Rest up and get a good night's sleep. Any thoughts welcome – tomorrow." She rubbed her forehead. The headache hadn't completely disappeared.

Lucas was by her side. "Aunt Muriel would like you to come to tea on Sunday afternoon."

"Oh, I don't think–"

"I was told not to take no for an answer."

"But–"

"She's an old woman, Miranda. You wouldn't want to disappoint her, would you?"

"That's emotional blackmail."

Lucas smiled the lazy smile that used to turn her legs to water. He held his hands up. "Guilty, your honour."

She had to laugh. It would be good to see Muriel again after so many years. They had bonded from the start.

"You're not exactly giving me a choice, are you? I still think–"

"I'll pick you up at two thirty. Don't keep me waiting." He picked his coat up from the back of a chair and left before she could think of more reasons why going to afternoon tea with his aunt was a bad idea.

CHAPTER EIGHTEEN

It wasn't the ideal way to spend a Saturday morning. Josh looked out of sorts. No doubt Lisa had given him hell about having to work on Saturday. Mandy had no sympathy with the woman. She should have known what the job entailed. The counselling they'd had last year helped to keep the marriage together, but Mandy wondered for how long. She'd caught him muttering apologies to his wife more than once when forced to work late. This morning, he looked particularly miserable. She was tempted to say something but, with Lucas in tow, decided to keep her mouth shut for a change.

Mrs Vixen's house was different in the daytime although the smell was still unpleasant. It would take some deep cleaning to remove that. They could see traces of fingerprint dust where the forensics team had been.

"If forensics have been all over the place, what do you think we're going to find?" Josh had the sulky little boy voice to go with the face. Mandy raised an eyebrow to warn him. Although Lucas had tried to blend into the team, they mustn't forget the purpose of his secondment. Professionalism required at all times, even though it was damned hard.

"I don't know. I'm not convinced this was a natural death. Too many people disliked Barbara Vixen and the connection to the weirdo church doesn't ring true. If Cassian is telling the truth, then we're looking for an envelope or something that would conceal photographs plus any evidence of tampering with her boiler or wood burner."

"Alan Jordan told her it was a liability. It's a pity she didn't listen to him. Faulty boiler and death by accident, don't you think?" Lucas was the voice of reason, but Mandy didn't want to listen.

"No. I've a gut feeling something isn't right. I don't know what, but I can sense things aren't as straightforward as you seem to think."

"Gut feelings aren't evidence, Miranda."

"I'm quite well aware of that, *sir*." She added emphasis on the last word. "That's why I'm here, looking for evidence. Now, either you help, or leave us to get on with things."

She shouldn't have said that in front of Josh. She'd just given Lucas another chance to report her for insubordination or put negative comments into his report. Oh, sod it. She had to do things her way and she was damned sure there was more to Barbara Vixen's death than was obvious at first glance.

Cassian had been upstairs. Did that mean he'd searched downstairs first? Instinct led her to believe anything hidden would be secreted in the bedroom where Mrs Vixen could keep a closer check. Mary O'Rourke had cleaned for her. Maybe she knew if there was somewhere she was forbidden to go. It would be worth asking. On the other hand, as detectives, they were trained to search and find.

Two hours later she admitted defeat. Josh was

right. Forensics had done a thorough sweep. Whatever photographs Father Michael had been anxious to find proved to be elusive. They had searched all the usual places and the more unusual places like the undersides of drawers, even pulling up ends of loose carpets.

Lucas found nothing in the wood burner or the boiler that looked obviously faulty.

"I think we need a professional to check them out," he said. "I'm no expert but apart from a fair bit of soot I can't see a problem."

"The outside flue?" she asked.

"Nothing obvious. It's got a bit of loose netting over the end to stop any leaves gathering. That can cause build up if blocked."

"Damn. We'll get someone down here on Monday. Meanwhile, I want a closer look at that dodgy church, at least Mr Carmichael, our sainted Father Michael. He must be up to something."

They were in a sombre mood when they got back to the station. "Anything? Anybody?" asked Mandy, with a hint of desperation.

"We won't be able to speak to the doctor until Monday," said Helen, "so I've been checking telephone messages. Nothing so far."

"I've been looking at Mrs Vixen's bank accounts," said Olivia.

"Please tell me you've found out she's been paying exorbitant amounts to that bloody church and Father frigging Michael."

"Well, no. That's what's so odd, see. She's got

her state pension like, here," she pointed at the screen, "and she's got a private pension too. But there's an extra five hundred a month going in and I don't know whose account that's coming from."

"Can you find out?"

"Well, it says, 'Relief Fund'. What do you think it means, now?"

"No idea but it's interesting, isn't it? We'll talk to her bank next week. Maybe get her brother to have a look. He might have some ideas. Okay. Good work everyone. We'll recap on Monday."

* * *

When she got home, Tabitha was sitting on the sofa with Luke. Mandy liked Luke. His Dad was in the force and his mother a nurse. Luke was sensible and caring unlike Daniel, the boy Tabitha had been seeing before Christmas. Drama club hadn't started after the break so the pair of them were watching something on Netflix. They both turned and smiled at her when she entered the lounge.

"Get you a cup of tea?" Tabs leapt to her feet ready to head to the kitchen. Luke had pressed pause on the remote.

"No, you're alright. Don't let me disturb you." Mandy rubbed a hand over her eyes and rolled her shoulders. "I'm going to have a nice long shower, get into my slobby clothes and chill for a while. Any news?"

"Mam rang. I told her about your bump on the

head."

"Yeah?"

"She said it would take a JCB colliding with you to break your hard nut." Tabitha giggled.

"She should know. I'll leave you two to your film and see you in an hour or so."

Mandy longed to lie down. The bump on the head had left her a bit out of kilter all week. It seemed the Couvade syndrome only worked one way as Joy hadn't reported experiencing any sympathy headaches. Bloody typical.

CHAPTER NINETEEN

On Sunday afternoon, Mandy made an effort with her appearance. She teamed a skirt and ankle boots with a flowery blouse instead of the usual trousers and plain-coloured tops. A quick lick of lipstick, a squirt of the perfume her sister had bought for her at Christmas, her padded jacket to keep off the chills and she felt tidy enough to meet Lucas's aunt again.

She remembered that Muriel was petite, charming and immaculate from the tip of her well-cut hair to the toes of the designer shoes she favoured. She always made Mandy feel like the survivor of a shipwreck. Although complete opposites in many respects, they used to enjoy each other's company. The break-up with Lucas had led to a parting of the ways so she hadn't seen Muriel for such a long time she didn't know what to expect.

"You look nice," said Tabitha. "The bruise on your forehead has almost gone. Luke's coming round for an hour. We're going to watch another film, if that's alright?"

"You live here too. You don't need to ask if you can use my Netflix account. Just don't let me catch you in a compromising position. I don't want a repeat of the Daniel situation. I know you'll be sixteen soon and you're sensible but..."

Tabitha blushed. "We mess about a bit but we're careful."

Mandy wasn't quite sure what 'mess about' meant although she could make an educated guess. Now wasn't the time to ask. She'd have to sit down with Tabitha again and talk. Tabs wasn't naïve but it would be all too easy to get caught up in a difficult situation. This was the sort of thing Joy should be doing instead of abdicating parental duties to her twin. Bloody Joy.

At the appointed time, Lucas pulled up the car outside. Mandy was out of the house before he had chance to switch off the engine.

"Punctual. Good. I don't like to keep Muriel waiting."

She hoped he'd make some comment on her appearance, but he said nothing, giving her a cursory glance before staring ahead. As they headed up Allensbank Road there was a long tailback behind a caravan. They were stuck in the queue, moving at walking speed. He drummed his fingers on the steering wheel.

The silence was oppressive. If Lucas wasn't going to say anything then she would have to try and engage him in small talk. Otherwise, Muriel would be able to sense the discord. She was very sensitive to moods and would be tempted to think she had two sulky teenagers in her home instead of adults. Lucas had music playing in the car. Not her style, but a safe area of conversation.

"What's the music?" she asked.

"It's syncopated jazz. Do you like it?"

"No. It's bloody awful."

He laughed then, turning his head to glance at her with a smile on his face.

"That's one thing I like about you, Miranda. You say what you think and to hell with the consequences."

"Only one thing?" Even to her own ears it sounded coquettish, and she wanted to kick herself.

The smile disappeared. "Don't flirt with me, Miranda. That boat sailed a long time ago."

Mandy could feel the colour rise from her neck and up her face. She looked out of the window and reflected on their convoluted relationship. She knew it wasn't going to be easy working together again. The professional basis was bearable at a stretch, but this was impossible. Time should have eased the pain they'd inflicted on each other but here he was, insisting she rekindle the relationship with his adored aunt and, at the same time, treating her like shit on his shoe.

She was nervous when they pulled up outside Muriel's house, Ty Newydd. She remembered it from all those years ago.

"Muriel's still living here? It's a big house."

"Yes, rattling around on her own since my uncle passed. Must be ten years now."

"I didn't go to the funeral. Work. You know." The truth was she didn't go to the funeral in case she bumped into Lucas. The Muriel who opened the door with a welcoming smile was still the same, despite being a little thinner and frailer, her back slightly bowed with arthritis. She was as articulate and charming as ever. A little Cairn terrier bounced around her legs and barked in excitement.

"Miranda, darling girl. Let me look at you." She held Mandy's arm as she studied her, head to one side. "A Detective Inspector no less. You haven't changed a bit since you were a rookie. Even the irrepressible hair is the same. Do you still like fruit scones? I made a batch especially."

"That's the delicious smell tickling my nose. I've never tasted better scones than the ones you bake."

With a twinkling laugh Muriel turned to Lucas. "Darling, take Miranda into the front room. Set out the little tables and then come to the kitchen and help me carry the tray. I'm not as steady on my feet as I used to be."

Lucas did as he'd been instructed, leaving Mandy alone in a room with patio doors leading to a substantial lawn enclosed with a beech hedge.

She remembered this room and the first time she'd been introduced to Muriel and Clive. They were the aunt and uncle who had become Lucas's guardians when both his parents and young sister had been killed in a road accident. He was thirteen at the time, away at boarding school. She often wondered why he'd joined the police after university. He could have carried on with his studies and become a solicitor like Clive, or even a barrister, but he'd opted for the police.

Her reverie was interrupted by Muriel entering the room, followed by her dog. The little terrier was obviously devoted to Muriel, trotting along at her heels. She came over to Mandy, sniffed and then licked her hand.

"She's a cutie. What's her name?"

"Clive." There was a mischievous glint in Muriel's eyes.

"But–"

"I know. She's female. Calling her Clive helps. I talk to her and imagine him still here. I'm a silly old woman, I know."

"You must miss him dreadfully." Mandy's heart went out to her.

"More than you could ever imagine, darling." A shadow crossed her eyes, then she pressed her hands together. "But we are not going to spoil this afternoon by being maudlin."

Although Mandy had been half-dreading this reunion, embarrassed at abandoning the relationship after the break-up, Muriel smoothed over everything with her endless questions. They chatted for an hour, while eating the mouth-watering scones, on various topics – about the city, policing and catching up on past lives.

"Lucas tells me you have a niece?"

"Tabitha. She lives with me. Joy's her mother but, well, Joy does what she wants to do. I try to give Tabitha a bit of stability."

Muriel gave her a speculative look before she said, "Tabitha is an unusual name. I had a cat once called Tabitha. She was a menace. Constantly ripping up furnishings, but I adored her." A twinkly laugh. "I'm sure you make a very caring and loving guardian for your niece."

After a while Mandy was aware of Muriel becoming less animated and decided it was time they left. "May I do the washing up?"

"Good grief, darling. No way. You are my guest. Lucas will sort it, won't you darling?"

Taking the cue, Lucas stood and proceeded to cram everything on to the tray before disappearing into the kitchen.

Muriel wasted no time. "I always liked you, Miranda. That Natalie he married on the rebound was a piece. All show but not a bone of humility or tenderness in her body. I told him he was making a mistake, but he didn't listen. He's still got feelings for you. I see the way he looks at you."

Mandy couldn't speak. Lucas had been a pain in the arse since he'd returned. An irritant. Even the invitation to tea with Muriel had sounded like a command. Maybe Muriel was losing her marbles.

"What are you two gossiping about?" The man in question was back in the room, saving her from making a reply.

"We were talking about you, darling. What else?" Muriel beamed at him.

"Aunt Muriel, you're very naughty. I'm glad Miranda seems to have cheered you up."

"Indeed, she has. You must bring her again." A moment's pause. "Soon."

She waved them off with a bright smile, Clive running in circles and barking goodbye.

Feeling full of lightness, Mandy said, "Thank you

for taking me. Muriel is wonderful, isn't she? I didn't realise you were living there while on secondment. It makes sense. I'll keep in touch and visit her when you go back up north. I should have–"

"She's dying. Cancer. She just found out a few days ago." Lucas interrupted before she could make any more excuses.

For once, Mandy didn't know what to say. Eventually she found her voice, "I'm so sorry, Lucas. I know how much she means to you. How important she's been in your life." She drew a breath before asking, "Do they know how long?"

"No definite timescale. It depends on her general health and what the drugs can do to help. She's determined to keep going, as you can see."

"I noticed she was flagging a bit but put it down to age."

Nothing more was said, a cloud hanging over both of them on the way back to Mandy's house.

"See you tomorrow," she said before opening the car door. No way was she inviting him in.

"I'm afraid you will have to do without my presence for a couple of days. There's something needs my attention at work so I'm heading to north Wales in the morning. I should only be a couple of days."

"Do you want me to check up on Muriel while you're away?"

She sensed rather than saw him smile in the gloom.

"That would be kind. I know what the demands

of the job entail. You aren't going to be able to fulfil the role of nursemaid but if you could give her a call?" It was a gentle query.

"I'll go up and see her one evening. I might even take Tabitha with me if I think Muriel would be able to cope with that."

"She'd love it. Thank you, Miranda. And try not to go off the rails while I'm in north Wales. I know you've been champing at the bit to push this investigation forward, but you need to be careful. And watch your back. That DS Gregory has it in for you. He's been talking to me. Trying to stir things up. He said he worked with you for a while last year on a missing baby case. He wanted to give me some background. He says you're difficult to work with."

"He's a shit-raker."

"Well, that's one word to describe him. I had a similar impression. Just take care. Don't do anything stupid while I'm away."

CHAPTER TWENTY

At Monday morning's briefing, Mandy was feeling tetchy. There was drizzle in the air, so everything seemed shrouded in a grey mist. It did nothing to raise anyone's spirits and she kept thinking of her sister. Joy was, no doubt, basking in the sun on the Costa del Sol and topping up her tan while pretending to look after their parents. Tabitha had looked washed out at breakfast. It made Mandy cross to see how her errant sister ignored everyone else's feelings except her own. How had Joy become so selfish?

She referred to the board to see what they had so far. Precious little in her estimation.

"We need to have a closer look at that creepy bloody church without making it too obvious. I'm not convinced Father Michael has turned over a new leaf or whatever. He's too damned smarmy for my liking. Even though I haven't met the man that website makes me want to vomit." Mandy concentrated on the notes she'd made about The Church of the Forgotten Souls.

"Well, he knows my face so I can't do any snooping." Josh omitted to say how uncomfortable he'd felt with Father Michael, but she could see him twisting his shoulders. A sure sign of his uneasiness. Too much Catholic guilt. Well, he'd have to live with that one.

"And I'm not exactly able to slip into the

background unless I pose as a lamppost." Mandy laughed at the thought of trying to make herself less conspicuous. Even if she patted down her unruly hair and wore a baseball cap, her height was against any hope of fading into the background.

"I could do undercover. Bit of fun, like." Olivia's face was alight with anticipation.

The reaction from Josh was immediate. "You haven't been trained and assessed properly. It's against the rules. You should read the guidelines. We'd need to do a risk assessment and–"

"For God's sake, Josh. She won't be infiltrating a known gang of murderers and rapists. It's a bit of low-grade snooping."

"I don't think–"

"Best if you don't do any thinking then." Mandy scowled at him.

"She could be in danger. We don't know if–" Josh was persistent, his face beginning to redden as he argued his case.

"She's got a black belt in judo. Isn't that right?" Mandy looked to Olivia for confirmation.

"Yeah."

"Are you going to clear it with Withers?" Josh had that stubborn look on his face, indicating he wasn't prepared to give in with any ease. There was tension in the air as the others waited to see what would happen next.

"You must be bloody joking. Withering would piss himself."

Olivia sniggered but tried to hide it by looking

away.

"So, you're going to send Olivia undercover without any authorisation or backing?" Josh stood up. "I don't believe it. Just as well DCI Manning isn't here. He'd have something to say about it."

The mention of Lucas was enough to annoy Mandy further. "Stuff that. The DCI is up north for a couple of days. It'll all be done and dusted by the time he's back. Olivia can go and attend prayer meetings and whatever. We just need to get a feel for what's really going on. If we could get into his computer, we'd be even better informed."

"Hacking is illegal. You're crossing too many lines. I want nothing to do with this."

Josh stormed out of the room, slamming the door on the way.

There was an uncomfortable silence. Mandy took a few deep breaths. Josh liked to do things by the book, but he was right. Both Superintendent Withers and Lucas would hit the roof if they had any inkling of what she had suggested.

"Josh is right. Olivia could be in danger. She can't go waltzing into there without proper training and a back-up plan." Helen seemed to be reading Mandy's thoughts.

"Damn. You're both right. Best forget about it all. Sorry Olivia. Another one of my hare-brained schemes. Too risky."

Olivia's disappointment showed on her face. "It would be a lot more interesting than my planned day off. Jaz wanted me to clean the flat. Deep joy."

They all laughed.

"Not my idea of a day off either," said Mandy. "Marigolds instead of handcuffs."

* * *

Mrs Hunter opened the door to Josh with a wide smile. "To what do I owe the pleasure?" She peered behind him. "No others today?"

"No, everyone is busy. I wondered if I could have a quick word." He nodded towards the house next door, still with the police tape across the door.

"Of course, although I'm not sure how I can help."

She ushered him into the house and offered refreshment, which he refused, despite the tempting aroma of toasted teacake. He was still furious with the boss and her latest nutty scheme. Mrs Hunter plumped up the cushions and indicated for Josh to sit down. She seemed unperturbed, settling herself into the chair. A pair of knitting needles with a ball of wool sat in a basket of old magazines and newspapers beside her. Josh produced his notebook.

"I wondered what else you could tell me about Mrs Vixen?"

"Not much. She's not been there that long and, as I told you, we didn't have much to do with each other."

Josh flicked open his notebook. "You said she'd always been a bully. It struck me as odd. The use of the word 'always' that is."

Yvonne looked a little taken aback and blinked. "Bullies tend to have been that way all their lives, don't you think?"

It was evasive and Josh persisted. "It seemed to me you knew more about the deceased than you told us. I'm just curious. Did you know Mrs Vixen before she moved next door?"

He could see her jaw tighten and she took a breath before she replied, almost reluctantly. "We were in primary school together. It was a long time ago."

"But you still remember she was a bully." He leaned forward a little in his seat. "Did she bully you?"

"She bullied everyone. I had pigtails and she used to pull them and shout 'Gee up.' It was a relief when she moved out of the area and attended a different secondary school. But all that is a long time in the past, sergeant. Over fifty years. One has to move on. I don't think it has anything to do with her death, do you?"

She still seemed tense, and he noticed shadows under her eyes but there was nothing further to be gained so Josh thanked her and took his leave. It wasn't much but seemed to confirm all they already knew about Mrs Vixen.

Outside the warmth of the house, an ominous black cloud hovered. His stomach rumbled again. Maybe the boss had come to her senses now. Helen didn't look too impressed with the undercover thing either. Perhaps she'd managed to persuade them it was a bad idea.

He went to the cafe for a bite to eat and a coffee. Best to have sustenance before returning to the station. He sat down and was startled to see movement out of the corner of his eye. A rather large woman had a small dog on her neck, using it like a fur collar. The dog, alerted to Josh's presence, moved and stared at him. He stared back, fighting the urge to laugh at the impish face. There was no sign of Mary O'Rourke.

The coffee, when it arrived, was accompanied by a sandwich filled with crispy bacon and peppery brown sauce. He bit into it, thinking about Barbara Vixen and wondering if the woman had any friends. She'd even bullied her own brother.

CHAPTER TWENTY-ONE

Mandy wanted to speak to Barbara Vixen's doctor. It wasn't as easy as she expected. The receptionist at the surgery was adamant. The doctor was very busy and would ring back when she had time. Didn't they realise the doctors were dealing with a lot of sick people and had no time to see a police officer? There was little Mandy could do about it. Turning up at the surgery was not an option but the patronising attitude of the receptionist annoyed her. With a face-to-face it was often easier to glean information from non-verbal signs. Still, the sick came first in the queue and Barbara Vixen, what was left of her, was going nowhere. Mandy had to be content with a promise that the message would be passed to the doctor who would ring when possible.

When the call came it was much sooner than expected; the doctor getting straight to the point after introducing herself.

"I believe you were seeking some background information about Mrs Barbara Vixen. I saw her tragic death on the news. I'm not sure how I can help." It was the voice of a young woman, pleasant and well-modulated.

"We believe, at present, it was death from carbon monoxide poisoning. Had you seen Mrs Vixen in the weeks leading up to Christmas?" asked Mandy.

"Yes. We all knew her quite well."

Mandy waited as it seemed as though the doctor was going to say more but she just gave a little cough. Without seeing her, it was difficult to judge if the doctor was withholding information.

"The lady in question is dead. We're investigating a possible suspicious death, so confidentiality isn't important to Mrs Vixen. We wondered if the poisoning occurred over weeks or was more sudden."

A definite sigh down the line. "I'm not sure how to say this without sounding unkind, but Mrs Vixen was what we might term 'the worried well'. She was such a frequent visitor to the surgery with one ailment or another. All the staff knew her. I've got her notes on screen now. In October she had a sore arm which she thought was a complication from the flu jab. November was the month for chest pains. In December it was headaches and dizzy spells. Possibly some of those symptoms were a result of carbon monoxide but when a patient presents so frequently, we tend to think it could be–"

"–Hypochondria."

"Exactly. The illnesses were so numerous it was difficult to know if they were genuine or a product of the mind. I had arranged blood tests for this month and considered offering some counselling. Perhaps I missed something." Her voice was laced with concern and Mandy tried to reassure her.

"Apparently not. I'm sure you did everything necessary. Her brother also said she complained all the time. She had painkillers next to her. You prescribed those?"

"Yes. She was very assertive, demanded something stronger than paracetamol." A pause. "She could be quite domineering with the receptionists too. Lucky they're made of strong stuff."

The irony made Mandy smile. She'd rather wrestle a Rottweiler than cross the receptionist she'd spoken to earlier. She thanked the doctor and hung up. Everything they found out about Barbara was negative. Didn't she have anyone who cared about her?

"Not much gained from that conversation." Mandy looked at Olivia and Helen. "She was a bit of a nuisance at the doctor's surgery. Let's hope forensics find something useful."

CHAPTER TWENTY-TWO

Olivia was brimming with a mixture of excitement and apprehension. This was certainly more thrilling than sorting through data. Way more exciting. Maybe a step towards promotion if it went well. She wasn't thirsty for promotion but on the other hand she didn't want to be slotted into a position like Helen without the opportunity to do something more adventurous. But, nevertheless, she was disobeying orders. What would the boss say when she found out? She'd emailed Helen with her plan just in case things went pear-shaped.

Hey Hel,

Decided the cleaning can wait so I'm gonna have a bit of a nose around the church place. Don't worry I've a plan. It's easier to make up a background story close to the truth so here it is. Like the title? Saint. Get it? Lol!

Operation Saint

Name: Livvy (Evans)

Background:

She was new to the city. Been a few times to gigs and shopping but a bit lost.

Lived in the valleys all her life.

Had a job doing cleaning (cash in hand) but given the sack. She took too long and gave back cheek.

Sofa surfing at a friend's flat down the Bay but needing to find something more secure.

Wandering around and someone told her about The Church of the Forgotten Souls.

Not keen on church although she used to go to Sunday school as a child.

At least it was somewhere warm. She was told she might get help, so she decided to have a look.

I'll text Fairy dust if there's any hassle. I'll say it's my drugs. Hope the boss won't be too mad at me.

Liv

Olivia was a bit uncomfortable in her disguise – but Jaz told her it was fine – when she'd stopped laughing that is. She coloured her hair beetroot and wore large loop earrings and dark glasses, despite the foul weather. She was wearing a puffer jacket, short tartan skirt, laddered tights and lace up boots. Chewing on bubble gum as the finishing touch of grunge, Olivia headed to Canton.

From the outside, The Church of the Forgotten Souls was unimpressive. An old corner shop repurposed she supposed. The main door was partially ajar, so she sidled in and looked around. It was a bit minging in her opinion. Damp, mixed with a sort of greasy spoon effect, tainted the air. She couldn't see a kitchen or anything other than this room with a wooden cross and chairs of different shapes and sizes. She wrinkled her nose in distaste.

She'd never liked churches, too sombre in the main, and this was no different. Which way should she go? She looked at the doors leading from the room.

"Hello." Her voice echoed in the empty room – no curtains to muffle the sounds.

Where was everyone? A door opened to her right and a man appeared. She recognised him immediately. Father Michael or M. Carmichael depending on your viewpoint. He was bigger than she'd imagined. More like a bouncer than a man of the cloth. He closed the door behind him, and she noticed it had a keypad for entry. Her senses prickled. What was behind there? She'd love to find out.

Father Michael didn't like being disturbed, judging by the surly look on his face. When he saw her, he switched expressions, putting a false smile in place.

Olivia popped a piece of chewing gum into her mouth, sniffed and cocked her head to one side waiting for him to make the first move.

"Can I help you?" His voice was cool but not unfriendly.

"Yeah, well. I dunno. Someone told me you helped people, like."

He spread his arms wide as if to embrace the space or emulate paintings of Christ on the cross.

"This, my dear, is The Church of the Forgotten Souls and I am Father Michael. Everyone is welcome here. This room is open for private prayer. We do have a meeting at six this evening which you are most welcome to join."

"Yeah, well, I was hoping for something a bit more practical, like." She squirmed, held his look and chewed her gum. "A job or somewhere to hang out in the warm." She allowed her eyes to fill with tears.

"We have a room where people come to meet. We run a youth club, after school hours. Young people are sometimes at a loss, perhaps at a crossroads in their lives. At times we provide shelter and food and try to help those lost souls."

Olivia sniffed. "My stepdad threw me out. Said I was a waste of space. I been doing a bit of this and that. Cash in hand. Know what I mean? A mate lets me sleep on her sofa sometimes but the work's dried up a bit." She looked at her boots and waited, moving her foot back and forth over a knot in the wooden floor.

"What type of employment are you looking for?"

"I'd like to work in an office, but I 'aven't got no qualifications." She sighed long and deep.

"Do I detect a valleys accent?"

Considering she was laying it on thick, it was about time he realised she wasn't local. She nodded in reply, not willing to give any further information. In her village everyone knew everyone else and if he wanted to check up on her it would scupper all their plans.

"Could you go home? You must have family who are worried about you."

"Yeah right. As if they give a toss. Apart from my aunt. She's okay is Helen." Best to mention there was someone who might be looking for her. It gave more credibility and made her feel safer.

Father Michael appeared to be thinking, his fingers steepled and pressed against his lips, as if in prayer.

"Hmmm. How are you with teenagers?"

"Okay, 'suppose. Not long since I was one myself."

He laughed. "And computers?"

"Yeah. Good."

"Well, what did you say your name was?" He raised an eyebrow as if perplexed because he couldn't recall.

She hadn't given him a name but now she smiled at him as if in gratitude. "It's Livvy. Livvy Evans. You got something for me to do then?"

"We can't pay much but if you can help with the youth group and the computer learners, we may be able to find something. On a temporary basis. To see how we get on. The lady who was helping us has sadly passed away but I'm sure you will have more in common with some of our youngsters than she did." He was smiling but the smile didn't reach his eyes. Olivia knew what Josh meant. There was something creepy about him despite the outer trappings of a kindly priest.

"How much?" Olivia narrowed her eyes as she looked up at him.

"Pardon?"

"How much you paying? Cash mind."

He named a figure and Olivia snorted. "You taking the piss? That's less than the minimum wage for teenagers and I'm twenty-three."

The priest's demeanour changed. The affected warmth was gone. "Your greed is unseemly. The church is poor, but you can eat and sleep here if you need a place of refuge. I'm trying to help you."

"Sorry." Olivia bit her lip and blinked, hoping she looked contrite. "Thanks. I didn't mean to sound ungrateful, like. Always being told I shoot my big mouth off too much, me. When do I start?"

He looked at his watch. "The young ones will be arriving now. Disaffected youngsters who find formal education discouraging for different reasons. We have a teacher who organises activities, but he is more inclined towards sports. The less physically orientated like to use the computer. We try to help them compose CVs and learn useful skills. We've only got three old computers donated by members of the church. Nothing exotic like laptops or iPads."

"They'd probably just nick them anyway."

His laugh was unexpected. "You're probably right, Livvy. You're free to use the computers for your own job search. We have Wi-Fi but some sites are restricted. For obvious reasons."

"No porn."

"Exactly."

The door opened and two lads tumbled through it laughing and play-fighting until they saw Father Michael. It was astonishing how swiftly their attitude changed. With a simple look he said everything. The laughter died and they stood, cowed.

"Stu, Leroy. This is Livvy. She will be helping

with the group. Take her to the community room, please. Show her where everything is kept." He turned on his heel and headed back to the door on the right. Olivia watched him punch in the six-digit code. She'd like to look in that room. What was so secret behind that door that it needed a coded lock?

CHAPTER TWENTY-THREE

"The forensics team think they've found something in the house." Josh's voice held a thread of excitement. It was the first time he'd shown any enthusiasm in the last two days. Withers was back in his office but seemed to be keeping himself to himself. Seemed his team, the Harlequins, had been defeated in a match so he was in a sour mood. Suited them. No questions meant no hassle and no need to tell lies.

"What have they got, Josh?"

"A USB in a bag of frozen strawberries. It might be damaged. We don't know how long it's been there. They'll have to dry it out and hope for the best."

"That could be where the photographs are stored. Barbara Vixen was a crafty cow if that's the case. Printed photographs would be hard to keep hidden but on a USB that's a different matter. Let's hope they can do something with that."

They knew it could be days before they had any results, but it was a step in the right direction.

"That's not all, boss. They found evidence that newspaper had been used to block the outside flue to the boiler. A scrap stuck far into the flue. Could have been missed."

"So, I was right. Some bugger had it in for her. This changes speculation into certainty. Death by intent. Let's look at who had most motive to kill her."

They gathered all the evidence together, starting

with the informal interviews.

"Right. One thing we know is that whoever did this didn't need to be present at the time of death. If the flue was blocked it could have taken weeks for the carbon monoxide to build up. Who had access to her house in the weeks before Christmas?"

Mandy stood, hands on hips, waiting to see what ideas Josh and Helen came up with. She loved this part of the investigation when her team bounced ideas and theories around.

"Her brother visited before he went abroad." Josh said. "But unless she was asleep, he couldn't stuff the flue without her seeing him."

"He has motive, doesn't he?" Helen offered while sifting through the documents. "He inherits everything. Who else had motive?"

"Just about everyone she crossed paths with seems to bear a grudge." Josh scratched his head. "Even the guy delivering the mail."

Mandy was deep in thought, gazing at a spot on the wall where the paint was cracked and ignoring the tick of the clock on the wall. Josh's comment had set her mind into action. What had Barry said? Something about a key.

"I wonder if she kept a key hidden outside. Did the forensic team find anything?"

Helen checked the list. She shook her head. "There was a spare key hanging by the back door and one for the gate to the lane. Both clearly labelled, strung together on a ribbon like a necklace."

"What about the neighbour? Did she have a

spare?" She waited for Josh to reply but his interest seemed to be focused somewhere outside the room. She sharpened her tone. "Josh, stop stargazing and stay with the plot. Did Yvonne Hunter have a spare key do you know?"

Josh shook himself out of his daydream. "No. I did ask her. She was a bit peeved by the fact Mrs Vixen didn't trust her with a key. I got the impression they didn't have a lot to do with each other. Strange in a way. You'd think they'd have something in common, wouldn't you?"

"Like what?" The scowl on Mandy's face showed what she thought of that idea.

Josh fidgeted from foot to foot. "I don't know. Women of a similar age might have similar interests. Women seem to make friends easier than men and–"

"Bullshit. Yvonne Hunter seems a pleasant woman. Barbara Vixen was a malicious bitch from all accounts and was involved in a weird church in some way. I wouldn't want to be friends with her, would you? Our job is to find out who hated her so much they were prepared to do something about it. Find the truth. Who had motive and opportunity."

"It's difficult, isn't it," said Helen, "because we don't know when the flue was blocked. It could have been anybody who held a grudge. Access to her garden was all that was needed. There's no CCTV in the lane and the houses at the back don't look directly into the garden."

"The garden gate was locked so maybe someone who came to work on the house had access to the back." Josh sounded a bit unsure but what he said made sense.

"Like the plumber, you mean? He had the knowledge and the opportunity but no motivation. He had no previous acquaintance with her. My bet's with that bloody priest. I wish we had something concrete to make a search. We can't go in like a group of stormtroopers without reason. Damn. We're no further forward."

Mandy chewed her lip as she contemplated the evidence in front of them. There was nothing else for it. They would need to talk to everyone again and see if any more information came to light. Better get the Super up to date before he came breathing fire and brimstone.

Superintendent Withers was staring at a file on his desk when she knocked on the door. He peered at her over his specs and made a sound somewhere between a grunt and a sigh.

"Well?" Not the most welcoming start to a conversation.

"I thought I'd come and report on the Vixen case, sir." Mandy tried to relax her face muscles as she felt herself tense under his glare.

"And?"

God, he didn't make it easy, did he? How to tell him the case was going nowhere fast? Not for the first time in his presence she was aware that perhaps her methods brought her more grief than anything else.

"I asked the forensics team to go back in." Withers sat forward and opened his mouth, but

Mandy forestalled him. "I know they'd been in after my assault, but they were looking for fingerprints. This time they may have found evidence the death was not accidental."

"I hope so, otherwise it's a waste of time and money. I'm the one who has to approve the budgets. What have you got?"

"We're still pursuing several lines of inquiry–"

"That's the line I give to the press when we've got nothing." He took off his spectacles and rubbed his eyes. "This job can be so frustrating at times. Sit down and close the door."

Mandy sensed a chill despite the fugginess in the office. Not another bollocking. Had Lucas given him an interim report before heading back up to north Wales? She felt more like running than sitting but did as he asked, back straight and hands clasped on her knee. She waited, counting the seconds.

"DCI Manning has been delayed. It seems a case he was supervising before he came south has hit a complication. He needs to deal with it. He hopes to be back by the end of the week. But he's asked for any new information to be sent to him so he can keep himself apprised of the progress in the Vixen case." He leaned back in his seat and stared at her.

"We're going back over the evidence and will speak to some people again."

"And The Church of the Forgotten something or other – Dogs?"

Mandy suppressed a giggle. "Souls, sir. We're convinced there's something going on there and we're looking into it."

"How's things with DCI Manning? Any tension?"

The question was unexpected. Mandy was taken aback. She thought of the afternoon with Muriel and hesitated before replying.

"We're managing, sir."

He perched his spectacles on the end of his nose again and peered over the top as if trying to gauge what the bland statement meant. Mandy kept a poker face and looked him straight in the eye. Another grunt before he waved a hand towards the door. She was dismissed.

CHAPTER TWENTY-FOUR

The idea of someone having access to the house was bugging Mandy. They needed to talk to Cassian again. How had he got in? She'd been so befuddled after the head injury she was more interested in what he was looking for. She read the interview report again. He'd worked for Barbara Vixen in the summer, helping in the garden. Did she give him a key? Had he kept it? They didn't get that information during the interview. Was Mrs Vixen the sort to trust anyone with access to her home if she wasn't there? Did she trust Father Michael? It seemed unlikely but anything was possible.

"Helen, do you leave a spare key with anyone? You know, in case you lock yourself out?"

"Yes, I do actually. The neighbour has a key and so do my in-laws. They sometimes look after the boys, so it makes sense. Not everyone has a trustworthy next-door neighbour though."

"Mmmm." Mandy thought about her neighbours. An octogenarian to one side and dope-smoking students on the other, even though they had a rather handsome cat. Certainly not the sort to trust with a key. She had given Kelly's mother a spare though. Just in case. You never knew.

"She didn't seem to have many friends. And she didn't get on with her brother," said Josh.

"He lives miles away anyway so not relevant."

Mandy interrupted Josh's musings. "But you're right, Josh. She seemed to get people's backs up. Except for the bloody church. We seem to end up back there a lot." She sighed. "I wish we could find out what's going on beneath the surface."

"What next, boss?"

"From what we know, Barbara Vixen was a pain in the arse. Lots of people seem to spend their days annoying others but it's not really a motive for murder, is it?" Mandy frowned. "Her brother is the only one to gain from her death, but he doesn't need her money. By all accounts he's done quite well for himself."

Helen agreed, picking up a file to check the information. "Olivia did a bit of background, and it seems he owns several properties outright. Bought shells, did them up himself and sold them on. Bit of a property guru by all accounts. He was right when he said he didn't need the money at the moment, but we'll dig a bit deeper."

"The gas engineer had the knowledge. He knew what would happen if the flue was blocked," said Josh, "but then how many times does anyone check their flue?"

"He also warned her about the danger. Plus, what motive did he have to knock her off? He doesn't gain anything. Helen, did you do a background check on Mr Jordan?"

Helen clicked on the keyboard and brought up the relevant information. "Yes, we looked into that. He was born and brought up in Hereford. Moved to

Wales about five years ago to live with his girlfriend. Set up his own business and works mainly in the Cardiff area up to Caerphilly and over Newport way too. He's got a website with glowing testimonials. Seems legit."

"The neighbour, Yvonne Hunter, recommended him to Mrs Vixen, and she says he's trustworthy. Still, it might be worth finding out what his movements were the couple of weeks before Christmas. I don't see him as a suspect but best cover all bases."

Helen nodded and made an action note. "My in-laws have a cleaner who knows where the spare key is kept. Do you think Mary O'Rourke was trusted with a key?"

"After being bawled out in public for pinching a couple of windfalls? Not bloody likely but we'd best have a word anyway."

The photographs of the interior of the house, now officially a crime scene, and the body were spread over the table. Who had access to the garden or the house?

"Josh, that back gate leading to the lane was locked, wasn't it?"

"Yes, but the frame was rotting. It wouldn't have taken much to push it open. But there was no sign of anything."

"Bloody hell. It's doing my head in. We must have something."

A ping indicated an email entering Helen's inbox. "Forensics report." She clicked open the document and scanned it, her eyes flicking from left to right as she read. "There might be something to help here, boss. As we know, they found a small piece of paper adhering to the inside of the flue. It was a bit wet so they're drying it out. They can confirm it's a newspaper and hope to be able to find a match. There's a number, possibly part of a date stamp."

"Not much to go on." Josh was in grumpy mode. Unsurprising as they seemed to be spending more time on speculation than anything else.

"A date would help. It might cut down on likely suspects. A fingerprint would be better though." Helen looked cheerful but Mandy wasn't so optimistic.

"We'll see what's what when they finish analysis. We can hope." Mandy grabbed her coat and scarf. "Meanwhile I think we should have another little chat with Mrs O'Rourke. See if she was trusted with a key at any point. It's easy enough to get a copy done which would provide ample opportunity for access."

* * *

Mary O'Rourke roared with laughter when they asked her if she had ever had access to any of the keys for Barbara Vixen's house.

"Her? Trust me with a key? You've got to be joking. She wouldn't trust me with a piece of toilet paper. She used to follow me around the house pointing out things and telling me to be careful. She'd tell me something was valuable, like a piece of jewellery and then the next time leave it out to see what I'd do. She wouldn't trust her own shadow that one."

"Was there anyone she did trust? What if she locked herself out by accident? It's easily done. Do you think there was anyone she could call on to help?" asked Mandy.

"From what I could see she seemed far too involved in that creepy church. For someone who pertained to being a Christian she had a funny way of showing love for her fellow human beings. She didn't have a good word to say about anyone. Shame really. People can be kind if you let them. You would think with my Emily and her screaming fits people would shy away from us. Once they know she has a problem they are all full of sympathy. The community here is good. Supportive. She just didn't fit in."

CHAPTER TWENTY-FIVE

Staying overnight at The Church of the Forgotten Souls wasn't exactly in the game plan. When Olivia was offered the chance of a room for the night it seemed an opportunity not to be missed. Only problem was she didn't have time to tell Helen or Jaz, her partner. Her phone had run out of battery. All attempts to recharge it had failed. A faint flicker but not long enough to do anything useful. Must have been at the end of its battery life she supposed. No worries. She'd leave after breakfast tomorrow. Maybe even earlier – before anyone had time to miss her.

Olivia scanned the room. Three sets of bunk beds so six occupants. Only one bed had a set of bedding unrolled so she assumed it was free. The others all seemed to have items stacked on top. A magazine; a carrier bag; an old t-shirt; a battered paperback swollen with water damage and a pair of battered trainers had been placed on or below the beds. Marking territory.

The room was painted submarine grey with the only relief provided by a mirror, speckled with age, and a framed photograph of Tenby harbour. Like downstairs, the smell of decay was masked by a plug-in air freshener dispensing fresh linen according to the label. Olivia wrinkled her nose. She was glad her fresh linen didn't have that fragrance.

Next door was a shared bathroom but in the

corner of the bunk room itself was a washbasin in avocado green. The tap was leaking. That constant dripping sound was going to be irritating if she couldn't do something about it. All she needed was a spanner to fit a new washer. She'd ask Father Michael, or Mike as he liked to be called, if he had anything suitable.

Olivia experienced a fleeting sense of guilt about lying to the priest. If she hadn't read his file and knew what sort of a sleazebag he was, she would have felt awful about the tales she'd told. Stories about sleeping on a park bench and in doorways and how scared she'd been. But this is what undercover meant. The offer of a bed for the night was unexpected but if a genuine case arrived before they locked the doors then she'd give up her place. Make some excuse and scarper.

A noise outside the door alerted her to an imminent arrival. Two girls, in their teens, came in together arm in arm. They stopped when they saw Olivia.

"Who're you then?" The accent was pure Cardiff with a harshness to it. Despite her obvious youth there was a defensiveness about the girl. The other one said nothing. Aggression came in waves from them both. How to defuse the situation? Olivia wasn't afraid of being overwhelmed physically despite her tiny frame. She was more than capable of knocking both these girls senseless but that wasn't going to help anybody. She adopted a friendly smile.

"I'm Livvy. Father Michael said I could bunk

here tonight. I… I've nowhere to go. I hope it's not a problem." She used a little girl lost voice, exaggerating her accent and waited.

After what seemed like minutes the first girl shrugged and relaxed. "Whatever. I'm Ceri and this lump," Pointing to her friend, "is Suz. You from up the valleys then? I got cousins in Merthyr like."

"Yeah. How'd you guess?"

They roared with laughter and the ice was broken. By the time the other three girls, all very young, returned, Olivia had made two new friends. They introduced Olivia to the others and the atmosphere warmed a little.

"That dripping tap is doing my head in." Olivia nodded towards the washbasin. "I'm going to see if Mike has a washer and some tools so I can fix it. Maybe there's something in that office of his."

It was as if she'd announced she was holding a live grenade. The silence in the room was so dense the dripping sounded more like seagulls drumming on the roof.

"I wouldn't do that, see." Ceri sucked in her cheeks." He don't like being disturbed unless he asks for you."

"Huh? I don't get it. What you on about? I'd be doing him a favour fixing that thing."

Another silence. Then Ceri shrugged. "He likes having private prayers with us at times." One of the others gave a nervous giggle. "Depends on the mood. You don't want to cross him mind. Rather listen to a dripping tap any day than… well best not."

Olivia's curiosity was aroused. Private prayers sounded like a euphemism for God knows what, but she expected it wasn't kneeling before a cross.

"Anyone fancy a ciggie?" Even though she didn't smoke Olivia had brought a packet of cigarettes with her. Going outside to have a smoke was a good excuse for escaping into the relative fresh air of the city and away from the already claustrophobic effect of being in the building.

"We're not allowed to smoke inside. The outer doors'll be locked now." Suz was matter of fact about it, but Ceri butted in. "I go out on the fire escape to vape. He don't like vaping either but what he don't know..." She winked at Olivia and nodded towards the door.

Leaving the others behind, they made their way along a corridor to a large window. The glass was opaque but when opened Olivia could see that it led out onto the fire escape. Olivia made a mental note in case she needed to make a fast getaway. There was a small space just outside the window, a sort of landing, where they could stand and smoke. Ceri sucked on the vape blowing out a cloud of what smelled like sugared strawberries. No wonder kids got hooked on those things. Bit like alcopops. Sweet, sickly and addictive.

Olivia lit a cigarette and pulled on it, hoping she wouldn't betray herself by coughing. The taste was foul. She wanted to spit but managed to blow the smoke out in a manner she hoped looked authentic.

"How long you been here, Ceri?"

"Not long. Couple of weeks before Christmas. Mam threw me out 'cos her new fella thought I was spoiling his pitch. Skanky bastard." Another long suck.

"And Suz?"

"Same time. I met her in Cardiff when I was looking for somewhere to kip. She looked after me, like. Brought me here. She's a couple of years older than me. Knows things. People. That's why we stick together. The other three are new – bit like you."

Ceri might have known Barbara Vixen. Olivia debated the best way to broach the subject.

"Father, I mean Mike, asked me to help with the youth group. Said the woman who did it before had died."

"Bitchy Barbara. Yeah. Pegged it over the holidays. Probably stuffing her fat face too much. I know I shouldn't speak ill of the dead, but she was awful to some of the kids. No tears shed over her. I heard her giving Mike a row as well."

That was interesting. Olivia opened her mouth wide. "Never. God I can't imagine that went down well. What were they arguing about then?"

"She told him she knew what he was up to, and he'd better watch his step. Dunno what she was on about. He didn't ask her for special prayers." A raucous laugh followed and then Ceri clamped a hand over her mouth. "Oops. Better not be caught out here. Come on." She clambered back into the corridor again.

Olivia stubbed out the cigarette, thankful she

didn't have to smoke any more, and followed her back to the room. The girls were all chattering and Olivia, feigning tiredness, lay down on her bunk and listened to them. It was mainly meaningless drivel about make-up, their families and the crap life had dealt them. Despite the situation they all seemed hopeful for the future. Maybe The Church of the Forgotten Souls had something going for it after all. As she was drifting off to sleep something alerted her to a change in the conversation.

"Told me with my figure I'd go far."

"He didn't try to shag you, did he?"

"Nay. Come on. Prefers boys, don't he?"

Suppressed giggles followed and Olivia smiled to herself. It was worth staying overnight to glean this information, whether it was true or not. Now, if she could get into that locked room downstairs it would be a bonus. Somehow, she knew the secret of Father Michael's shady dealings, whatever they were, lay concealed behind that door.

CHAPTER TWENTY-SIX

"Jasmine rang. Olivia didn't go home last night." Helen was distracted. "She hasn't heard from her, and her phone is switched off. I've tried ringing as well. Nothing. I'm worried. Olivia is clever but what if something has happened to her?" She swallowed. "She decided to go to The Church of the Forgotten Souls yesterday on her day off. I should have told you. I thought she'd go and have a quick look but..."

"Bloody hell's bells. What was she thinking? I shouldn't have even considered the daft idea of letting her go incognito. You should have told me she'd gone and done something so stupid. I thought she'd have more sense. Bugger. Now what?"

Mandy paused and thought about things for a moment. Olivia wasn't flaky. She was bright and resourceful. There were all sorts of reasons why her phone was switched off. However, it still didn't feel right.

"Jasmine said she'd fallen asleep about ten. She thought Liv would be back later. But when she woke up this morning, there was no sign of Liv and no message."

"Shit, Helen. Okay. Go down to that church and see if you can find anything out. Where's Josh?"

"Here." Josh appeared looking tired, his nose red with the cold. "What's up?"

"Olivia's gone awol. Nothing from her and her

phone is switched off. She went to that bloody church yesterday on her day off."

"Crap."

"Helen's going to speak to Carmichael in guise of a worried aunt. If she can't find anything out, we'll follow up and ask a few more questions." Mandy bit her lip. "We'll have to use a softly, softly approach though. She could be okay. We don't want to break her cover if it's just a flat battery in the phone. After all, we don't know what her situation is. Bloody stupid thing to go off on her own like that. I'll give her a shitload of grief when I see her. Helen, talk to some of the folk who hang out there. They have a drop-in centre or common room as well as the prayer room, don't they?"

"It's quite a large building," Helen was pointing to her computer. "Three floors and a basement. Unusual in that area but ideal for setting up a church and related activities."

"It's the activities that creepy bastard is up to I'm concerned with. If he's hurt Olivia, I'll make sure he's singing soprano."

"What about Withers?" Josh nodded towards the superintendent's office. The door was closed, and the lights switched off.

"He's not in yet. Let's get to hell out of here before he appears."

As they drove to The Church of the Forgotten Souls, Mandy said nothing. Her stomach was a tight knot of fear. This could be the end of Olivia's career, and possibly hers too, if the Super found out but what was more important was ensuring Olivia's safety. She glanced sideways. Josh had been right. It had been foolhardy to even think about sending an officer unexperienced in undercover work into a potentially dangerous situation. They wouldn't even have discussed the idea if Lucas had been there, and Olivia would be safe at her desk. Maybe a few prayers wouldn't go amiss after all.

A couple of streets away from the church, Mandy pulled into a parking space.

"We'll wait here, Helen. If you aren't back within fifteen minutes, we'll follow you. Any sign of danger or any hint of trouble just get out of there. Okay?"

Helen nodded but didn't speak. Mandy wasn't sure if she was nervous or just worried. They watched as she disappeared around the corner. Silence filled the car as neither Mandy nor Josh wanted to voice their concerns.

* * *

Helen took a deep breath as she approached the church. What was the worst that could happen? If she didn't see or make any contact with Olivia it would lead to a more serious situation. Superintendent Withers would have to be told, all hell would break loose, and DI Wilde would be in the firing line. It would be more than a shouting match, that was certain.

The front door was locked so she went to the

side. Someone was coming out, an untidy looking youth. He didn't make eye contact or move out of the way to let her pass. She caught the door before it closed again and entered the narrow hallway. She could smell bacon cooking so followed her nose to a room with tables in rows. She could see a hatch at the end of the room where a rather overweight man seemed to be dishing out food. No one took any notice of Helen. A quick scan of the room confirmed Olivia's absence. She wound her way past the tables to the hatch.

"Yes?" The man stood with a spoon in one hand, a slice in the other, hovering over a pan of baked beans. A frying pan held eggs. Behind him a grill with bacon and sausages sizzling away completed the scene. He was young and looked, with his rotund figure, the perfect example of someone who enjoyed his fried breakfast.

"What can I get you, darlin'?"

Helen realised he thought she wanted breakfast. This must be the drop-in centre, open to everyone. The website had stressed the caring nature of the church and the welcoming spirit of the community. She didn't feel welcomed. In fact, fat boy had a definite air of aggression as if questioning why she was there.

"I'm looking for my niece. She said she was coming here but we've heard nothing from her. I'm worried."

He stared at her for a moment. "Nothing to do with me, darlin'. I just cooks the grub. You need to speak to Mike, Father Michael." He indicated with the slice the way she'd come. "Through there and he'll either be in the prayer room or his office this time of day. He might be in the common room, but I doubt it."

She could feel his eyes follow her out. So far so good. The place was like a rabbit warren and much bigger than she expected. It looked as if they had knocked through to the building next door as there was certainly more space leading back from the narrow hallway. It was all in need of a lick of paint and some repair work.

She opened a door to her right. It had to be the prayer room as a huge cross dominated one wall and the painted windows were those she'd seen as she approached. Empty. She turned and almost bumped into a tall bulk of a man. Father Michael. She recognised him from his photograph but was a little taken aback by his presence. She hadn't heard him approach. He wasn't wearing clerical clothing preferring jeans and a t-shirt with 'God is Love' across the front. His muscular arms were tattooed.

"Can I help you?"

"Oh, I do hope so. I was looking for Father Michael." Helen managed to sound a little breathless.

"You've found him." He gave her a crocodile smile.

"Oh. I thought… I wasn't expecting…"

"Someone who looks like a boxer?" He threw his head back and laughed at his own joke. "Well, I used to live a different sort of life before I found God. Or I should say He found me."

"Well, I'm looking for someone too. My niece Livvy. She's so good at keeping in touch with me but I haven't heard anything for a few days. Last time she spoke she talked about this place, this church. I wondered if she came here. Her phone is off and I'm beside myself." It was true in one sense. As she stood in his shadow, Helen could feel her gut clench with anxiety. There was something unsavoury about this man.

"Your search is complete. Livvy is here. She's a bit of a wild one, I'm guessing." He raised one eyebrow.

"You can say that again. Gives her Mam hell. I'm the only one in the family she talks to. It's a responsibility." Livvy was alive. Relief. The knots in her stomach started to relax.

"She's past the age when an aunt should be looking out for her." It was a statement but phrased like a question.

"She's had," Helen took a breath, "problems in the past. Drugs. Sorted herself out I think, but I still worry."

"You don't sound as if you come from the same neck of the woods. She's quite the valleys girl."

"And I sound posh?" Helen gave a little pretend giggle. "I live in the city. My mother and Livvy's mother were cousins. I suppose that makes us second cousins, but she's always called me auntie."

The extended conversation was making Helen uneasy. Was Olivia here or not? She was about to ask him directly when, screeching with laughter, Olivia emerged from what Helen later found out was the common room.

"Hel. What you doing 'ere then?" To Father Michael she said, "It's my aunt. One I told you about?"

"I remember. She's been worried about you."

Taking the cue Helen said, "Worried sick. I didn't know where you were. I even rang your mam."

"Oh, gimme a break. As if she cares and as for that scrot she's livin' with–"

"Livvy." Father Michael's voice was stern.

"Sorry. I'm alright, Hel. My phone's bust. Father Michael gave me a job and I'm bunking down with five other girls. It's a laugh." Livvy blew a bubble with her chewing gum, seeming unconcerned.

"I'd rather you came back to my place until you get something more... more suitable workwise." Helen was conscious of the priest watching and listening to their interaction. She wished he'd clear off and do some more praying or something.

"I think your aunt has a good solution to your immediate problems. Perhaps if you can help with the youth club today again, we shall consider our arrangement is complete. You will have worked to pay for your bed and board."

"But–" Olivia's protestations were cut short by a look from the priest. She lowered her eyes to the floor.

"Thank you, Father Michael."

For some unknown reason, automatic good manners perhaps, Helen extended her hand. The priest grasped it in both his large hands and held her hand captive, pressing too tightly for her comfort.

"Bless you. Helen. And bless you too, Livvy."

CHAPTER TWENTY-SEVEN

Helen walked past the car and checked behind her before retracing her steps and diving into the back seat. She took out a hand wipe and mopped her hands.

"Olivia's fine. Promised she'd go home to her auntie's flat after youth club. Seems her phone died and couldn't be revived." Helen smiled and strapped herself in. "I got the impression she was enjoying herself. She can certainly act the stroppy individual. I think Father Michael is a creep. He enjoyed seeing me squirm."

"He would. I think he's a nasty piece of work. So, she's going to report back this evening?" Helen nodded. Mandy revved the engine. The sooner they got out of the area, the less danger of being spotted.

"Youth club finishes at five I was told. I expect she'll come to the station after that. But you'll never guess who I saw lurking on the street corner?" Helen sounded quite animated. For someone who was used to being liaison officer most of the time the little subterfuge in the church seemed to have provided some excitement.

"Cassian?" It was a fair guess, although Josh was wrong.

"None other than Tod Blakeney."

"What?" Mandy braked and the driver behind blew his horn in frustration. "What the hell is that bugger doing around there?" She thumped the steering wheel and carried on driving. "Does he know we're sniffing around too?"

"I don't know, boss, but I think he recognised me. He did a double take, but he didn't say anything."

"Shit. Shit. Shit. That's the last thing we need. Poking his nose in where it isn't wanted. What the hell."

"You could give him a ring and ask him. You've got his number on speed dial, haven't you?" Josh tried to keep the smile out of his voice. He didn't succeed.

"Ha bloody ha, smartarse."

The fractious relationship between Mandy and Tod was a constant source of amusement to Josh and a constant source of annoyance to her. They'd just reached the station and parked when her mobile rang. Josh picked it up from the console and handed it to her. The name flashed up 'Scumbag'.

"Looks like it's Tod calling." Josh was grinning from ear to ear. "He must be missing you."

Fury made Mandy even less patient than usual as she accepted the call.

"What do you want?"

"Now, now, Mandy. That's not the tone to use with an old friend, is it? Here I am trying to be helpful, and a good citizen. You aren't being very encouraging now, are you?"

"Look Tod. I'm busy. Say what you have to say and get on with it."

An exaggerated sigh from Tod before he spoke again. "You're hurting my feelings. I thought I'd be a good friend and share with you what I know about a certain priest."

Those words stopped her from flinging further insults and cutting the call. Confirmation he was investigating The Church of the Forgotten Souls. Mandy was conflicted. She hated the gutter press. On the other hand, Tod had been helpful when they had the missing baby problem. He'd been true to his word and not printed anything that could have harmed the family further.

"Why should I be interested?"

"Maybe because you've planted that cute little detective constable of yours in that dodgy church."

That made Mandy draw breath. If Tod knew Olivia was undercover, he could spoil the whole operation. It sounded as though he might have valuable information. Swallowing her antipathy, she agreed to meet. "Okay. Downstairs in the museum in half an hour. It's my shout."

"As you say inspector. Your turn. Our second date."

Before Mandy had a chance to say anything he hung up. Josh and Helen had heard the exchange and were creased with laughter.

"Our second date." Josh could hardly get the words out. Helen's eyes twinkled. Mandy glowered at them both for a moment before she saw the funny side too.

"I'd rather date Trump. Or on reflection, maybe not. Better the idiot you know."

"And you know what they say about the third

date?" Josh was almost squeaking with the effort of talking.

"Fuck off, Josh. It's not a bloody date."

"He's not that bad-looking and he's got a nice car." Helen tried to sound serious, but her voice wobbled.

"Enough of this bullshit, both of you. Back to work. We have a murder to solve."

* * *

Tod wasn't in the museum when she got there. She scanned the room for a quiet spot and sat down. This rendezvous was against her better judgement. She'd need to make sure she didn't divulge anything Tod could latch on to. He was like a tick, gripping with hidden teeth. Her animosity seemed to amuse him. Well, she wasn't in the mood to be amused. Whatever he knew it had better be worth her time otherwise she'd give him the hard shoulder.

She thought about Helen's words. In a different life would she have considered Tod as dateable material? It made her smile, so she didn't see him until a voice said, "Is that a smile or have you got wind?"

Ignoring the remark, she pointed to a cup and saucer. "I got you a flat white."

"You remembered, Mandy. How sweet." Tod beamed at her as if she'd presented him with a large cheque or the keys to a Lamborghini.

God, he was so annoying. Mandy clenched her

fists and took a deep breath. "This had better be good. I haven't got time to piss away. What do you know about The Church of the Forgotten Souls?"

"Always direct and to the point. My kinda girl."

Mandy moved to stand up. She wasn't in the mood to play mind games, especially with this slimy slug.

Tod must have thought she was going to attack him as he put his hands up, ready to defend himself. "Okay. Okay. I'll tell you what I know. And you needn't worry. I haven't blown your little mole's cover."

There was no way to answer that without exposing herself, so Mandy said nothing and waited, one finger tapping the edge of her saucer.

"I've been interested in The Church of the Forgotten Souls for a while. You know, of course about Father Michael's credentials." He didn't wait for a nod of confirmation before ploughing on. "There's money going in there from somewhere and I don't know where. I've got a couple of lads who pass on info. They say he's got a back room he uses for something, but they haven't been able to find out what it is. There's a keypad door lock or something."

"So, I've been told."

"His files are encrypted–"

"Hacking's illegal." Damnit. Tod had already found out more than they knew and by the same illegal methods they had toyed with. Ironic really.

Tod laughed. "I take it you aren't interested in the Relief Fund? He had to skip the States, you know.

It was all hushed up, but he was up to his old tricks. Scamming people out of money where he could; property scams; selling porn; gambling sites; anything he could turn a fast one. We managed to get access to some of his bank records."

"I don't think I should be listening to this. I'm not going to ask how you found out. In fact, I should go before you incriminate yourself."

Tod ignored her and carried on. "It seems there's a substantial so-called Relief Fund in bitcoin. We haven't been able to follow the money yet or to figure out where it's coming from in the first place."

"And you think I know? I wish."

"But you're interested in him, hence your little valleys girl in there." It was a statement and Mandy couldn't ignore it. Tod had been upfront and given her more information than she hoped, so time to do a bit of sharing. The Relief Fund rang a bell somewhere. She couldn't quite remember where.

"I knew there was something about him, but his dodgy dealings aren't my main concern."

She waited for a few seconds to see if Tod made the connection.

He quickly realised what she was implying and whistled. "You think he's involved in some way with the death of that woman, Barbara Vixen."

Her silence gave him the answer. Tod sat back in his seat, rocking a little as he thought about it.

"Really? Come on, Mandy. Scamming old ladies and gullible people I can believe, but if you're thinking he's a killer I can't see it. Can you?"

CHAPTER TWENTY-EIGHT

It was her chance. All was quiet and the priest had gone out to 'tend to the flock'. Olivia remembered seeing Father Michael entering the office and memorised the code. She keyed the numbers in and entered. In contrast to the shabby appearance of the rest of the building, this room was totally different. It had recently been replastered and painted judging from the fresh smell. It contained a desk with double monitors, a state-of-the-art computer and an industrial sized printer which filled a lot of the space. The office chair was the one she'd eyed with envy in John Lewis with a price tag almost the same as her monthly salary.

Olivia wished she'd been able to hack into the server. She'd tried, despite the boss's warning, to do so from the old computers in the common room. All security coded. It would have taken ages and aroused suspicion if she attempted it. For the same reason, all she could do was gaze wistfully at the equipment and check what else was in the room. A filing cabinet, surprisingly unlocked, yielded little of interest. Nothing incriminating anyway. A door led to the back of the building. It wasn't locked either. Father Michael must have guessed that the locked office door was sufficient to keep snoopers out.

When she went through her eyes lit up. It was a photographic studio of some sort, set up with a low stage, screens, reflective lights and stands where expensive looking cameras were poised. What the hell?

She closed the door behind her and set off to investigate. Beyond the screens was what looked like a walk-in wardrobe with racks of various costumes. Olivia picked up one or two of these and shook her head when she realised their purpose.

This side of the building seemed to stretch. Another door brought her to a small bathroom with a shower, toilet and washbasin. Here too was an opaque glass window. It opened out to a yard surrounded by high wooden fencing. A gate led, she hoped, to the street. Another way out.

Closing the door, Olivia made her way through to the office. She'd better get back to the common room before she was missed, and questions were asked. She'd need to be there.

As she cursed the fact her phone wasn't functioning, she was just about to re-enter the prayer room when she heard voices. Father Michael and Cassian.

"Why did they not charge you?"

"Dunno. Mam told them I used to work for her. They had no real evidence, did they?" She could hear the tremor in his voice.

"You're a bloody fool. Where's that new girl got to? Seems she's got relatives looking out for her not like those other little wannabes. She's too old for my purposes anyway." He stopped and there was mumbling. Olivia couldn't make out the words clearly enough. Then, "Go and tell that Ceri bird I'm ready for special prayers. I'll be in the office."

Olivia's heart was thumping wildly. What would Father Michael do when he found her in his inner sanctum? There were two alternatives. Brazen it out or hide? She could hear him entering the numbers in the key lock and made up her mind. She slipped into the studio, closing the door just as the office door opened.

A few minutes later she heard a timid knock on the office door and could hear Ceri's voice.

"Father? You called me for special prayers."

"Yes, my child. You want fame? You want to be a big movie star? Suz has explained it to you?"

Olivia could hear the smile in his voice and could imagine that speculative look in his eyes.

"Yes, Father Michael." The words were spoken with a breathless quality. Different from the girl vaping with her last night. What was going on? Was all that bravado? Ceri didn't sound so sure of herself now she was confronted by the priest. Olivia sympathised with the girl. He was formidable in many ways. She remembered his commands to the lads and their instant responses. Not a person to disobey.

"We need to work on your portfolio. I have contacts in the States. We'll do a screen test and see what they think. Come on now. Into the studio."

From her hiding place in the walk-in wardrobe Olivia could hear Ceri's gasp as they entered the room.

"Wow! It's really professional."

"I do what I can. If this works and my associates like you, they may ask for you to go to LA to do a proper test."

"LA like–"

"Los Angeles. The city of angels and how appropriate. You have the look of an angel. The camera is going to love you."

Olivia could sense Ceri's excitement. It quivered like a bird in flight, unsure of direction. He really was a clever bastard. Ceri was vulnerable. Olivia knew, if things got out of hand, she'd have to intervene. Without her phone she'd be on her own. It wasn't a comforting thought.

Father Michael said nothing until Ceri asked, "What do I do?"

He was all business now, issuing instructions. "Behind the screen you'll find racks of clothing. I suggest you change into something more age appropriate. We are trying to portray innocence combined with growing awareness of... the world." He cleared his throat. "Perhaps the schoolgirl outfit and take off your underwear too. We don't want to spoil the lines, do we?"

Olivia slipped into the bathroom; thankful the hinges didn't squeak in protest.

"Oh, and Ceri..."

"Yes, Father Michael?"

"Wipe all that muck off your face. They want to see the real you. Not some painted doll. Okay?"

"Sure."

No escape for Olivia unless she went through

the window. She waited behind the door until Ceri entered and then grabbed her from behind, placing a hand over her mouth. She whispered into Ceri's ear.

"It's only me. Livvy. Okay? You're not going to scream or anything, are you? He'd kill me if he knew I was here."

Ceri nodded her assent and Olivia released her.

"What the fuck are you doing here, Livvy?"

"Long story. Wash your face and do as he tells you. If he tries to assault you, I'm on it. Okay?"

Pale as a nun's nightie, the girl nodded and went to the wash basin. She scrubbed her face with the liquid soap until she looked about twelve which was probably closer to her real age than the fifteen she claimed to be. She was shivering when she went back to the wardrobe, pulling off her clothing and dressing in school shirt, tie and pleated mini skirt.

"I'm ready," she said, her voice quivering.

"Come on, my dear. Let me see you." As Ceri appeared from behind the screens Olivia could hear the priest sigh.

"Perfect. The screen is going to love you. Now, go over to the spot where you see a cross painted on the floor. Perfect. Kneel facing the camera."

A series of clicks as he took some photographs. For about fifteen minutes he issued instructions for Ceri to follow. At last, he said, "Beautiful. You *are* a natural. I'd like to do a little video now. How are you with that? Not too tired?"

His tone was hypnotic. Olivia understood how he had people in his power.

"No. I'm fine. What do I do?"

As she listened to the instructions, Olivia realised what this was all about. Grooming. Porn. Movies with underage girls. He asked Ceri to open the blouse and then remove it. Ceri hesitated at first so had to be persuaded. He asked her to lift the skirt and expose herself.

"I… I'm very cold. I think we should stop now." The girl's voice was trembling. She wasn't going to be compliant with the order. Olivia was ready to intervene. Then, a knock on the studio door.

"Damn. Okay Ceri. That will do for today. We will carry on tomorrow and perhaps one of the little choir boys can join us."

It sent a chill down Olivia's spine. What was he planning? She'd seen the choir. Most of them under twelve. Cassian was an exception, but he looked young anyway. Is that what Suz had meant when she said that Father Michael preferred boys?

They could hear him entering the office, then opening the door into the prayer room. His bad temper was evident.

"Why have I been disturbed when I expressly informed you no one was to enter?"

"I'm sorry Father Michael but there's a reporter here who insists–"

A familiar voice boomed through the closed door. "Tod Blakeney. I don't believe we've had the pleasure before. I'd like to interview you about The Church of the Forgotten Souls and the concepts behind it. All good publicity for you. A little tour perhaps?"

More mumbled voices and then silence. Olivia crept out from behind the screen. Ceri had pulled the shirt back on and was slumped on the floor, shivering.

"Come on. Let's get you into your own clothes again."

Ceri was like a robot, needing Olivia's help to get up and get dressed. All the time Olivia's mind was working overtime. Should she keep the girl in here or send her out through the bathroom window? Now she knew what was going on behind the scenes she needed to get out herself before Carmichael realised that she wasn't who or what she pretended to be.

"Look Ceri. We can get out through the bathroom window. Away from here. I have friends who can help you."

"No. I can't leave Suz. She's my friend. She told me some of what 'special prayers' meant. Mike has promised her he will send the photographs to his friends in America. Make her into a big movie star." The girl's eyes were huge and filled with tears. Olivia had her own theory about Suz. She thought she'd been recruited to entice other young girls into this so-called opportunity for fame.

"Look. If I'm found here, I don't know what Father Michael will do to me. I've got to go. You didn't see me, okay?" Olivia hoped Ceri understood the gravity of the situation.

Ceri nodded.

"There's a reporter talking to him in the prayer room. If you just walk out of the office and through the room while the reporter's there, he won't try to stop you. Go upstairs and see if Suz will come with you. Okay?"

Another nod.

"Meet me in the park around the corner at five. I'm going to scarper. Promise you'll be there. By the swings. I can help you. I promise."

Ceri shivered. Her voice was a whisper when she agreed. Olivia guided her through the office to the door leading to the prayer room. She could hear the men's voices.

"Go." She propelled Ceri towards the door not waiting to see what happened next. Escape was essential. She dashed back to the bathroom ready to climb through the window. The yard was no longer empty. The cook, fat boy, was standing by the gateway to freedom.

CHAPTER TWENTY-NINE

As she entered the office, Mandy ignored Josh's smirks. He was typing up his report, so she left him to it.

Helen raised an enquiring eyebrow. "Anything useful?"

"Maybe. He says there's something odd related to the church. He's going to talk to Father Michael, but he said something about a Relief Fund and bitcoin. It struck a note with me but I'm damned if I can remember why."

"I think Olivia was working on Barbara Vixen's bank records. I'm sure she said something about a Relief Fund. Let me pull the relevant information and see if I can make sense of it." She clicked the keyboard for a few seconds. "I've got the records up now. I'll have a skim through. You think he's scamming old people again?"

"God knows. He's up to something." Mandy frowned. The conversation with Tod had been useful although she wasn't sure how they could use the information or even authenticate it. "I'm going to do a bit more background digging into Mrs Vixen's past. She moved to Llandaff, or that address anyway, a year or so ago. I think we may need to do a bit more background. See if there's any reason why she moved in her late sixties. Let's find out about her employment history too. Did someone hold a grudge?"

"Yvonne Hunter was at primary school with her. She said something about Barbara always being a bully," said Josh.

"Her brother said much the same thing. Maybe someone decided to knock her off for terrorising them."

"Bit extreme, isn't it?" Josh pulled a hand through his hair and yawned.

"Lisa keeping you up at night then?"

He reddened and Mandy laughed. "You have a look at her early days then. See if any of our suspects," she made quotation marks in the air, "knew her in school. I'll investigate her working life. And her ex-husband. I should speak to the brother about that to get a bit more family dynamic."

"Got it." Helen raised her voice above the background hum. "Barbara Vixen had five hundred every month from something called the Relief Fund. That's the church money. It doesn't make sense. If Father Michael was involved in some sort of scam or shady dealings, she'd be paying him, wouldn't she?"

"Not if she knew what he was up to and decided to blackmail him. Five hundred a month. Bloody hell. We've got our motive."

"But no evidence, boss," said Helen.

"Not yet." She pointed to the clock. "Olivia should be back soon. She might have something we can use. I'll give Charlie Forbes a call. I think he's still in Cardiff."

"I've just had a look at his listings in Company

House. It looks as though he's changed the name of the company every couple of years. Assets are in the hundreds. Odd."

"He might be lying about his financial security. Can you get someone to look a bit deeper into that one, Helen? Crafty bugger might be trying to fool us into believing he had no motive. I'll speak to him tomorrow and see if I can shake him up a bit. Where the hell is Olivia? I thought she'd be here by now."

* * *

As Olivia watched, the cook smoked a cigarette while scrolling through his phone. How long did it take to smoke a cigarette? It seemed like hours. She expected Father Michael back in the studio any minute and if he wanted to use the bathroom, she'd have some explaining to do.

Helen's appearance hadn't helped, except to make her feel more vulnerable. The death of the iPhone hadn't been something any of them had planned for, but she'd hoped to get a message out somehow. Even if it meant just walking out. Something she couldn't do now the way was blocked. The way Father Michael looked at her after Helen left had made her feel uncomfortable. It was as if he could read her mind. As if he knew Helen was police. If he suspected, no amount of bluffing would convince him she wasn't a plant.

A voice from the back door called to fat boy. He dropped the cigarette as if it was on fire and hurried inside. Olivia hefted herself up to the windowsill and dropped down the other side. She hoped no one noticed her as she slunk across the yard to the gate. Locked. An industrial sized padlock ensured no one could get in – or out.

What was the purpose of the lock? From what she'd seen of the interior of the building the only expensive equipment in the whole place was the computer set-up. Even the studio apparatus wasn't up to that level from what she'd seen. Father Michael was paranoid. Wanted to keep his dirty secret. There had to be a way out.

The yard was relatively tidy with bins for the rubbish and recycling pushed to one side. Olivia eyed them. If she climbed on top, she could probably drop over to the other side. Providing nobody spotted her. She glanced up at the windows. She could pick out the room she'd slept in last night. No faces at any of the windows. Time to go.

She heaved herself up to the top of the bin. It was almost full so steady enough with her weight. From that position it was easy to pull herself up on the fence and swung her legs over. As she poised to lower her body down the other side, she could hear the back door opening again. Without pausing to look she dropped onto the pavement and ran.

Her heart was thumping double rate by the time she reached the park. Would Ceri turn up? Would she tell Suz about their conversation? A church clock struck quarter to the hour. Olivia settled on the swings to wait for the five o'clock bell. It was already dark.

She didn't have to wait long. Ceri almost ran to the swings, threw herself at Olivia and burst into tears. Where was the self-assured and streetwise girl from the previous evening? It seemed the video making experience had shaken her, or was it something else?

"Suz?"

Ceri shook her head. "Dunno where she is. When I went back up all her stuff had gone. I asked the others, but they said she'd decided to go back home. She packed up as soon as I'd gone for 'special prayers'. I thought she was my friend." Snot was mixing with the tears running down her face. Olivia gave her a hug.

"Look Ceri. I know you had a row with your family, but do you have somewhere to go?"

"Yeah. My sister said I could go there but I guess I just wanted them all to pay for being so shitty to me. I can ring her."

"You do that. And don't be afraid to report what's been going on in that place." Olivia didn't want to tell Ceri she was in the police. The details would go into her report. No doubt Vice would be interested and Social Services. "What happened when you went out of the office into the prayer room?"

Ceri wiped her nose on her sleeve. "Father Michael was fuming, like. I could see it on his face. The other bloke didn't say nothing to me. He was still there when I left."

"Did you hear what they were talking about?"

She shook her head. "Nuh. Scarpered. Got to ring my sis now." She moved away and Olivia sat swinging gently until she'd finished. The girl looked much happier after the call. "She's going to take me to her place. How do I get to Cardiff Central? She works in an office close by. I just need to go to reception and ask for her. She's going to wait for me."

"I've a friend who can pick us up and drop you there. Can I borrow your phone to ring?"

Twenty minutes later Olivia and Ceri were in Mandy's car. Mandy didn't recognise Olivia at first. She raised an eyebrow but said nothing, suppressing a smile at the disguise. She drove to Cardiff Central railway station and pulled up. While Mandy waited on double yellow lines, Olivia ensured Ceri was safe with her sister. In a few days she'd check up on the girl but for now it was enough to have helped her escape from Carmichael's clutches.

"Well," she said, when back in the Juke, "that was an adventure."

"A bit of a mad thing to do, Olivia. You went against orders. If I reported this you'd really be in trouble. You and I need a serious talk."

"Sorry, but I think it was worth it."

Olivia reminded Mandy of her younger self. Ready to go the extra mile and not afraid of anything or anyone.

"Do you? It was bloody stupid, Olivia. You had no authorisation, no backup and you were entering a potentially dangerous situation. Madness. You and I will need a little talk when this is over." She took a breath. "Now, tell me what happened."

Olivia briefed Mandy on what she'd seen and heard. It was disturbing and raised more questions. Had Barbara Vixen found out about the filming and used it to blackmail Father Michael? It seemed a reasonable assumption. Olivia's little escapade had unearthed more than they suspected and now Mandy would have to come clean about the undercover. She would take responsibility. The last thing Olivia needed was a bollocking from the Super. Withers was going to go ballistic.

CHAPTER THIRTY

Mandy had promised Lucas she'd look in on his aunt, so she was determined to keep her promise. She sent a text to Tabitha to let her know what time she'd be home. It was already past six and dark by the time she got to Muriel's house. The scent of flowers she'd picked up on the way tickled her nose, making her want to sneeze. The security light wasn't on when she rang the doorbell. Nothing happened for minutes although she could hear Clive barking. Mandy was about to ring again when the porch light went on and a rattle behind the door indicated Muriel was there. As soon as she saw the older woman's face, she knew something was wrong. Muriel was grey and almost bent double.

"Oh Miranda, darling. I'm so glad to see you. I don't–" With that she crumpled at Mandy's feet. Clive ran in circles barking and whimpering in turn.

It seemed ironic to be ringing 999 but after establishing that Muriel's pulse was weak and erratic there was no alternative.

"It could be an hour or more," the operative said. "There's been an accident on the A48."

In fact, it was just over half an hour before the welcome flash of blue lights.

"I can't... Clive." Muriel waved a weak hand. Clive was lying under the hall table watching everything with interest. The little dog seemed to realise things were not right and had calmed down after the initial barking.

"I'll look after her. Don't worry." Mandy had no idea what Tabitha would say but it was essential Muriel went with the paramedics.

"Her food, bed and everything, are in the kitchen. Spare key in the drawer. Thank you, darling." Muriel closed her eyes and allowed the paramedics to carry her out on a stretcher. Clive wasn't happy, running in circles again and whining. Mandy watched the ambulance leave and then collected what she thought she'd need. Clive had retreated to her bed and watched. When Mandy was sure she'd gathered everything into the boot of the car, she bent down to talk to the little terrier.

"Come on, Clive. You're going on your holidays." No movement. She rattled the bag of treats and Clive lifted her head. There was nothing else for it. Hoping she wouldn't be bitten, Mandy picked her up. Clive seemed to cuddle into her and didn't protest when Mandy put her on the back seat of the car. She checked the house and locked up.

At Brithdir Street, Mandy made sure she had the lead attached before letting Clive out of the car. Losing her would be a disaster. She opened the front door and called out.

"Tabs. We've got a visitor."

Tabitha came out of the lounge. Her eyes opened wide, and she dropped to her knees beside Clive.

"This is Clive who is going to be our house guest

for a little while. I hope you can entertain her."

Tabitha frowned. "Clive? But–"

"Yeah. I'll explain later. I need to get up to the hospital and see what's what. Can you look after her? Maybe a walk around the block to make sure she's done her business?"

The smile on Tabitha's face told it all. Clive was going to be spoilt until Muriel got out of hospital. Just as well school hadn't started yet.

* * *

It wasn't Mandy's first time in the emergency department but, as always, it struck her how busy the place was. Like a war zone someone described it, with people in various states of trauma slumped on seats and sprawled on the floor. Space was limited. She asked at reception and was told to wait.

Hours later a nurse came to tell Mandy they were keeping Muriel in for a couple of nights. Observation. Even though it was well past midnight she knew she'd have to ring Lucas. It wasn't an easy conversation.

"They wouldn't let me stay with her as I'm not a relative. I've given them your contact. She's in no immediate danger but it was a bit–"

"Distressing. I can imagine. Thank God you were there." Lucas's manner was very matter of fact. "I'll be back to Cardiff later today."

"You'll let me know how she is? When you see her? By the way, Clive is with us."

"Yes, I'll be sure to let you know. Thank you, Miranda." There was a warmth to his voice this time. "I'll see you soon."

* * *

The Oasis ringtone seemed to sound almost as soon as Mandy had dropped her head to the pillow. She groaned, swinging her feet to the floor. God it was cold. Her head was light. Tabitha had been asleep when she'd got in, Clive on the bed with her. The guilt at abandoning her niece was bad enough. Having to face Withering this morning and confess to Olivia going undercover was the pits. Best get it over with as soon as possible.

Mandy could hardly open her eyes. They felt gritty and tired. She wondered if crying, when the Super delivered the inevitable bollocking, would be a strategy that would gain some sympathy from him. Somehow, she doubted it.

The rest of the team were in place when she got into the station. A sickly-sweet smell greeted her as she entered the room.

"Helen brought in some doughnuts. Fancy one?" Josh pushed the box under her nose. Her stomach heaved at the sugar scent.

"Got to go and see Withers. The information Olivia has discovered is relevant to our murder inquiry, but Vice will need to be informed too. He's not going to like the undercover bit."

A sigh.

"And, by the way, DCI Manning is back today. His aunt is ill." She didn't tell them about the hours spent pacing in the hospital, the conversation with Lucas or the two hours' sleep she'd enjoyed before the alarm brought her back to reality. Mandy straightened her back, brushed down her jacket and patted down her hair before marching to the Super's office and knocking on the door.

"Come."

The lump in Mandy's chest expanded. This was it. Come clean. Take the banshee yells and grovel.

"DCI Manning expects to be back later today. He told me what happened and expressed his gratitude. Well done." The Super had a benevolent look on his face.

Oh God. It was going to be worse than she expected. Her voice seemed to be strangled when she managed to speak.

"Sir–"

"You've been up half the night, Wilde. Sit down before you fall down. What do you need to tell me?"

Mandy closed the door and sat. In a flat tone she explained the undercover operation taking full responsibility for what had happened. How they discussed the possibility of sending someone in undercover. How it had been discounted because of the potential dangers involved. How DC Wyglendacz decided to take the initiative and go incognito to the church. Mandy stressed the importance of the intelligence gained and waited.

Withers said nothing for minutes, his head

rocking backwards and forwards as he glared at her over his specs. That was scary. Shouting was expected. Withering in quiet mode was dangerous. Much more threatening. Mandy could hardly breathe. At last, he broke the silence.

"Have I understood correctly? Are you telling me a constable, untrained in undercover work, snooped around a community church with no prior evidence there was anything to uncover in the first place?" A calm controlled and quiet tone.

"Yes, sir." Was that squeaky voice hers?

Another long silence. Mandy watched fascinated as the Super's nostrils flared, and his eyes bulged.

Then an explosion. "What the hell did she think she was doing? I know you use unorthodox methods at times, Wilde, but this is beyond comprehension. I could have you thrown off the force. A junior officer put herself in danger without any permission. Without any information being shared with you or your superior officer. It's beyond belief. You're supposed to set a good example to your team; not encourage them to follow some half-baked scheme because you've got a hunch. A young officer put herself in danger because she witnesses your maverick ways on a daily basis and thinks it's how the force works. This is your fault. Get out!"

Mandy almost ran out of the office. The team was standing open-mouthed.

"You heard it all?" It was a redundant question.

"I expect the whole station heard. It's a wonder

he hasn't had a stroke." Josh was concerned. They were used to the odd rant, but Withers had surpassed any previous reprimands by miles.

Mandy slumped into a chair. "If he calls in Professional Standards, I'll probably be thrown off the Force."

"I don't think he'll do that. After all it worked. We've got inside information about The Church of the Forgotten Souls and the shady operation. Thankfully Livvy didn't hack the computer as well." Josh seemed to be on her side this time.

Mandy groaned. "I'm sorry. I suppose we'd better carry on with the investigation until he decides what to do with me."

"Are Vice going to look into the child pornography thing?" asked Helen.

"It seems they were already alerted and were keeping an eye on the place. They'll go in and seize the equipment later today and talk to everyone involved."

"What if he's our killer, now? They aren't taking over our case? That's not fair." Olivia sounded indignant.

"Priority for us is finding Barbara Vixen's killer. We have no evidence to link Mr Creepy Carmichael with her death. Anything on that USB we found?"

"Naw. Corrupted it was." Olivia shrugged. She was more subdued than usual since Mandy had spoken to her about her lack of judgement. Shocked as well, no doubt, knowing that the screaming match she'd just heard should have been directed towards her.

"No evidence. No case unless he confesses. I think that bogus priest is a sleazeball, but I'm also inclined to think he may not be our killer after all. We need to find out what hold she had over him. You don't give five hundred a month to someone who helps out with the youth club." Mandy sighed, long and deep. "There are too many threads unravelling in this case. Too many possibilities."

CHAPTER THIRTY-ONE

Charlie Forbes was staying in an Airbnb in the Bay. He didn't want to stay in a hotel, preferring a bit of space. Not that there was a lot of that in the tiny flat. Minimalist. Muslin drapes covered the windows making it seem dark and drab and the prints of dead movie stars on the walls did little to cheer the place up.

Mandy could smell fresh-brewed coffee and knew Josh would accept when it was offered. She declined and settled herself on a dining chair, turning it around to face Charlie who had taken a place on a cord-covered sofa. Josh lowered himself into what looked like a deckchair which creaked. His eyes widened in alarm, but it held firm.

"We thought we'd keep you up to date on the investigation so far and perhaps get a bit more background information from you, sir."

Charlie sipped his coffee gazing at her over the top of a mug with the slogan 'You're the best!' emblazoned on the outside.

"Why is that relevant?"

"Your sister seemed to have a reputation for assertiveness–"

His laughter interrupted Mandy's words. "I told you my sister was a bully. Right from primary school she had to be the leader. If she'd been born a man, she'd probably have been one of those gangland leaders. You wouldn't want to cross her. I never heard her express remorse over anything she did either."

"I see. Is that why you moved to Hereford?" asked Mandy.

"Oh, I didn't move there. She moved away. Anything to avoid being involved in caring for our elderly parents. My mother was a tough cookie too."

The bitterness in his voice was clear. Mandy was confused. Yvonne Hunter said she was in school with Barbara, but Yvonne had always lived in South Wales.

"I thought you were both from Wales."

He nodded. "It's a long story. We were both born and brought up in South Wales. When Barbara was ten my father had the chance of a better job, so we moved to Hereford. I loved it. She hated it. She was teased about her accent at first. She soon put stop to that."

There was a sense that he wanted to elaborate so they waited. "One of the girls in her secondary school had a bit of a reputation for being a bully." A slight smile as he remembered. "Until she met my sister. The school took them for swimming lessons every week. Barbara nearly drowned the other girl. Held her under the water until she went limp."

"Didn't the teacher intervene?"

"She didn't see anything until Barbara screamed that Milly needed help. Barbara helped to get the girl out of the pool and was treated like a hero. Poor Milly was so shocked she gave her a wide berth after that."

Josh leaned forward to ask a question and the

chair creaked as the legs moved on the wooden floor.

"Did Milly not tell everyone what Barbara did to her?"

"It seems she was too scared. Barbara told her she'd kill her next time if she told anyone. She was proud of standing up for herself. Milly moved schools not long after." He sipped his coffee.

"And your sister became queen bee."

"Exactly." He smiled. "Not long after she finished A levels, she left home. She could see my mother was ailing and didn't want the responsibility of looking after Dad. She applied for an admin job with some law firm in Swansea and off she went. It was a relief to be honest."

"Did she do well in her exams?"

"Yes. She was clever. She could easily have gone to university, but I think she wanted her independence. She really wanted to get away from mother."

The picture they were building of Barbara Vixen was fascinating.

"When we last talked, you said the deep animosity between you came after you were married. Is that correct?"

"She didn't like Jean, my wife. But by that time, she didn't like me much either."

"Was there a reason?" asked Mandy.

"I think she was jealous. I went to university and did a degree. Then I set up my own business designing websites and IT provision for companies, plus a bit of property management. As the company grew and became more successful, she became more envious." He sighed. "Even after she married Chris. There was always tension in the air on the odd occasion we did meet up."

Mandy glanced at Josh. He was busy making notes and action points while they talked. He checked his notebook, "Christopher Vixen. Divorced. Do you have a current address?"

"Australia somewhere. Perth maybe" He shook his head. "It lasted less than three years. She made his life hell. He was such a nice bloke too. I thought he'd knock the edges off her, but it turns out she bossed him around so much he left. She got a good lawyer and ended up with the house, the car and everything. He was virtually penniless."

"Why didn't he oppose the settlement? Appeal." Josh was interested now. The previous year it had looked as if his marriage was going to end.

"Poor guy was so ground down by that point he just wanted out. He was lucky to escape."

Partners and ex-partners were often the one most likely to be the perpetrator in a killing. Imagine going to the other side of the world to avoid an ex, thought Mandy. Did Barbara have any redeeming features?

"You also said she'd bullied some woman into a nervous breakdown. Really?"

Charlie tapped his fingers against the side of his mug. "She was proud of herself as well. It was a long time ago. She moved from the Swansea office and there was a promotion in the offing. Barbara knew she was in with a chance. One of the others, who had just joined the firm, had a degree and was studying for some other qualification. She was a threat." He made a sort of puffing noise as he told the story. "Barbara undermined her in all sorts of ways. She started making up stories behind her back. She made comments to this woman about not fitting in and asides about the poor quality of her work. All this when no one else was around, mind you. No witnesses. When the woman complained she laughed in her face. No remorse. Crowing about it."

"What happened?"

"The poor woman became so anxious and depressed she had a complete breakdown. My sister got the job. I was appalled when she told me. 'All's fair in work and play,' she said. As if it was all a game. I think it was to her. She didn't care about other people's lives."

He put his mug down on the floor beside the sofa. "Now you know why I'm not sorry she's gone. She was clever and had the potential to do some good in the world. Maybe working for this odd church was her penance for a lifetime of nasty behaviour. Who can tell?"

CHAPTER THIRTY-TWO

When they got back to base, Mandy was surprised to see Lucas. He looked weary. She wanted to ask him about Muriel, but not in front of the team. Too personal. He probably didn't want to share his private life with people he didn't know that well. Instead, she called them together to disclose what they had gleaned from the interview with Charlie.

Olivia was back at her desk looking her normal self although Mandy thought she acted now with a little more confidence. She had confessed to a feeling that she could be interested in working in Vice sometime in the future. A chance to make a difference. She'd certainly made a difference to Ceri's life.

"It's a long shot," Mandy told them, "but there's a slim possibility someone from Barbara Vixen's past has somehow caught up with her."

"Karma, it is," said Olivia.

"Whatever. We need to look a bit deeper. She bullied a girl in school. Well, more than bullied her."

"According to Charlie, she almost drowned a girl called Milly in secondary school. That was when they were living in Hereford about fifty years ago. Could be some sort of connection there." Josh sounded doubtful. It was history as far as he was concerned. Long before any of them were born.

"Well, they say revenge is best served cold," said

Helen. "Hang on a minute. Didn't that plumber say he'd moved from Hereford?"

"Alan Jordan. Yes. You're right. He's in his forties. I suppose it's conceivable he had an older sister bullied by Barbara. Plus, he had the knowledge and access to the house," said Mandy. "See what you can find out, Helen. Maybe we need another word with him."

Mandy drew a question mark beside his name on the board and wrote 'sister – victim?' It was good to have something to pursue.

"Mr Forbes also mentioned again the woman his sister bulled into a nervous breakdown. No names to go on, but we know it was someone she worked with in the Cardiff office." She gave them the name of the law firm. "This woman had a degree and was tipped for the office manager role that Barbara wanted. She got the job after the woman left. No other opposition."

"What? They gave her promotion after she'd driven someone to a breakdown. Well, that's one firm not to use now, innit?"

"Come on, Olivia. Bullying is part of the culture in lots of workplaces." As she spoke, Mandy recalled DS Gregory's threats and attempts to undermine her. It was said the only way to deal with a bully was to stand up to them and hope they would stop. She hoped it was right. It seemed it hadn't worked for Barbara's victims. "Can you find out where she was working? She started a job in Swansea, would have been around 1970s, I suppose. Transferred to Cardiff a few years later. I'm assuming it was the same firm she has her occupational pension from."

"Bit of a wild goose chase all this, isn't it?" Lucas spoke quietly but his words carried.

"Maybe, sir, but we need to explore these possibilities. Father Michael is still my favourite. She was blackmailing him."

"Has he been interviewed yet?"

Withers appeared like the ghost of Christmas past interrupting the discussion.

"I've had word. It was from a DCI whose team in Vice was keeping an eye on that church place. It seems your Mr Carmichael has scarpered. Must have got wind we were after him and done a runner. It appears he took a private jet to Amsterdam last night and from there to God knows where. He had this planned it seems. He didn't even use an alias. So, not a hope of getting him anytime soon."

"Bugger."

"Wilde?"

"Sorry, sir. How did that happen?"

"Good question. It seems he was spooked by something and decided to take his leave of the so-called Church of the Forgotten Souls. The team from Vice isn't happy."

Mandy took a deep breath. Was he accusing her of something? She tried to distract his train of thought.

"We were just exploring other possibilities, other suspects, for the murder, sir."

Withers gave her a look and turned towards Lucas. Something unspoken passed between them and Lucas gave an almost imperceptible nod.

"Sort it. Now. We need something to redeem ourselves." Withers threw the words over his shoulder as he stomped out of the room. They all seemed to be holding their breath.

At last, Olivia spoke. "When I left, Father Michael was talking to that reporter guy. Do you think–?"

"I don't think Blakeney would give him the heads up. He's a shit but not that corrupt. But something, or someone, spooked Carmichael. If Tod Blakeney had anything to do with that–"

"You'll roast his balls on a platter." Lucas was half-smiling as he said the words. "Isn't that your form?"

"Maybe I'll just cut them off and feed them to him, slice by slice."

Mandy could feel her blood pressure rising as she thought about it. Maybe Olivia's presence had been recognised. Or possibly Helen looked more like a cop than a desperately worried aunt. But, if Tod was there and Carmichael disappeared not long after, she had to know what went on. Mandy grabbed the phone and dialled.

"Mandy." Tod sounded delighted. "How lovely."

Mandy pressed the button, so they were on speaker phone. The others stood waiting to hear what Tod had to say.

"Don't you give me your smolt, you arsehole. What did you tell Carmichael?"

"Tell him? What are you talking about? It was an interview. I was doing the questioning. What's got you so annoyed?"

"The bugger's skipped the country and you were talking to him not long before that happened. So, I'm going to ask you again. What did you tell him?"

"Hey, Mandy. You've got the wrong end of the stick. I was trying to deflect him from your little mole. I asked for an interview. I said I wanted to do an article on the church and how it was filling a much-needed gap in society."

"Don't give me any bullshit, Tod. I'm not in the mood."

"I promise I did nothing to indicate we were on to him. He was very open until I asked how the church was financed and if he'd asked for council funding or lottery money. He was a bit reluctant to say much. Then a young girl came out of his office looking a bit flushed. It seemed to throw him off balance a bit. The interview finished not long after. I had a little scout around, but the place seemed quiet – even the drop-in centre. I didn't see your little mole. Is she okay?"

Mandy slammed the phone down. She didn't know what to believe but she didn't believe in coincidences.

"You should try to keep on the side of the press. You never know when they might come in useful." Lucas seemed to be serious. As if he'd know.

CHAPTER THIRTY-THREE

"I've spoken to the firm Barbara worked for." Helen put the phone down before speaking to Mandy. "Seems she retired at sixty-three even though she didn't get her state pension then. She sold the house in Radyr about a year later and rented for a while before she bought the Llandaff property."

"Can we find out about the rental? Any disputes with neighbours? Problems with the landlord? Anything which could give rise to a killing."

"Sure, boss. I'll get onto it."

"I think I might have found Milly." Josh looked up from his screen. "We know which town in Herefordshire they lived in. There's only one secondary within a ten-mile radius."

"Unless she went to private school."

Josh didn't argue but ignored the remark. "They don't have a list of past pupils on the website, but they do have photographs of the teams. The swimming team has a Millicent Jenners in what was Form One, Year Seven now, but she doesn't appear in any of the later pictures."

"Maybe she wasn't good enough to make the team."

"All the others are there, including Barba Vixen. I think it's Milly. I thought I'd give them a ring and see if there's anything they can tell me." Josh seemed convinced he was on to something.

"Bloody good luck with that one. Most of the staff will be dead I'd imagine. This is like working on a cold case."

Undeterred, Josh rang the school. They could hear him mumbling away and scribbling something down on a piece of paper. He finished his conversation and was jubilant.

"Not totally fruitless after all. The secretary has a house in the village and has lived there all her life. She knows the former deputy head. Says she's been there since the year dot. Miss Ruth Peters. She said she couldn't give me her telephone number, but I do have an address. Should be able to trace her." His expression said, 'told you so'. He settled down to find Ruth Peters' contact number.

"Nice one, Josh," said Olivia. "This is interesting, boss. Charlie has recently remortgaged one of his houses. Seems he needed some ready dosh. Makes you wonder, don't it now?"

"It certainly does. Forensics turn up anything else? Fingerprints on the newspaper for example? That would be very useful."

Olivia shook her head. "Apart from identifying it was The Western Mail there was nothing."

"And God knows how many people in Llandaff buy that paper." Mandy rubbed her forehead. She glanced over to Lucas. "Any gems of wisdom? Sir."

"I think you are pursuing too many lines of inquiry. Means, motive and opportunity. Why chase old enemies? How could something that happened fifty years ago have an impact on a recent killing?"

"With respect, we've reached an impasse. Carmichael has done a bunk, so all suspicion is on him. I can't see him as a killer. And I don't see her giving him access to her home without watching him like the proverbial hawk. Okay, I agree, the Hereford connection is a wild card, but you never know."

Josh hadn't heard their conversation as he was on the telephone again. They listened as he reasoned with the person on the line.

"Yes. I do realise it could be a scam. You are quite right to be suspicious, Miss Peters. How about I give you the police station number? You can ring the switchboard and ask to be put through to DS Josh Jones. Yes, it is a common name. You check it out and ring me back. That's fine. Thank you, ma'am." He put the phone down and then hit the palm of his hand on his forehead. "I blame the television. They have old folk so scared they trust no one."

"Better that way. It's good she's on the ball. I keep warning my parents not to respond if they get unusual phone calls," said Helen. "What age is she?"

"Nearly eighty and as sharp as a shark's tooth."

They laughed as the phone rang again.

"Ah, Miss Peters. Thank you for ringing back." He flicked to speaker phone. "We are investigating the death of a former pupil of yours. It would have been quite a long time ago. Nineteen sixties."

"Ancient history." She chuckled. "Or so I'm told. Seems like yesterday."

"We've been informed there was an incident between two of your pupils in the swimming pool. A near drowning. The girls involved were–"

"Millicent and Barbara. My goodness. It was my second year of teaching. I didn't see what happened. One of the others had got out of her depth and was screaming the place down."

"But you remember the incident?"

"Indeed. Barbara was quite a big girl and Millicent almost her equal. The first I knew was when Barbara yelled for help. She was pulling Millicent into the shallow end and the poor child appeared to be unconscious."

"What do you think happened?" asked Josh. "I believe there was quite a fuss."

"A fuss." A brittle laugh. "My dear young man, you have no idea. I was terrified. Nearly had a heart attack. I administered CPR and Millicent was alright."

Josh cleared his throat. "Was that the end of it?"

"Good grief, not at all. There were rumours that Millicent had accused Barbara of trying to drown her. I hadn't witnessed anything and there was a conspiracy of silence between the other girls. I think they were afraid of Barbara. She did like to throw her weight about. Millicent's parents put her in a private school after that. I believe the family moved to Scotland after a couple of years. No, not Scotland. Canada. So why do you want to know all this past history?"

"We are investigating the death of Mrs Barbara Vixen. You knew her as Barbara Forbes. We thought her death could be linked to something untoward in her past."

"Is it a murder investigation? How exciting. I suppose I should be surprised or upset at hearing about the death of a former pupil. A few of them have dropped off the perch but I'm still here. Carpe Diem. Seize the day." She sounded quite cheerful, and they reckoned she'd be gossiping with her friends and neighbours before the day was out.

"Another dead end." Mandy wrote 'no known connections' beside Alan Jordan's name. She was relieved. Good plumbers were hard to find.

CHAPTER THIRTY-FOUR

"Someone to see you."

Out in the kitchen, radio playing, and about to prepare the evening meal, Mandy didn't hear the doorbell. It was Tabitha who alerted her to their visitor.

"He's in the lounge." Tabitha indicated with a thumb to the tall shadow standing in the bay window. Lucas.

"How?"

"He said you'd want to see him. Your friend." Tabitha was all innocence.

That was a matter of opinion, although she had asked Lucas to keep her informed about Muriel's progress. She hoped it wasn't bad news, otherwise why hadn't he rung? Her stomach lurched.

"Lucas?"

He turned and smiled. Muriel must be alright otherwise he wouldn't look so cheerful, would he?

"Is everything alright? The hospital?"

"She's stable." The smile was wider now. Genuine relief evident in his relaxed stance.

"I didn't hear the doorbell. How–"

"Oh, don't worry. Your niece is very well trained. She didn't take my word for it and insisted on seeing my warrant card before I was allowed over the threshold. I was also asked to remove my shoes."

It was true. He stood, looking a bit odd wrapped

in a heavy winter coat and scarf but in stockinged feet. Mandy's lips twitched and she could see the merriment in Tabitha's eyes.

"I'm just preparing a vegetable curry."

"Sounds wonderful."

Mandy opened her mouth to say something sarcastic but the weariness under his cheery look made her change her mind. "I'd better microwave some more rice then. Tabitha can keep you entertained while I cook. Make yourself at home."

As she watched he removed his coat which Tabitha took to hang up. He almost threw himself onto the sofa and leaned back, closing his eyes. She saw his chest heave as if in relief before she disappeared into the kitchen.

What the hell? Why did she not tell him there wasn't enough food or just give him some excuse or a cup of tea and send him on his way? A drink. She could offer him a drink at least. Maybe if she spent long enough in preparation he'd clear off.

To Mandy's surprise, though, Tabitha was deep in conversation with Lucas.

"Your niece has been telling me all about the drama club. Great way to keep youngsters involved and off the streets."

"She's got hidden talents, has our Tabs." Mandy beamed with pride at her niece. "I should have offered you a drink, Lucas. I'm afraid I haven't got any wine but there's the medicinal gin and orange juice. I've no tonic."

"And no wine?" He lifted his hands as if in mock

horror. "That's not the Miranda I know."

Tabitha giggled.

"Things have changed." Her response was sharper than intended and she needed to temper it with an explanation. "I've responsibilities and going to work with a hangover doesn't always provide the best start to the day."

He nodded, his look appraising her. "Just orange juice is fine. I have to drive back to Muriel's afterwards."

As she chopped the vegetables Mandy's head was racing. She calculated how much more she'd need to put into the pan deciding to double the ingredients. Men ate a lot, didn't they?

In automatic pilot she peeled and chopped two onions which made her eyes water. No matter what advice she read on ways to stop it happening the enzymes released on cutting the onion irritated her eyes. She was soon streaming and sniffing. She recalled the angry tears when she'd broken up with Lucas. Funny how time had eased the pain and yet how swiftly she recalled the agony.

A bigger knife was needed to cut the butternut squash. She scooped out the seeds. If she remembered, she'd roast them and feed the birds. She only had one sweet potato so took an ordinary white potato as well, chopping into neat cubes. If only life was so easy to separate. With Lucas back, her life was an emotional quagmire again.

She opened the fridge to see if there was anything she could add to bulk out the meal. Nothing.

The store cupboard next. Chickpeas were a good staple. She'd throw in a tin of those with the tomatoes and spices and hope it all worked out.

Since Tabitha had become her responsibility, Mandy tried to make sure they ate a balanced and healthy diet. Left to her own devices she would have succumbed to fast foods and ready meals, eating on the hoof when it was necessary. But providing a secure home for Tabitha was a priority these days and cooking part of that stability. No excuse to resort to takeaways – except as an occasional treat. Meals out were also a rare occurrence. Work was all consuming. As she stirred the pot of curry, Mandy wondered what it would be like to have an ordinary job. Probably boring, but not as stressful. As always, her thoughts strayed to her twin. How did Joy manage to cope?

The hum of conversation reached her as the warm spicy aroma started to fill the kitchen. With everything prepared all she'd need to do was set the table. She would need to disturb the flow of conversation in the main room. Somehow, she was reluctant to do so. Would he want to talk shop? God, she hoped not. The thought of that putrefied body was enough to put anyone off eating.

As soon as she put the cutlery on the table, she knew there was no excuse not to be sociable. She perched on one of the dining room chairs rather than cross the room to the tub chair under the window.

"Food won't be long."

"Smells good. Better than the scrambled eggs I

was going to have tonight."

Lucas had dark rings under his eyes. She wondered how much sleep he had managed in the last couple of days. Should she press him for further information about his aunt? As if reading her mind he said, "They are hoping to discharge Aunt Muriel over the weekend. She's had some blood and is itching to get home again."

"It's good you're here to keep an eye on her."

"Yes. About that–"

He was interrupted by the ping of the microwave.

"That's the rice. Meal's ready. I'll dish it out." She escaped to the kitchen.

Whatever Lucas had been about to say was lost as Mandy leapt to her feet and scurried to the kitchen.

The usual form was to put the meal straight on to the plates but, not knowing how much Lucas would eat, she decided to use the serving dishes. She placed a huge bowl of curry and another of rice in the centre of the table. Tabitha opened her mouth to say something then bit her lip.

"The plates are very hot. Be careful," she warned them as they sat down.

"This looks delicious. Thank you, Miranda." He gave her one of his devastating smiles which made her feel a little light-headed. He oozed charisma and, despite herself, she was charmed.

"Why do you call her Miranda? Everyone else calls her Mandy or Mand." Tabitha broke the spell.

"Because Miranda is a pretty name. It means to

admire. It's much more distinctive than Mandy. A bit out of the ordinary. Like your aunt, don't you think?"

Tabitha giggled. "Oh yes. No one could call Auntie Mandy, I mean Miranda, ordinary. That's for sure."

CHAPTER THIRTY-FIVE

"Still threads to pull together on the background. What have we got so far on the victim? Finances. Olivia, what have you found out?" asked Mandy the following day when the investigation resumed.

"No money worries. The dosh from the church Relief Fund was bunce, like. She spent mostly in John Lewis and Marks and Spencer. She took out about two hundred in cash every month. No idea what that was spent on, now. Her purse had about fifty quid in it."

"She may have paid people in cash. We know she employed Mary O'Rourke for a while and that was cash. And Cassian. Pretty sure she'd have given him cash."

"Speaking of Cassian, have you decided on the assault charge? You've got the photographs for CPS, haven't you?" Lucas was watching her face as she touched her temple.

"I think he's learnt his lesson. He needs focus though. The Church of the Forgotten Souls is without its leader so I expect that will go tits up." Mandy was thinking. "I'll have a quiet word with one or two people and see if there's something he could join. Keep him out of mischief. Get his mam on the case too."

"Scary. She'll sort him." Josh laughed.

"I think I'd like a look at The Church of the

Forgotten Souls myself. See if there's any other bugger there to shed a light on things. Maybe we can catch Cassian while we're there."

"Bit late for anything else." Josh looked glum. "A team has already been in and seized the computer and cameras. Latest I heard was that the hard drive had been removed. Don't suppose they'll get much from what's left."

"He was a right clever bastard, wasn't he? I wonder what, or who, gave him the nod to scarper."

From the corner Lucas intervened. "From your screeching at your friendly reporter guy, I doubt if it was him."

Mandy ignored him and grabbed her coat. Time to pay a church visit.

"Olivia. With me to The Church of the Forgotten Souls. I want to see the place for myself. You can be my guide. I suppose you want to come too?" The question was directed towards Lucas. He shook his head.

"I need to speak to Superintendent Withers. I'll catch up with the team later."

For a split-second, Mandy was disappointed. Olivia seemed relieved to be going out. Mandy observed her whistling softly to herself as she skipped down the steps.

Everything looked normal at The Church of the Forgotten Souls. The door was open and, when they entered, they could hear music and laughter from the common room. It appeared to be some sort of exercise class with a group of people in mismatched clothing and various states of disarray.

"It's the homeless lot." Olivia smiled. "The teacher, the tall skinny guy with the long beard at the front, slept in his car for six months after he split from his wife. He likes doing something for these guys."

"I wonder if any of them realise Father Michael has gone?"

Olivia pouted and shrugged. "Let's ask him." She made her way around the group to the front. "Hey, John. Did you know the priest has bolted?"

"Heard a rumour. Something about dodgy photos?" He had a high voice which seemed out of place with his stature.

"Yeah. That's what I heard too. Who opened up today? Any idea who's taking over the place?" Olivia wasn't giving much away including her status as a detective.

"Think it was the big bloke in the kitchen. He had keys to come in early to do breakfasts. He's organising a community get together this evening. They need to keep this place open. It's a lifeline for some people."

"Seen Cassian?"

"Prayer room."

Cassian was sitting on one of the chairs staring at the cross. He didn't look as if he was praying, just a little dazed. They sat down either side of him.

"Can't believe he's gone." His voice was a little forlorn. "Talking about making it a community hub. Suppose the cross an all will go."

They each stared at the rough wooden structure.

Mandy wanted to pull it down herself. Such hypocrisy. This place had given some people solace and purpose but for others it was toxic. Those youngsters who had been exploited for their innocence and money-making potential were victims of Carmichael's greed.

"Cassian. I want to ask you again about Mrs Vixen's house. It's okay," she put up a hand as Cassian moved as if to stand up, "you're not in trouble over that. You said something about a key. Did Mrs Vixen give you a door key?"

The lad coloured and looked at the floor.

"No. Key to back gate so I could get in to do the garden."

"But you knew where she kept a spare key?"

He picked a spot on his chin and nodded, still examining his feet. They waited for further information. "Found it one day while doing her garden. It were in a stone. Looked like a stone but rattled, like. Key was inside."

"The night you were looking for the photographs," Mandy paused, watching his face. "Did you use the key that night?"

"Yeah."

"Did you put it back?"

"Yeah. After the pi–police had cleared off. I didn't take nothing, you know. I'm not a thief. She paid me to do the garden. Honest. I try to keep out of trouble. This place helped me a lot." He sniffed.

"I know a pretty good drama club you might like to join," said Mandy, grinning. "I'll be in touch."

They had another look around the premises. The cameras were gone and the rails with the range of skimpy costumes was missing. All evidence to be used when they caught up with Carmichael. Olivia pointed to the window she'd escaped through before they headed upstairs. The bedroom Olivia had shared was empty. No sign of the previous occupants except a lip-gloss which had rolled under one of the bunks.

CHAPTER THIRTY-SIX

Lucas wasn't around when they got back.

"He's gone to the hospital." Mandy hadn't asked but Helen seemed tuned to her thoughts. "He was a long time in with the Super and they called in DI Blake as well."

That wasn't good news. Last time DI Blake had been in discussions with Withering she'd been landed with DS Gregory and his not-so-subtle threats. Something was afoot and she'd have to be patient. She spent an hour going through the interviews and statements with Josh.

"Okay. Devil's advocate here. Is there any way Barbara Vixen's death could be accidental?"

"No. If the flue had been blocked with leaves, I might have believed it but newspaper? No way. Someone put it there deliberately to poison her. Not a doubt in my mind." Josh sat back in the chair and folded his arms. "Plus, Carmichael has to be the killer. We've thought it all along. The fact he's left the country proves it."

"'Fraid not, Josh. Evidence is what stands up in a court of law. Doing a runner makes him look guilty. Circumstantial at best. We know the bugger had motive and means, but opportunity? She was canny. No way she'd have given him the chance to do anything. We still don't know who stuffed the flue."

"Wouldn't Alan Jordan have cleaned it out? When did he say he'd been to service the boiler?" Josh started looking through his notes.

"September. We didn't ask him specifically about the damned flue, did we? Maybe worth giving him a call. He's got the knowledge but motive?" Mandy shrugged. "Barbara didn't spread malicious gossip about him like she did with Mary O'Rourke. Just threw him out on his ear when he told her she needed to upgrade the boiler."

Olivia was clicking away on her computer, eyes fixed on the screen.

"Boss, I've been digging again into Charlie's finances. On paper he has plenty of assets but he's cash poor, now."

"What do you mean?"

"He's broke. He got two houses but no money. Well, nothing substantial coming in. Want me to dig a bit deeper?"

"Do you need to ask? Hell's bells. Why does everyone seem to have secrets they think we can't find out? Pricks." Mandy scratched the back of her head making her unruly mop stick out further.

"Secrets?" Lucas came back into the room. He looked less stressed than earlier. Mandy hoped it meant that Muriel was on the mend.

"Seems everyone's got one. Charlie isn't as flush as he makes out. His sister's money would probably get him out of what those wankers, I mean bankers, call a cash flow problem."

"She wasn't loaded though, was she? The house

would be her major asset. Selling houses takes time. Do we know why he's got a cash flow problem?"

It was a reasonable question from Lucas. Mandy had to admit not much passed him by.

"Looking into it, sir." Olivia's eyes didn't leave her screen. They waited a few minutes, but she just shook her head. "Nothing yet."

Mandy sighed and went to the kitchen to make a cup of tea. Lucas followed. It was the first time they had a chance to speak privately since the meal the night before.

"You have a delightful niece." The words were spoken sotto voice. "You've been a good influence in her life, and she adores you. That's pretty obvious."

"She's one of the reasons I get up in the morning."

"And the others?"

"Bringing justice to the world. Doing a good job and what's right."

It sounded pompous and defensive, even as she uttered the words. But it was the truth. She could have ended up going a bit off the rails, like Joy. Or even got involved in some of her dad's dubious dealings. Joining the force was almost an act of rebellion.

The constant scrutiny was making her tetchy. Lucas was making her doubt herself. And the fact this case seemed to be going nowhere. Every corner they turned led to another dead end.

"Why did you join?" she asked him. "You did a law degree. You could have been a solicitor or even a barrister, like your uncle. What possessed you to get your hands dirty by policing? It must have been hard in those early years when we were training and pounding the pavements."

He didn't answer. She'd never asked him the question before. Even when they were in training, almost living together. They'd shared the trials and tribulations, the exams, the difficulties of being out on patrol and also the satisfaction of doing the job. Lucas had been a star pupil, and it was obvious from the start he was destined for higher office. Mandy had dogged determination to succeed and show her family there were better ways to get justice than beat the hell out of your competitors. She pulled herself out of the reverie. No time for the past. Time to push on.

"Let's have another chat to Mary O'Rourke. She was lucky to be taken on at the cafe after Mrs Vixen pulling her to shreds in the middle of the village."

"Do you think she knew about the hidden key?" asked Lucas.

Mandy shrugged. Another unanswered question.

* * *

She was impatient on the drive to Llandaff, tapping her fingers on the steering wheel at every set of traffic lights or slow-moving vehicles. Lucas declined to go with them. He said he had some personal business related to his job in North Wales to sort out. Josh was quiet on the way. Mandy wondered if there had been a tiff with Lisa, but he volunteered nothing. She didn't want to ask. She wanted her team to be content but really, she wasn't a counsellor. If he didn't want to share the reason for his moroseness then she wasn't going to force the issue. There was enough crap to deal with already without adding personal angst.

Out in the back garden they hunted for the stone Cassian had told them about, lifting and shaking anything that looked big enough to hold a key. At last Josh held something in the air.

"Listen." He shook the stone. It rattled. When he turned it over there was a sliding panel. Inside a key. "Got it." He waved it in the air, triumphant. "Boss?"

Mandy hadn't responded. She was wandering around the garden.

"Josh. Come here." She pointed to a panel in the fence separating the garden from that of Mrs Hunter. "What does that look like to you?" She pulled an overgrown piece of hedgerow out of the way.

"A gate. I hadn't noticed that before. Yvonne said her friend used to live here. Maybe they spent time in each other's gardens. Easier to have a gate through if that was the case." He pushed against the edge of the panel and a click indicated some mechanism had been released.

"Interesting."

"Doesn't look as though it's been used much recently though. Bit rusted." Josh wiped a finger over the catch.

Mandy wandered a bit more. She tried the back gate. "Locked as well."

As she stood looking up at Barbara Vixen's

house, she seemed lost in thought. Then, with long strides she marched up the garden and stared at the back wall of the house. She stretched up her arm towards the flue.

"Josh, try to reach the flue."

"If you can't do it then I won't be able to, will I?"

She grinned. "So, it would take someone well over six foot to be able to stuff newspaper in there."

"Unless they had a stepladder."

"Or something else to stand on." Once more her eyes scanned the garden. "The bloody garden table. Of course. If someone stood on that they'd be able to reach. It's aluminium, lightweight and could be put back in place. Mrs Vixen would never know."

"You'd have to be agile to climb up on that."

"Not if you used one of the chairs as a step. Let's get forensics to dust these for fingerprints."

"Doubt there'd be any trace of anything after all the rain and frost."

Josh was so negative sometimes she wanted to slap him. "Not on the top. But think about how you'd move a table." She mimed lifting the table without touching it.

She could almost see Josh's brain processing before he answered, "Your fingers would be underneath."

"No shit, Sherlock. We don't need a forensic team. Just one person with fingerprint dust who can go away and do some checking on the quiet. Ask that nice girl who gives you the moon eyes."

"She doesn't–" Josh was blushing again. "Okay.

I'll ask Gemma."

"Tell her we want it quick and on the quiet otherwise Withers with have my guts for garters for spending too much money. He's already been moaning about budgets."

CHAPTER THIRTY-SEVEN

A few minutes later, after a mumbled conversation with Gemma, he said, "Sorted. She's actually off today but she only lives down the road. She said she'd bring the gear and do it within the hour."

"Bloody brilliant. You'd better take her for a drink to say thank you."

"I.. I can't. She'd–"

"Think you wanted to get into her knickers."

"Bet you wouldn't have said that if DCI Manning was here."

"Maybe. Maybe not. He wouldn't be shocked." She laughed. "Apologies if I overstepped the mark."

Emboldened by the apology, Josh asked, "What's the deal with you and him? There's a bit of tension in the air. Liv reckons he fancies you."

Mandy stiffened and scowled at him.

"We trained together a long time ago. He moved away and got married. End of story. Basically, it's none of your bloody business."

Josh took a step back, mumbled an apology and went to see if Gemma was on her way. He returned a few minutes later with the woman in question and her box of equipment. Gemma was petite with a mop of blonde hair and big blue eyes, almost doll-like. She gazed at Josh in obvious admiration. He explained what was required. She wasted no time. Mandy paced. Bloody Barbara Vixen. It was a horrible way to die. Something you wouldn't wish on your worst enemy. And she had so many enemies.

"Got a few beauties here," said Gemma after a while. "I can check them on the system in the morning and let you know if anything comes up."

"You are a star." Mandy's good nature had returned with the little bit of hope this latest development afforded. "Look why don't I treat you to tea and cake in the cafe? I want to talk to someone who works there anyway, and Josh is always willing to sample the delights of the Cardiff cafe culture."

"Cool. Never say no to cake. I should be the size of a house."

Considering the young woman was like a stick insect, it was a silly remark. Despite his earlier protests, Josh was animated on the way to the cafe. Mandy walked ahead and they followed. She could hear laughter and pondered again on his home circumstances. Oh well. None of her damned business as long as it didn't impact on his work.

The cafe was quieter than last time. Mandy ordered and asked if Mary was about. They were out of luck. She'd left half an hour early to collect her daughter. They'd have to call on her at home. From what Mary had said about her daughter it was likely to be challenging.

* * *

The house in Fairwater was rented, so Mary told them. They were hoping to buy a house outside the city but couldn't quite afford it. Mrs O'Rourke was reluctant to let them in at first.

"It's Emily. She's not good with strangers."

Her daughter was sitting on a chair with a tablet, playing a game. When she saw Mandy and Josh, she disappeared up the stairs without making eye contact or uttering a word.

"She'll sulk all night now." Mary O'Rourke rolled her eyes. "I love her to bits, but she can be really hard work."

"We wanted to talk to you a little more about Mrs Vixen and your relationship with her. How did you get the job in the first place?"

Mandy didn't want to start questioning her about the key, preferring to have Mary in a relaxed frame of mind. They might learn more.

"It was Yvonne Hunter. We're distant relatives. We hadn't seen each other since I was little. In fact, it wasn't until we got talking one day that we discovered the relationship. Yvonne's very understanding. She asks me to help out – usually when the family is coming, and she wants everything sorted. She's a busy lady and housework isn't her priority she told me." Mary laughed and waved a hand around her home. "As you can see, I'm not house-proud. I'm too exhausted after work and dealing with my daughter. She's quiet now but some days she can have real temper tantrums. Plus, I like cleaning for others. It's something I can control."

Mandy didn't quite understand that remark and frowned. Mary noticed her puzzlement.

"Life can be chaotic but if I can wash a floor or clean a window then I can see I've made a difference. I walk out and the customer is left with a clean house, and I don't see them make a mess of my hard work."

"Until you go back again."

"Yes." She smiled. "I like working in the cafe too. Debbie is a great boss. Very considerate and flexible. Her sister has a boy who's autistic so she's sympathetic. Understands the problems."

"But Mrs Vixen was a different calibre."

"God, yes. I know I went off on one when I saw you in the village. I'm sorry. But some people were saying "oh poor woman, dying alone like that.' As if any of them cared. I don't believe the dead achieve sainthood and all their nastiness is forgotten because they're dead. That's bullshit. She was a nasty piece of work."

Mandy wanted to avoid getting Mary too worked up. She changed tactics.

"Did you see the lad, Cassian, at all? He worked a bit in the garden, I believe."

"Yes, he did. Cass can be a bit wild at times. Likes smoking weed. His mam got him involved with that cult church which supposedly helped keep him occupied. He's a good lad at heart but teenage years are hell, aren't they?"

Mandy nodded. She thought about Tabitha and how turbulent her teenage years were proving to be. Adolescence was hard enough without an errant mother who skipped off when she got bored with family life.

"Did you work in the garden as well, Mrs O'Rourke?"

"Not really. She got me to brush up the leaves a couple of times. Waste of time that unless you put them in a bin."

"Did you know she had a key hidden in the garden?" Mandy held her breath, wondering about the response.

"Did she now?" Genuine surprise. "I know Liz, the previous owner, hid one out there in case she ever locked herself out. Yvonne and Liz were good friends. Spent a lot of time in the garden on summer days." She shook her head. "I can't see Barbara Vixen leaving a key outside."

Josh was right. That's why there was a gate between the gardens. It was so Yvonne and her friend could spend time together without traipsing through each other's houses.

"Did Mrs Vixen ever leave you alone in the house or garden?"

"You've got to be joking. Didn't trust me an inch. Told you. She'd leave things out to see if I'd take them. And those bloody rotten apples. Friggin' joke."

"You mentioned you always came and went through the lane access at the back."

Mary nodded.

"Did you have a key to the back gate?"

"No. She'd unlock it before I arrived."

"There was never an occasion when you were alone in the house or garden?" Mandy persisted.

Mary shook her head and then stopped. "No...

Hang on. She had a phone call one day and went upstairs to take the call. Must have been gone for about twenty minutes. Other than that, she was like a conjoined twin."

CHAPTER THIRTY-EIGHT

"Let's see what our plumber has to say." Mandy rang the number on the business card Alan Jordan had given her.

"Perfect plumbing" He sounded upbeat, almost jovial.

"Mr Jordan. It's DI Mandy Wilde here. We've got a couple of technical questions for you."

"Oh now, that sounds a bit serious. How can I help? New boiler? Heat pump? Washer?"

He laughed as if any of those things were funny. Mandy wondered if he'd been to the pub or was on something. The heavy grey skies did nothing to lift her mood. Why the hell was he so cheerful?

"Where are you working? Could we meet you somewhere?"

"Urgent, is it?"

"It is a murder inquiry." Her tone was severe.

He sniffed, the jovial attitude gone. "I'm in Caerphilly. Could meet you top of the mountain in an hour. Got to finish off here and then I'll be ready for a bite. See you outside the cafe." He was gone before she could agree.

"Is he still a suspect?" asked Josh. "I thought we'd discounted him once we found he had no prior knowledge or connection to Mrs Vixen?"

"Nothing discounted until we find our killer. You know that."

On a summer's day the drive up to the top of Caerphilly mountain would have been pleasant. On such a dismal day all Mandy was worried about was getting there and back in case it snowed. The mountain could be treacherous in bad weather.

Alan Jordan wasn't there. No sign of his van. As they got out of the car the wind seemed to whip around them from all sides. A weak sun winked through the clouds and then disappeared again. They could smell chips and Josh's stomach rumbled in response.

"For God's sake, Josh. Can't you control that bloody stomach of yours?"

"It's the lure of the chips."

"Bloody hell's bells. Go and get some if it will keep you happy."

He trotted off in the direction of the cafe and Mandy looked around. It was bleak. She wondered how long before even this part of the mountain became another housing estate. She remembered coming up here with her parents and sister for picnics in the summer. Not often. There always seemed to be a stiff breeze on the top, even on the warmest day.

At last, she heard the rumble of an engine and saw the little green van approaching. Alan got out just as Josh appeared with his chips and can of coke. It wasn't ideal, interviewing someone with a bag of chips in your hand instead of a notebook. Mandy regretted telling him to go ahead. He could have waited until after they'd spoken to Mr Jordan. Then Josh's stomach growled again.

Alan Jordan heard and laughed. "Sounds like you need those, mate."

"Can you explain how you ensure the flue for a boiler is clear?" she asked.

"That's an easy one. Going for the pub quiz, are you?"

Mandy gritted her teeth.

"Not exactly. Perhaps you could just answer the question."

"Alright, love. Keep your hair on." A definite snigger from Josh although he tried to cover it with a cough. She didn't need to imagine how wild she looked with her mad hair being blown in fifty directions at once.

"I poke something through from the inside. If there's a blockage, I'll be able to feel the resistance."

"Do you check the outside too?"

"Course, I do. Most flues have a sort of grid to stop leaves and things blowing in. Sometimes they get dislodged, or an accumulation of leaves and stuff causes a bit of a blockage."

"Would the boiler switch off automatically if that happened?"

"Modern boilers should do. Some of the older models are a bit cranky, like my missus, and might carry on for a while. That's dangerous. The fumes leak back into the house instead of out." He was serious now, unsure why she was asking the questions.

"That's what I thought. When you serviced Mrs Vixen's boiler did you notice anything amiss with the flue outside? You did check, I take it?"

"Always do, love." He met her eyes, aware of what she was asking. "There was nothing blocking her flue. The grid was a bit loose. I wanted to fix a new one, but she wasn't having any of it. Would have cost a couple of quid but one of those mean buggers I reckon. Watching every penny."

The grid being loose would have made it easy for someone to stuff newspaper in there and then replace it. To the untrained eye everything would have looked normal.

"How did you reach the outside flue?"

"I've a step stool. I used hers inside. She didn't want me dragging mud from the garden through the house. Had to take my stuff out the back way. Tradesman's entrance." He pulled a face, then grinned again.

"One final question. Could you give us a sample of your fingerprints for elimination purposes?"

The pleasant face slipped to be replaced by suspicion. "Why? You trying to fit me up for summat?"

"Not at all. On the contrary. Elimination means just that. We know you were in Mrs Vixen's house in the months leading up to her death. When exactly did you work on her boiler? I think you mentioned September."

"Now you think I'm flippin' Encyclopaedia Britannica. You'd have to ask my missus. She keeps the records. I just do the work. Now, if you're not going to share those chips I need to go and eat. We finished?"

"Just the fingerprints." She took Josh's can from him, wiped it down and handed it to Mr Jordan. "This will do. Save you coming to the station. Just grip."

She didn't know who looked more surprised – Josh or Alan Jordan. He paused, eyes narrowed, before gripping the can as requested. Mandy produced an evidence bag, opened it and he dropped the can inside.

"Reckon she owes you one, mate," he said to Josh with a wink before heading into the cafe.

Josh stared at the bag. "That's mine."

"Don't look so pissed off. I've a couple of bottles of fizzy water in the car. You can have one of those to wash down the chips. Better for you than all that bloody sugar.

"Are you my mother?"

Josh shoved a couple of chips into his mouth and grunted before climbing into the Juke.

Mandy closed her eyes and counted to ten. Bertha was going to stink of grease and vinegar now. She was tempted to drive back with the windows open. A heavy shower put paid to that idea, huge raindrops making it difficult to see far. Bloody rain.

* * *

Withers appeared as soon as they were back in the office. He stood and waited until all eyes were on him. Lucas was standing by his side. Despite the cold day Mandy could feel sweat trickle down her neck. She was tempted to sniff her armpits as she was sure she must be reeking. What was it all about? The Super was going to announce something. She could see it in his stance, shoulders back and head held high. When he was sure he had everyone's attention, he spoke.

"DCI Manning came here for a month to observe this team at work."

This was it. Interim report. Things not good enough. Not following protocol. Poor leadership. Mandy braced herself.

"Since then, there have been various developments in er, shall we say circumstances."

Nobody spoke, waiting for information about the developments. Withers coughed. Prolonging the agony.

"DCI Manning has requested an extension to his secondment. His commanding officer has agreed in principle to this move if we are able to facilitate it. It will leave a space for an officer from Cardiff to take a secondment in North Wales."

Josh took an audible breath. Had he been approached? Had they poached her best detective? Mandy opened her mouth to protest but caught some warning in Lucas's eyes.

"In discussion with DI Blake it has been decided that this opportunity should be offered to someone with no family ties to Cardiff. DI Blake has spoken to DS Gregory, and he has accepted. He will have an acting DI post and the chance to add something to his CV."

God, Gregory would be bloody impossible

when he got back. Had they offered Josh the chance to go to North Wales? Whose idea was it? In a way she should have been pleased but annoyance with the system won. As soon as the Super had left, she grabbed her coat and stormed out.

CHAPTER THIRTY-NINE

By the time she'd reached the steps outside the station, her burst of bad temper had dissipated with the cold wind. Mandy intended to just walk around the block and do some thinking, but it was too cold for that. Her steps took her to the museum cafe where she mulled over things while she had a cup of tea. She needed to speak to Josh and see what he thought about things before she started stirring up trouble. What did it mean? Was Lucas going to observe or be part of the team? He'd be her next in command so everything would have to go to him first. Mandy realised how lucky she'd been. Withering might be a miserable old sod at times, but he would always have her back. Would Lucas do the same? Realising time was passing and there were more pressing matters than her personal worries, she headed back to the station.

As she reached the foyer, she recognised a familiar figure.

"What the hell do you want now, Tod?"

"Tut, tut, Mandy. That's no way to talk to friends. Just wondering if you could confirm something for me. Is it true Carmichael went down in the crash?"

"What?"

Tod got out his phone and scrolled down to a news item. "There was an air crash over Thailand. It's rumoured Michael Carmichael, otherwise known as

Father Michael, was on the flight."

Mandy was dumbstruck.

"You didn't know?" Tod was closer now, head to one side as he studied her.

"Who told you he was on the flight anyway?"

"I've a friend who got hold of the passenger list. It should be released later today. He said an M. Carmichael, described as a British citizen, was on that list."

"How the hell did he do it?"

"Our friendly priest had connections. Laying a trail in one direction while he was actually heading somewhere else. You know how they do it, Mandy."

"Slimy bastard. Well, he's with his God now, I suppose."

Mandy took a deep breath. Damn and blast. There was no way they would get any details about the blackmailing by Barbara Vixen now. No bloody evidence. She needed to be careful what she said to Tod. He'd grasp any morsel and use it to embroider his story. She needed to get upstairs and talk to the team.

"I know nothing. No comment."

Tod grinned. "Glad I'm ahead of the game. See you around DI Wilde."

When she got upstairs it was obvious the team already knew. There was a buzz in the office with everyone talking at once. She was glad to see Lucas wasn't present. She didn't feel ready for that just yet.

"What does it mean to the investigation?" asked Josh.

With a sigh, Mandy said, "Well, we can remove him from our second trawl of suspects. I doubt if he's going to tell us anything now."

"Gemma rang. There's a match. You'll never guess whose prints came up." Josh seemed animated but Mandy wasn't in the mood for guesswork. She raised an eyebrow.

Josh swallowed. "Cassian Jones."

If he was expecting some animation from Mandy, he would have been disappointed.

"He's fourteen. Hardly killer material either. And he did work in her garden."

"But Carmichael could have put him up to it. Forced him to stuff the flue."

"Really? That's your theory? We'd better have a chat with our juvenile delinquent then." She couldn't stop the sarcasm in her voice.

Josh looked put out. "Kids younger than that have been convicted as killers. Think of the Jamie Bulger case. They were ten at the time."

"True. There is always a possibility. We'll see what he says for himself."

* * *

Cassian looked sheepish when he came down the stairs. His hair was wet and there was the faint whiff of shampoo, coconut or something similar. Sweet and clean.

"It's best you stay, Mrs Jones, while we ask some questions. It's a bit more relaxed here so maybe

Cassian will be more forthcoming."

Mrs Jones sat on the sofa and patted beside her. A spring protested making a creaking noise. Cass sat down, rubbing at his mouth with the back of his hand, wariness in his body as he waited.

"First of all, I'm not sure if you heard that Mr, that is Father Michael, has been killed in that flight you'll have seen on the news."

Cass's eyes opened wide. Mrs Jones sniffed. "Such a shame. I thought it was a good place for Cass to be, a church and that. Then we hear he's bunked off with all the cash and he's been kiddie fiddling to boot." She shook her head as if in disbelief. "Is that all true? If you can't trust a priest, then who do you trust?" She didn't expect an answer, just sat shaking her head.

"Cassian, we need to ask you a bit more about your work in Mrs Vixen's garden. You did a bit now and again, didn't you?"

"Yeah."

"Did you move the patio table and chairs at any point?"

"Yeah. Had to get at the flower bed. She wanted me to cut down a bush. Proper spikey thing it was. Cut my arm on thorns. I put it back after and helped her put the cover on for winter, like."

Mandy looked at his face. He seemed earnest enough, meeting her eyes without flinching.

"Do you like school?"

"Wha'?"

The change of tack had unnerved him, just as

she hoped. She repeated the question and waited for an answer. He just turned up his nose and shrugged. His mother intervened.

"He don't always go. Thinks I don't know. That's why I got him into the choir at the church. Keep him out of mischief. He had a lovely voice before it started to break."

Looking at the spotty teenager it was hard to imagine an angelic voice. From what information Olivia had gleaned the choir was a small group with someone playing guitar and another on tambourine with a number of young boys in the main. Father Michael had tried to introduce a sort of 'happy clappy' ethos in the church to encourage the youngsters to join.

Mandy pressed on.

"What subjects do you like? What's your favourite?"

"Sport. And art sometimes." He was hesitant, glancing at his mother as if for help.

"What about science?"

"Nah. Brainy kids do that."

"Do you know what carbon monoxide is, Cass?"

He nodded. "Yeah. We breathe it, don't we? It's in the air, like."

"And carbon dioxide?"

He frowned at her as if she was asking something stupid.

"Same thing, yeah? Just sounds a bit different. Like those things you find in caves. Stalisummat."

"Stalagmites and stalactites." Josh volunteered

the information.

Cassian beamed. "Yeah. Like that. Same thing, different names." He sat back looking pleased with himself. Either he was an exceptional actor, or he really didn't have a clue.

"Did you ever have a look in Mrs Vixen's flue? That's the pipe sticking out of the wall. It leads from her boiler to send the gas outside."

Another frown. "Why would I want to do that? I just did the garden." He wrinkled his nose and pressed a knuckle to one nostril. "I didn't see no pipe."

"Did you like Mrs Vixen?"

His mouth turned down as he shrugged. "She were okay, suppose. Bit fussy but always had squash and cake for me."

From what everyone else had said about Barbara Vixen this was a revelation.

"What about others at youth club? She helped with stuff there, didn't she?"

"Sometimes. She didn't take no crap from anyone. If anyone messed about, she'd yell at them." He wrinkled up his nose. "But she were fine if you did as you were told. Gave me a row over the smokes," a sideways glance at his mother, "but paid me for doing the garden."

There was nothing further to be gained. They told Mrs Jones they might need a formal statement at some point and left.

Deep in thought, Mandy hardly registered Josh was speaking to her.

"Not the sharpest tool in the box, is he?"

"No. I suppose he's not a bad kid at heart. Can't see him being the one to stuff that flue. Can you? Too dumb."

"We don't have anything, do we boss?"

"Circumstantial evidence that could link Cassian to the death of Barbara Vixen. We need to find out the owner of the other set of fingerprints but even then… shit. Doesn't look as if we will find out who did her in. I hate unsolved cases. Bugs me. Let's see if we can get Mary's prints now. Strikes me that every bugger in Cardiff that had any dealings with Mrs Vixen wanted to do her in. It was refreshing that Cassian wasn't in that group."

CHAPTER FORTY

Once back in the car, Mandy decided to confront Josh. "What did you think of Withering's announcement?"

"About Luc... DCI Manning joining us for six months? I think it should be good. We can learn a lot from someone with his experience."

"Did you know about this before? Were you offered the opportunity to go to north Wales for six months?"

Mandy could tell the way Josh was wriggling in his seat that he had known something. Obviously, he'd been alerted to the changes but didn't know how to tell her. She suppressed the desire to slap him and waited, seething.

"Eh, yes. DCI Manning mentioned there could be an opening."

"And?" She tried to keep the accusatory tone out of her voice. Josh could be so annoying without even trying.

"Lisa didn't want me to go. She's got her job to think of too."

"Bloody hell, Josh. It's north Wales, not the bloody moon. You could have arranged to come home for breaks. I'm sure Lisa could have had a sabbatical if she couldn't bear to be parted from you. You've passed the exams. You're ready for promotion. I thought she wanted you to climb the greasy pole. A flaming golden opportunity pissed away."

Mandy could feel herself sweating. It was beyond frustrating. Lisa wasn't exactly the supportive spouse.

"DS Gregory has been a sergeant for years longer than me. He deserved the chance."

"Don't be so bloody stupid. DS Gregory is a lazy bugger. He's a nasty piece of shit. They probably gave him the job to get rid of him for a while. I know I shouldn't speak in an unprofessional manner about a colleague but believe me, he's poison. Do not get drawn into his web."

Josh wiped the inside of the car window and peered out. "I don't like him either. Besides, there may be other opportunities closer to home."

That made Mandy think. This observation review that Lucas was part of. Did it involve restructuring? She knew she overstepped the line at times and was headstrong, but could her job be at risk? It wasn't a happy thought, especially as she had Tabitha and her future to think about.

* * *

Mary O'Rourke proved elusive at first. She wasn't at the cafe, so they went to her home. No reply. They were just about to give up when they saw her turning the corner. She stiffened when she saw them, gripping her daughter's arm more firmly than was necessary judging by the yelp from Emily.

"What now?" She was weary, her face drawn with the strain of the day evident.

"We've a couple more questions. Best indoors." Mandy indicated the house and Mrs O'Rourke plodded to the door, never letting go of her daughter's hand until she turned the key. She let the girl go in first with instructions.

"Drink first. TV after."

Turning to Mandy and Josh she said, "If we don't follow her routine there will be hell to pay. I'll put the kettle on. Come into the kitchen."

Apart from a pile of crockery on the draining board the place was neat and clean and smelled fresh. Despite her protestations that she wasn't house proud she ensured hygiene essentials were addressed.

"Well, whatever it is make it quick. If I don't feed her on the dot, there will be a paddy. Believe me, you don't want to witness that."

"Okay, we'll get straight to the point. Did you ever move the garden furniture in Barbara Vixen's garden?"

"The patio set?"

"Yes. It's covered in tarpaulin now but would have been on the patio when you were working there."

"I don't remember. I don't think I moved it."

"But it's possible?" Mandy persisted.

She rolled her eyes. "For God's sake. I have three part-time jobs, a demanding child to look after and a home to maintain. Am I supposed to remember every little detail of every day?" Her tone was more aggressive now, tiredness making her tetchy.

"We've found fingerprints on the table. We'd like to eliminate you from our enquiries. Would you mind giving us a sample of your prints, please? DS Jones can do it here so there is no need for you to come to the station."

"What if I say no?"

It felt like an impasse. Neither Mandy nor Josh said anything and waited as she almost snarled at them. Mandy met her eyes, unblinking, staring her down. At last, Mary's shoulders sagged. "Whatever."

"Josh? Kit?" He shook his head. Mandy pursed her lips. She stood, picked a glass from the drainer and wiped it clean, holding it to the light to ensure there was nothing on there, no smudges or grease.

"If you can just grip this firmly in your hand pressing your fingers on the glass it should do. If we need anything more detailed, we'll come with a kit. I'll make sure you get the glass back."

Mrs O'Rourke did as instructed. Then, like Alan Jordan, dropped the glass into an evidence bag. Josh dated and labelled it.

"That it?" Mary was on her feet, already pulling food from the freezer. "She'll only eat fish fingers and chips. Not a good diet, I know." She shook her head. "Some days I could run away. I'm bone tired."

They left her to it and made their way back to the station to check against the rogue prints on Mrs Vixen's patio table.

CHAPTER FORTY-ONE

"Any updates?" Lucas asked when they got back.

"I'm just taking some samples to the lab for comparison," said Josh, making a quick exit.

"We found prints on the patio table in Barbara Vixen's garden. It's possible the patio table was used to access the flue. We've spoken to Alan Jordan, the gas engineer, and he said the flue was clear at servicing. He used his own stepladder to access the pipe outside. It's about eight feet off the ground so, whoever stuffed it had to have the means to climb up there."

"And Mr Jordan?"

"Clear. We've had confirmation he was outside the area for the whole of December."

"Cassian Jones's prints have been identified. We interviewed him at home today. Unless he's got a scholarship to Rada or had a brain transplant, he hasn't got the knowledge or intelligence to even think about poisoning someone by carbon monoxide. Stupid little… I mean he thought it was the same as carbon dioxide. Not a bl… clue, sir."

"Next steps?"

"We are looking into any other links to the victim."

"Word in private?" Lucas nodded towards the kitchen which was empty. They might have a chance to speak uninterrupted.

As she followed him, Mandy couldn't help seeing the exchange between Helen and Olivia. God, that's all she needed. Office gossip. If they got wind of her previous engagement to Lucas, she'd had it. Rumours would be rife.

"Sir?"

Lucas sighed. "For God's sake, Miranda. I'm doing my best here, but you keep putting up barriers. It's not about work now. Can I speak freely without you getting into a mood?"

Mandy felt like a disobedient teenager with a Victorian parent as Lucas waited, displeasure evident.

"Sorry."

"I know why you're in a sulk."

She opened her mouth to protest but Lucas held his hand aloft to stop her interrupting.

"I should have spoken to you first. Superintendent Withers rather took me by surprise with his announcement." He exhaled. "I went up north to see my Superintendent to arrange things. I need to be here for Muriel. You understand why."

Mandy's chest constricted. She swallowed while Lucas continued with his explanation.

"The only way they would let me come for a protracted period was if I could send a body, anyone really, to cover some of the work. It was obvious I wasn't going to get a DCI to do it, so we had to think more widely. It was only fair to ask DS Jones in the first place. You understand that?"

Mandy nodded.

"I could see DS Gregory was a thorn in your side.

A dangerous man to have as an enemy. The stuff he spouted to me showed him as both unprofessional and vindictive. Rather than create any more problems for you, I was the one who suggested he was offered a secondment to my division in north Wales. I've pre-warned my Superintendent about his tendencies, but we all hope a temporary promotion will ease his resentments."

"Am I supposed to thank you? You try to poach my best detective, make him think you're the best thing since bloody chocolate massage cream, and then think I should be grateful to you because he didn't fall for your little trap. Bullshit to you, sir."

No response. Mandy could feel herself redden. When all things were considered, Lucas had acted in her best interests. Why did she feel so confused? As the silence lengthened, she realised she was in the wrong.

"I'm sorry. I felt... I don't know. Marginalised. Josh said something about restructuring. It made me feel insecure. I know I push things too far. I don't always play by the rules, but I need this job. I've got Tabs to think about and besides, I'm good at what I do." She lifted her chin up, met Lucas's eyes expecting opposition but finding only kindness and understanding.

"You are an outstanding detective. Dogged and determined. I'd hate to be a criminal in your sights."

It was unexpected praise, and Mandy experienced a glow of pride. Lucas lifted a hand as if he was going to touch her and then changed his mind. "I'm going to the hospital to collect Aunt Muriel now. Once I've got her settled, I'll give you a buzz and collect Clive. She's already pining for her dog. Thank you for stepping into the breach like that. I don't think Clive would appreciate kennels."

"It's been good for Tabitha. No thanks required. I hope Muriel will be alright."

Lucas bowed his head. "See you later, Miranda."

* * *

Helen was waiting with some news.

"Boss, I've some information from Mrs Vixen's previous employers. I spoke to one of the partners in the firm. He said she was very competent, meticulous and ran a tight ship. Apparently, as the office manager, she oversaw all the secretaries and kept the wheels running 'like clockwork'," Helen made quotation marks in the air, "according to him."

"I'll bet. What about the people she supervised? Can you talk to any of them? And this woman her brother told us about. The one who had the breakdown. Dig a bit more. You never know what crawls out of the woodwork when you look further."

"I did ask, but he said we were looking at ancient history." Helen had a faint smile on her lips. "They have quite a high turnover in the firm. He's given me the number for the HR manager. I rang and she's going to ring back when she's had a search through the files. Not everything has been computerised so it could be a couple of days before she can access the relevant information."

"More bloody delays. With Carmichael dead we're running out of suspects. Alan Jordan. Anything there?"

"Yeah." Olivia piped up. "We got his work timetable from his wife. I rang all his customers for confirmation. Glowing references from everyone, like everyone." She sounded surprised. "An' all the dates match. No chance he was there in the month before she died. Reckon we can knock him off the list – again."

Mandy put a line and a question mark against Alan Jordan's name on the board.

"We spoke to Cassian. I don't think that dumbwit is capable of killing anyone. Two brain cells working alternative days. Plus, we only have circumstantial evidence linking him to the scene. He has a valid reason for that. He's the only one I've met who had a kind word to say about Mrs Vixen."

As Mandy sat and stared at the list of suspects she kept asking herself again – who could have hated Barbara Vixen so much?

The phone rang and Helen picked up. They could only hear her side of the conversation. She was making notes and asking questions.

"And this was when? Did anyone visit this person? Anyone remain in touch with her? Yes, I understand. Do you have an address? We can possibly trace her through that. I'm sure she will have moved on after so long but it's a starting point. Thank you. Much appreciated."

She put the phone down and smiled. "That was the HR department for the firm Mrs Vixen worked for. They sifted through their files and there had been a complaint made against Barbara Vixen way back. It was still on her file. Company policy to keep detailed records."

"Do we have a name for the complainant?" asked Mandy.

"We do. It was a Miss Yvonne Grey. She reported that she was being bullied. The complaint was investigated and dismissed, and Miss Grey left soon after. We have an address so I can check on the electoral roll who lives there now."

"Yvonne isn't a common name in Wales. I wonder how many we'd find. Bit of a coincidence that Barbara Vixen's neighbour happens to have the same first name." Mandy was deep in thought. "Before we do anything else let's see if it's the same person. If it is the same woman, we could be on to something. Olivia, check out marriages with Yvonne Grey and John Hunter. About forty years ago."

"Bit of a long shot innit, boss? I mean, even if it is the same woman."

"Could be a coincidence but if Yvonne Hunter was the woman driven to a nervous breakdown it could give her a motive."

"After all these years? And they've been neighbours for over a year. Don't you think she'd have done something before now if she was intent on revenge?" Helen was dubious, vocalising what Mandy was thinking.

She had a valid point. It didn't make sense. On the other hand, nothing about this case appeared to make sense. Yvonne and Barbara knew each other in primary school. Could the torment started at an early age have continued through life? They'd need to ask Yvonne herself, once they had confirmation of the relationship.

Josh was almost skipping as he entered the room. "We've got a match to the other set of prints."

"And it's not Alan Jordan."

"How the…?"

"Let me guess. Mary O'Rourke."

"Got it in one, boss. She lied to us."

CHAPTER FORTY-TWO

Mandy could feel that tingle of excitement when things took a turn for the better. Before confronting Mrs O'Rourke about the fingerprints, she wanted to delve a little deeper into Yvonne Hunter's history. If Barbara Vixen had hounded her to the point where she had a breakdown, surely it was something she would have volunteered when Josh spoke to her. On the other hand, perhaps it was something she was ashamed of. Even with discussions about mental health becoming more open, there had been a stigma attached to these things when Yvonne was younger.

It didn't take long for Olivia to find the marriage record. Yvonne Grey had married John Hunter three years after she left the law firm where Barbara Vixen had bullied her.

"Bingo. Damn. It's too late now to research the rest of her employment history. We'll have to leave it until Monday. Helen, what was the name of the person they told you had kept in touch with Yvonne Hunter?"

"A Mrs Amy Wright. She stayed on at the firm after Yvonne left but they had been friends so kept in touch. She retired six years ago. Last address was in Whitchurch. I've checked. There's no record of the property being sold. Chances are she still lives there."

With a glance at the clock, Mandy decided to call it a day. She wanted to speak to Amy Wright, but it would have to wait. Everyone looked weary and a bit disillusioned. Plus, Lucas was calling to collect Clive. She checked her mobile. Nothing from him yet. She had time to get home and flick a duster around before he arrived. She hoped Tabitha had taken Clive out for a walk. The little dog needed a lot of patience. She missed her mistress and her home. Tabitha was going to miss Clive too. Mandy could imagine the pleas to get a dog. Maybe they could compromise and arrange to take Clive out for long walks on the weekends. Lucas would be there at weekends too until… she tried not to think about Muriel's demise.

Clive greeted her with sharp barks. The little terrier couldn't be satisfied with just wagging her tail as her whole rear end wobbled. She tried to leap up to lick Mandy, but it proved impossible and provided much laughter. Tabitha calmed the little dog with pats and treats.

"Lucas will be collecting her later. He's gone to the hospital. Muriel is desperate to get home and see Clive."

"It's such a silly name for a girl dog." Tabitha was grinning as she cuddled Clive on the sofa.

"Muriel's husband was called Clive. I think it's a comfort to her."

Just then Mandy's phone pinged. A text from Lucas.

Be down in about half an hour to collect the mutt. Okay? X

She wondered if the X was deliberate. In fairness he had been kind and supportive to her since his return. All the problems had been of her own making. It hadn't been as bad as she expected. She still pondered over Muriel's words. Did he regret their break-up? Too many years had passed. They were different people now although she couldn't deny his attraction.

When the doorbell rang, Tabitha answered. Clive jumped up Lucas's legs, her sharp barks echoing around the narrow hallway. Mandy joined them.

"Cuppa?"

"Thanks, but I'll take a raincheck on that one. I don't want to leave Aunt Muriel too long. She's anxious to see this little lady." He fondled the dog's ears.

"How is she?"

"Remarkable. As always. The problem is, she won't rest so I need to make sure she puts her feet up. The doctors are in awe of her tenacity and stoicism." To Tabitha he said, "Thank you for looking after Clive. Muriel wants to express her gratitude to you in person. What about Sunday afternoon?"

"Oh, I don't think–" Mandy was stopped by his look.

"I've had my instructions. She wants to thank Tabitha, personally. I thought we could take Clive out for her afternoon W-A-L-K. I dare not say the word." He laughed and Tabitha giggled. There was no way Mandy could refuse.

"I'll bake a cake," she said, instantly regretting it. When was the last time she'd baked anything? Oh crap. She'd talked herself into another mess.

"Lucas is nice," said Tabitha, after he'd left. "Is he going to be your boyfriend?"

"What?"

"Don't think I haven't noticed how you are around him. Sneaky glances. Dreamy eyes. Bit soft on him, are you? He's got your number too."

It was time to put Tabitha right before she became too enamoured of the idea.

"Lucas and I were engaged a long time ago. He married someone else. It's history. End of story."

"Really?" The word held the weight of disbelief as Tabitha went upstairs to her room humming to herself. Mandy rolled her eyes. Bloody Teenagers.

* * *

Saturday morning brought early post including a letter with a Spanish stamp. Joy's handwriting. What couldn't be said on the phone? Their last conversation had been a few days ago and this letter was posted not long after. Maybe even on the same day.. She shoved the letter in her pocket and headed to the station.

First task of the day was to speak to Amy Wright. They rang her in advance and Mrs Wright opened the door at the first knock. She was dressed smartly and fully made up despite the early hour, her dyed light blonde hair expertly arranged, laughter lines etched beside her mouth and eyes. She inspected their warrant cards and invited them into a living room at the front of the house, overlooking the compact garden and a quiet road. The room was furnished with two sofas, one grey, the other teal velvet on which perched a large black and white cat. Mrs Wright sat beside the cat leaving the other sofa for Mandy and Josh. She offered refreshments which Mandy refused before Josh had a chance to open his mouth.

"How can I help? I heard about Barbara's death of course. I worked in the same firm as her for several years."

"We're looking into her life. Trying to establish some sort of history. She was the office manager I believe. 'Ran a tight ship' was how one of the partners described her management style," said Mandy.

"That is probably an understatement. Micro-management is a better term. We had quite a turnover of staff. But the partners thought she was wonderful. She was always efficient and so pleasant towards them."

"I believe you were there for years. You had no problems with her?"

Amy Wright gave a rueful laugh. "My brother-in-law is one of the partners. She was aware of that so didn't pick on me. George says she was the best office manager he's ever had the pleasure of working with. Brought him his coffee every morning with a smile and never complained." She raised one eyebrow.

"What about Yvonne Hunter? Can you recall what happen there? I know it was a long time ago, but you remained friends with her after she left, didn't you?" A slight drawing up of her shoulders was the only indication of wariness. The steady gaze and enigmatic smile stayed in place.

"We still meet for coffee now and again. About a year or so ago she told me Barbara was her new neighbour. We laughed about it."

"Yet Yvonne had accused Barbara of bullying her before she left the firm. She had a breakdown because of it."

A definite intake of breath.

"I think, Inspector Wilde, that is something you need to talk to Yvonne about. It wasn't pleasant and it was very personal. I've never been one to gossip. I prefer to keep my own counsel." The faint smile had gone. Amy Wright looked uncomfortable, stroking the cat as she stared at them. Mandy wondered for a moment if all retired women had cats as companions. She let the silence stretch a little to see if Mrs Wright would elaborate but she remained tight lipped.

"We'll be talking to Mrs Hunter again, but it's always useful to get the outsider point of view. Did the incident damage Barbara's job prospects? It would seem it didn't," said Mandy.

"On the contrary. She applied for, and got, the post of office manager less than six months later. She was, in my opinion, the reason why we had a such a turnover of junior staff. She terrorised the youngsters. A formidable personality."

It fitted the profile they had of Barbara Vixen as a selfish and vindictive woman. It was predictable that the partners in the firm had a different viewpoint of the woman. Efficiency valued above sentiment or staff welfare. They needed to speak to Yvonne Hunter. Had she held a grudge for all those years? Mandy thought how easy it was for Yvonne to access the garden through the secret gate. The work of minutes to get on a step ladder and shove something into the flue. Conjecture and theories. No evidence.

"Time for a coffee?" asked Josh after they left Amy Wright.

"Hmmm?" Mandy was distracted. "Where?"

"Follow me." Josh marched off and Mandy followed, still reflecting on what they'd just heard. She wondered why Barbara had considered anyone else was a threat when she was the obvious candidate for office manager. It was strange.

The cafe was warm and fuggy, with condensation streaming down the windows. The air was filled with the aroma of fresh brewed coffee and sweet pastries. She'd forgotten about the letter until she delved into her pocket for her debit card. A frown. Joy wasn't the world's best communicator. What the hell?

As Josh wolfed down a Danish pastry, she ripped open the envelope. She read the contents and swore, oblivious to the disapproving looks from an older couple on the next table.

"Hell's bells. Unbloodybelieveable."

"Boss? Are you okay? You look a bit pale."

Mandy pushed the letter towards him. He stopped chewing as he read. When he'd finished, he pushed it back to her. "Well, that's something else."

CHAPTER FORTY-THREE

The letter was brief and to the point.

Hey Sis,

I know this is going to come as a surprise, but it's amazing how a few days in the sun can focus thoughts. I don't mean to be flippant. I appreciate all you've done for me although I know it doesn't always look that way. Those months living with you and Tabs got me wondering about my life. Now that I'm here and I've had time to think more clearly, I've decided.

I could see the way Tabs adored and looked up to you as a role model. Yes, I know I'm her mam and she loves me too, but she's a bit wary of me at times. Can't say I blame her. I've been a crap mother. With you she has stability. When we were both there she was confused, unsure who to turn to when she was upset. I could see how difficult it was for you too. We both love her to bits. I only want what's best for her. So – big ask. I want you to become her official guardian until she's eighteen. Deep breath, Mand. It's not far away but I'm not in a good place right now. I know if anything happened to me, you'd be there for her, always. I just want to make it official. Please understand.

I love you both.

Joy

Xxx

"Typical Joy. Selfish to the core. I need to speak to her. We'll leave Yvonne Hunter until Monday, Josh. I need to deal with this pile of crap today."

As he wiped his fingers and mouth on a paper napkin, Josh attempted to defuse Mandy's anger.

"You're already looking after Tabitha, boss. Maybe–"

"Maybe bullshit. Self-pitying. What's 'not in a good place'? She's lying in the sun without any responsibility having abdicated from motherhood several years ago."

"But the miscarriage. That wasn't good. Maybe Joy's still grieving after losing the baby." She didn't think he was so tuned in. It made her take notice.

She rubbed her temples where a headache threatened. Perhaps Josh was right. She needed to be a bit kinder towards her twin. Still, they should have discussed it before now. Joy lived with them for months during the pregnancy, termination and aftermath. Ample time to talk about Tabitha's future. Hadn't she wanted Tabitha to go with her to Spain? What the hell was Joy up to now? None of it made sense.

She scraped back her chair and stood. Even when Joy wasn't hanging around, she was causing trouble.

* * *

Josh was surprised when the boss had shown him the

letter from her sister. Work always came first. This was big time stress for her. From his perspective, he couldn't see what all the fuss was about. She was already looking after Tabitha and doing a pretty good job of it by all accounts. It was just a way of making things legal. Maybe it was a cry for help? God knows. Not his problem. He had enough worries of his own.

* * *

All was quiet as Josh approached Yvonne Hunter's house. Any doubts he had about interviewing her by himself were balanced by the thought he was taking the initiative. If the boss didn't like it, she could come back and do the job again. Maybe he'd just warm things up a bit. See what he could find out without giving any information away.

Mrs Hunter opened the door with a smile on her face.

"Well, this is a surprise. And I'd just put the kettle on." She looked past him to see if anyone was lingering behind. "No DI Wilde?"

"Not today. She was called away."

As predicted, she offered him refreshments and rustled up tea. To Josh's delight, she produced a plate of Welsh cakes with that faint hint of cinnamon.

"How are things with the investigation? I hear there's been a bit of a hoo-ha down at that church place. Father Michael has absconded. An admission of guilt, do you think?" She seemed relaxed and interested.

Josh knew better than to speculate on anyone's guilt with a member of the public. "I'm afraid I can't comment on the case."

"Of course. I understand." She sipped her tea and nibbled on a cake, appearing unconcerned.

"How did you meet your husband?" He tried to steer the conversation on to more personal matters without alerting Mrs Hunter to the purpose of his visit.

Her face softened as she gestured towards the wedding photograph. "We met at a yoga retreat. I had been quite ill. I thought a week away from everything was what I needed. John was the teacher. I was hooked on yoga and even more hooked on him." Her giggle was almost girlish. "I trained as a yoga teacher, and we ran quite a successful business until he died. Such a shock. Massive heart attack." She dabbed at the corner of one eye, took a breath and then made an effort to brighten up again. "I still teach yoga, would you believe? I'm just as supple as I was in my thirties. Or that's what I tell myself."

"So, it was a change of direction for you."

"Let's say I had different ambitions after university. I was a sort of legal secretary before I met John. Stultifying work really. Mind numbing and lacking in any creativity. I was bored but my parents thought the legal stuff was a good solid career. My mother thought the yoga thing was a fad and a waste of my education. It wasn't."

Josh's phone buzzed. He ignored it, pressing on with his questions.

"You worked for the same firm as Barbara

Vixen."

A flash of alarm showed in her eyes for a second before she regained her composure.

"Goodness. Have you been looking into my murky past? Am I a suspect?" She attempted a laugh. "If you have, then you know what happened. It was the best thing for me. I never wanted to have anything to do with the law. Barbara did me a huge favour. Without her I'd never have met my John. We shared a wonderful life."

"Did she remember you?" asked Josh,

"Goodness, no. It was a lifetime ago and people like her don't remember the misery they caused. Too self-centred." Her voice held an edge.

Josh's phone buzzed again. He pulled it out of his pocket making his apologies to Mrs Hunter as he did so. It was a text message from DI Wilde.

> Where the hell are you? Something kicking off at the church.

He made his excuses and left.

* * *

When Josh got to The Church of the Forgotten Souls, Mandy and Olivia were already there, standing outside talking to the uniformed officers.

"What's up, boss?"

"Report of a break-in. Gogo called me because he knew we'd been investigating here. Uniform had a cursory look around but apart from a window at the back being levered open there's no sign of anything being disturbed."

"Why are we here?"

"Because I've got one of my gut feelings. You can take that look off your face, Josh. Think. Why break into a building when you know there's nothing of value?"

It was a good question. Josh puzzled a moment before he replied. "To hide something? Recover something that was hidden?"

"No shit, Sherlock." She patted him on the shoulder. "It's a big building. Olivia knows the layout and can spot if anything's different. I suggest we proceed with caution. We don't know if there's anyone still here."

The uniformed police officers had obtained the key from the cook so the main door to the prayer room was open. The door to what had previously been the office was ajar and the room beyond. Everything had been removed. Computers, cameras and costumes were gone.

Mandy spoke in a whisper. "I expect this will be put to a much less seedy use now."

A sound coming from the floor above made them all freeze. Mandy put her finger to her lips. She indicated for Olivia to go to the back window as that's where the intruder had gained entry. Uniformed police were lingering at the front and side doors and in the street. Whoever was in the building was trapped. When people were trapped, just like rats, they would lash out and she didn't want another shiner. Whoever was in the building could be armed and dangerous. She pulled out her baton and indicated for Josh to follow as she made her way back to the hall.

They crept along to the bottom of the stairs. In these old buildings the wood was often warped, and they needed to make as little noise as possible. She stepped to the left of the stairs, avoiding the centre of each step. Josh followed.

Another sound. They could hear footsteps towards the front of the building and a hinge squeaking. Mandy could feel her heart beating in her ears. She was sure Josh must feel the same as they slunk up to the first floor, silent. They identified which room the noise was coming from and made their way towards the closed door. One at either side.

Their breaths came in shallow waves. They didn't know who was in the room or if they were armed.

With gestures, Mandy managed to tell Josh they would go in on the count of three. She was going first. Bit late in the day for a protective vest. She held her hand up. Three fingers. Two. One.

They burst into the room.

"Stop. Police. Hands above your head." She brandished the baton but nearly dropped it in surprise when she saw who was in the room.

They were looking at a dead man.

CHAPTER FORTY-FOUR

"Mr Carmichael. Now this *is* a surprise. Last we heard you were on a flight out of the country. Then the news came through that you were on a flight which crashed. Welcome back from the dead." Mandy couldn't help grinning. They would find out how Carmichael had managed his escape during interviews. For now, the return of their chief suspect was more than welcome.

Carmichael looked behind him and then at Mandy and Josh, assessing his chances of escape.

"We've people at every door so, even if you got past us there's no escape." The threat was enough. His shoulders slumped and he sighed.

"Nothing to say, Father?" Mandy put emphasis on the last word and waited. Carmichael sneered but remained silent. "Okay Josh, read Mr Carmichael his rights, cuff him and let's get back to the station. It could be a long night unless we get some truths."

While they processed Carmichael, Mandy looked at the charges against him. Vice would want to question him, and she didn't have much time before he was taken out of her hands. She just hoped he'd talk. A confession to killing Mrs Vixen would wrap things up very nicely.

The duty solicitor was called – a drab man in his fifties, with a bald head and neck thick as a bulldog. After conferring with his client, they were ready to start the interview.

They put Carmichael in one of the smaller interview rooms. His bulk seemed to fill half the space. He looked well, in contrast to the tired solicitor with the pallid complexion. Before they started recording the interview, Mandy leaned across the table and looked the bogus priest in the eye.

"You know you're going to spend a long time behind bars, whatever happens. Let's not waste everyone's time here today. Okay? None of this 'no comment' crap."

The solicitor opened his mouth to protest but Mandy fixed him with one of her 'don't mess with me' looks. Carmichael stared back, no emotion showing on his face. When they started recording, Mandy leaned back in her seat, exuding confidence. All they needed was his confession.

"We know why you killed Barbara Vixen and how." Mandy allowed herself a smug smile. "Nobody's mourning her death. I suppose she deserved it. Blackmail. Not a nice thing to do. Tut. Tut."

Stalemate. Carmichael said nothing. He stared back at her as if finding it all boring. In fairness, she didn't expect an answer as it was more a comment than a question.

"When did you decide to kill Mrs Barbara Vixen?"

"I didn't kill her." His voice was firm. His gaze unblinking.

"But she was blackmailing you. We know all

about your little porn business. Some of my colleagues in Vice will be talking to you in more depth about that little game. You've been a naughty boy, haven't you? What hold did she have over you? Did she find out about the girls?"

Carmichael glanced sideways at his solicitor. A nod from that direction. "She said she knew what I was up to. If I didn't pay her, she'd tell the police. She said she had evidence, photographs." He stared at them, waited a moment. "I don't know what she had. I know she'd been in the office one day while I was out. I was careful but maybe she found something. It was easier to pay her while I figured out what to do."

"When to kill her, you mean."

"Look inspector. I've done a lot of bad things and I admit that. Look at the website. I'm not a killer. I can't say I'm sorry she's dead, but I'm telling the truth when I say I didn't kill Barbara Vixen. You might not believe me, but I do have genuine faith. What I did with the photographs," he swallowed, "was try to raise some money." He lifted a hand as he saw Mandy's mouth open. "For the church. If you look past the things I've done wrong, you can see the difference I've made to that community. Lost souls came to our church and found solace and friendship. It was the wrong way to raise money, but I swear by my God and all I hold sacred, I did not kill Barbara Vixen." He placed a hand over his heart. His eyes shone with sincerity.

They questioned him for another hour. He was surprisingly candid about everything, realising openness was the best policy in his situation. He explained about the false trail he'd left and how the crash provided him with the means to start again. He'd hidden cash in the church and false passports. A precaution in case some of his former enemies came looking for him. He'd gone back to retrieve them. His ultimate plan was to disappear somewhere like Mexico and start up a new church there. It was fascinating. Mandy could see how people were drawn into his web. The questioning was going nowhere. They had no hard evidence to connect him to Mrs Vixen's death, so they turned him over to the Vice team for questioning about the porn movies and the bitcoin.

"What do you think?" Josh asked, with a yawn.

"I believe the bugger. I don't think he did it. Maybe I'm just going daft but we've nothing we can pin on him. He had motive, possibly opportunity but without something placing him at the scene we're scuppered. Nothing but motive." Mandy yawned too. "It's been a long day. Let's pack it in for tonight."

"Are we going to see Mary O'Rourke on Monday?" asked Josh.

"And Yvonne Hunter."

"That's why I didn't answer my phone. I was at her house. She said she was grateful to Barbara as she left the firm with a lump sum and went off to be a yoga teacher. That's where she met her husband too. What had been a horrible experience turned out to be positive for her. No grudges held."

"Well, we did say it was a long time ago. Cassian

didn't seem to hate Barbara Vixen either. Maybe she had a soft side to her. Good with youngsters. No threat to her. God knows. I've other problems to deal with now."

"Your sister?"

"That as well. My immediate problem is having to bake a bloody cake. Me and my big mouth as usual."

CHAPTER FORTY-FIVE

When she got home to Brithdir Street, Tabitha was working at the dining table. She gave her aunt a smile.

"You look tired."

"Thanks, honey. It helps to know I look as bad as I feel."

"I'll put the kettle on."

Tabitha leapt to her feet while Mandy flopped on the sofa. She was tempted to show Tabitha the letter, then thought again. Her niece was not a parcel to be shoved around from one to the other. Life was disruptive enough for her without stirring things further. A few minutes later, Tabitha brought in two mugs and sat down beside Mandy.

"What are you working at?" Mandy pointed towards the table.

"Project. It needs to be finished by Monday and as we are out tomorrow afternoon, I thought I'd better crack on with it."

"Oh God. And I said I'd bake a cake. I must have lost my marbles."

Tabitha laughed. "You could cheat and buy one from the bakery on Crwys Road. They do great cupcakes."

"That would be very naughty and not what I promised to do. I'll look up some failsafe recipes when I've drunk my tea." She sipped from the mug. "Your Mam rung today yet?"

"Yeah. While you were out. We didn't talk long. She was going shopping or something. Said we might catch up later."

There was a flatness to Tabitha's voice. It was hard to tell what she was thinking as she didn't make eye contact. Mandy thought of the letter again. She'd have to try and speak to Joy when Tabitha was out. She picked up her iPad and started flicking through recipes.

"We don't have any caster sugar, and all these recipes call for it."

"That's no excuse." Tabitha laughed. "I'll go down to Lidl. I could do with a break anyway." She finished her tea and got her coat. "Won't be long."

As soon as the front door closed after her, Mandy rang Joy.

"Hey Sis." Joy sounded dull, sleepy. A wave of anxiety washed over Mandy. She hoped Joy wasn't into drugs again. "How's work? Lucas still there?"

Ignoring the questions, Mandy plunged straight in. "I got your letter. Bit left field, isn't it? What about your daughter in all this? First you want her to go to Spain to live. Now you want to fob her off. For God's sake Joy. Get a grip on reality. Think of Tabs."

For moments it seemed as though they'd been cut off. No sound from Joy at all. Then, a faint noise, almost a moan.

"It's not easy, Mand. What have I got to give her? An ex-druggie – no I'm not using before you ask. I've no home, no job, no prospects. You've got it all. Nice house, good job, solid career and the stable background she needs. I *am* thinking about Tabs."

It was said with conviction. Mandy couldn't argue with the facts. It wasn't her decision though.

"You need to get a grip and speak to your daughter about what *she* wants. She deserves to be consulted about her future. She's not a puppy you can give to the dogs' home because you're fed up. Grow up, Joy." She cut the call, her headache worse now. Bloody Joy.

* * *

Tabitha balanced the cake on her knee on the way to Muriel's house. Between them they'd managed to produce a loaf of banana bread. It looked and smelled okay so they hoped it didn't have a soggy middle. No doubt Lucas would have expected a Victoria sponge or similar, but cake baking was not a skill Mandy had time to practise. Tabitha was full of questions.

"Will I be able to take Clive out for a walk? Is Muriel very old? How come you haven't mentioned her before if you've known her for years?"

Mandy managed to avoid anything too intense, telling Tabitha she would soon find out and to be patient. It was Lucas who answered the door. No sign of Muriel or Clive.

"Is everything alright? I mean if Muriel's too tired or anything it's fine. We can go home again." Mandy half-hoped she could leave before her poor cake baking skills were exposed. Although, at the same time, she wanted to see Muriel.

"Not at all. She's looking forward to your visit." He turned his attention to Tabitha. "Is that the cake?"

With a nod, Tabitha pressed the tin into his hands. "Banana bread. We made it together." She smirked at her aunt.

Excited barking ceased further conversation as Clive emerged wagging her whole rear end. Tabitha dropped to her knees to cuddle the little dog.

"You've made a friend, I see. Come in both of you. Muriel's in the front room."

They followed him into the room where Muriel was sitting with her feet up, a rug draped over her knees. She looked better than when she'd been taken into hospital, her cheeks a rosy colour. As always, she was immaculately made up and Mandy wondered if Lucas had helped to style her hair.

"You must be Tabitha. I can see the family resemblance. Miranda darling, come and sit beside me." She watched Tabitha playing with Clive on the floor. "I see Clive has an admirer." Muriel's eyes still held a sparkle, despite her fragility.

"I've been nagged about getting a dog ever since we looked after her."

"Oh dear. I hope that hasn't caused you a problem, darling."

"With the hours I work it would be difficult to manage." Mandy changed the subject, not wanting to talk about the job while her superior officer was present. "You're looking better. How are you feeling?"

"A little weak but enjoying having my wonderful

nephew look after me. He's a saint. He never complains, even when I'm grumpy. Isn't that right, darling?"

Lucas looked at his aunt with such love and devotion it almost brought tears to Mandy's eyes.

"It's my pleasure, Aunt Muriel, and a privilege to be able to look after you. You looked out for me when I was a boy, and I know at times it was hard."

"Oh, you were a nightmare, darling. Teenage years." She rolled her eyes. "No wonder my hair turned white." Her tinkling laugh was infectious, and they all relaxed under her spell.

While Tabitha took Clive for a short walk, Lucas prepared a tray with tea and the banana bread. Muriel kept Mandy entertained with stories about the people in the ward in the hospital – the cheery cleaner, the grumpy phlebotomist and the caring nursing sister. After Tabitha returned, they had tea and the banana bread which turned out to be delicious. Lucas challenged Tabitha to a game of Scrabble, so they sat at a table under the window laughing and talking. Clive dozed by Muriel's side. It was all unexpectedly relaxing. Muriel was reflective, her gaze lingering on Lucas.

"When are you going to tell him, darling?" Her voice was low. She leaned forward, closer to Mandy's ear so as not to be overheard.

Mandy was puzzled. "Tell him what?" She wondered for a moment if Muriel was referring to her previous comment about Lucas and his feelings for her. She hadn't processed her own emotions properly. She was still attracted to him but the hurt he had caused ran too deep to dismiss.

"Tell him he's Tabitha's father, of course."

It was as if time stopped. As Mandy observed Lucas and Tabitha together, she saw the veracity of Muriel's remark. She gasped. Muriel put a hand on her arm.

"Oh, darling. You didn't know, did you?"

CHAPTER FORTY-SIX

The room was spinning. She had to get out.

"Excuse me a minute." Leaping to her feet, Mandy almost ran out of the room. She made it to the cloakroom and threw up. Sixteen years. Her sister and Lucas. What a bloody fool she'd been. Why hadn't she guessed? And Joy? She'd kill her.

After rinsing her mouth with water, Mandy took a few deep breaths. Was she dreaming? Five minutes passed before she came to her senses. She pinned on a smile and re-entered the room. Muriel gave her a speculative glance but said nothing. Lucas and Tabitha had just finished their game.

"This girl is good. Tabitha Wilde, I challenge you to a rematch."

Tabitha was glowing with pride. Mandy was desperate to leave.

"Not today. I think Muriel needs to rest now. We've taken up enough of your afternoon." She leaned over and gave Muriel a hug. "Don't get up. You need to take things easy."

"Thank you for a lovely afternoon." Tabitha stood in front of Muriel; her head slightly bowed.

"It's been a real pleasure, my darling. I'm sure Lucas enjoyed it as much as I did. You will come again, won't you?" asked Muriel.

"Please. I love playing with Clive." She turned to Lucas, her eyes lighting with a shy smile. "I enjoyed our game as well."

Once again, Mandy was struck by how innocent her niece was. Innocent and natural with people. She exchanged a silent message with Muriel. They would talk again. She knew Muriel wouldn't say anything to Lucas. Not yet anyway. But how long would she stay silent? Lucas deserved to know he had a daughter. She'd have to confront Joy. She suppressed her inner fury. Just as well Joy was in a different country.

Mandy brooded on the way home. She remembered only too well when Joy had announced she was pregnant. Their parents weren't too shocked until she said she didn't know who the father was. Sixteen years ago. All this time her twin sister had been lying. She'd lied to their parents, to Mandy and worst of all to Tabitha. Now Mandy had seen for herself the truth of Muriel's statement. A paternity test would prove it. Damn Joy to hell and back. She was so quiet, Tabitha asked what the matter was.

"Nothing. I'm fine. I'm glad you had a good afternoon."

"Muriel is lovely, and I had a good game of Scrabble. Are you… is Lucas your boyfriend now? He fancies you and I can tell you like him too."

Despite the inner tension, Mandy had to laugh. "Oh yes, Miss Matchmaker. I told you before, it was all over a long time ago. What makes you say that?"

"He keeps looking at you and there's a sort of tension in the air when you two are together."

"Oh my God. You are so funny. He's my boss, presh. I have to watch my Ps and Qs when he's about."

Tabitha said nothing for a moment, contemplating the situation. "I think it's more than that. I wouldn't mind, you know. If you wanted him to stay over or anything."

Mandy nearly choked. "Tabitha Wilde. What are you saying? I don't know where these crazy ideas are coming from. I can assure you that whatever Lucas and I had together was over a long, long time ago. He will not be staying the night – ever."

"So you say." Tabitha grinned.

* * *

It was difficult to keep up the pretence of being normal. Every time she looked at Tabitha, she could see Lucas. The mannerisms: the way she tilted her head; her searching eyes and her intelligence were all the signs required to confirm Muriel's suspicions. It was vital to speak to her sister, the anger bubbling inside Mandy ready to explode. Was that the true reason Joy had skipped off to the continent? She thought back to the day she'd told Joy about Lucas coming south to observe the team for a month. Joy had been quiet and made little comment at the time. The next day she announced her plans to move to Spain for a while. Coincidence? At the time it was unremarkable but in hindsight…

Mandy had to wait until Tabitha had gone to bed before ringing her sister. She took a few deep breaths before dialling. It was late but she expected Joy was still up. She was a true night owl.

"Hey, sis. What's up?" Joy sounded flat again, lacking in any enthusiasm. Mandy had little sympathy for her.

"When were you going to tell me? More to the point, when were you going to tell your daughter?"

"What are you on about? Have you been drinking?" The confused voice didn't fool Mandy.

"Don't give me any bullshit, Joy. We've spent the afternoon with Lucas and his aunt. She's the one who noticed. I've been a bloody fool. We all have. You've lied to everyone for years. You betrayed me. Worst of all you've betrayed Tabs."

A silence at the end of the line stretched until Mandy wondered if they had been cut off. Then, she could hear Joy breathing. She waited. When she interviewed criminals, the silences unnerved them. It forced them to fill the gaps. Maybe it would work with her sister too.

At last, Joy spoke. "It's not what you think. It wasn't deliberate. I didn't–"

"You never bloody think. That's half the problem. I could slap you. All the pain you've caused over the years. Mam, Dad, Tabs and me. Where to even start? You've been a total selfish arsehole all these years. We've put up with all your crap and now this. Frankly, I'm ashamed to call you my sister. To think we shared a womb, and you slept with the man I was going to marry."

"Listen. It didn't happen like that, Mand. It was when you went through that patch. You know, when you broke up with Lucas. He was devastated. I saw him out one night. He was blind drunk. He… he thought I was you. I was wearing one of your dresses."

"Oh yeah. Another one of your little habits. Borrowing things without asking. Borrowing my fiancé was a step up. Lucas never got blind drunk. He always knew when to stop." Mandy couldn't keep the resentment out of her voice. The break-up had been bitter, and she was reliving that feeling as she spoke to her twin.

"I think someone must have slipped him something–"

"Cut the crap. If anyone slipped him something it was probably you. This story just gets worse. What next? What shit are you going to tell me now." In a way it was fortuitous they were separated by hundreds of miles. A physical anger filled Mandy. She wanted to punch something or someone, preferably her sister. "Come on, Joy. Give me the rest."

"I asked him in and..." another pause as Joy gasped a little, obviously unsure how to continue. "He asked for another chance. He really thought he was talking to you. Begged for it. I… he was so drunk I didn't know what to do with him. I thought he needed to sleep it off, so I took him into the bedroom. He insisted I stayed with him. In the middle of the night–"

"You absolute bitch." The hot anger had turned into cold hatred. Mandy wanted to end the call but couldn't. For some reason she needed to hear it all.

Now the truth was out, she wanted the details.

"He never knew it was me. He always believed he was with you that night. I swear. I left before he woke up and I tried to forget the whole thing. Believe me, I felt really bad about it. When I found out I was pregnant and did the maths I was horrified. I considered a termination, but Mam found out and the pressure was on to keep the baby."

"That baby is now almost sixteen and has been deprived of knowing her father for all her life. You need to tell her."

"But sis–"

"Don't you sis me. As far as I'm concerned, we're finished. No more running after you and picking up all your shit. You spread nothing but crap and worry everywhere you go. The only joyful thing about you is your name."

Her heart thumping, Mandy ended the call.

CHAPTER FORTY-SEVEN

The morning meeting was subdued. The case was as difficult as climbing a monkey puzzle tree – not that Mandy had tried that. She was late into the office, after a sleepless night. It wasn't the best way to start any day. She kept glancing at Lucas. It was up to Joy to tell Tabitha the truth – and Lucas too. He'd demand a paternity test, of course. She wondered how he would take the news that he had a daughter. The memory of the two of them laughing as they played Scrabble came into her head. She called the team to order.

"Right. It seems we've ended up with a lot of loose ends and nothing conclusive. We've still got Mr Carmichael in custody though Vice will be hauling him off for further questioning. He's adamant he didn't kill Barbara Vixen. I'm inclined to believe him. We have motive but no evidence. Where do we go from here?"

"Mary O'Rourke," said Josh. "Her fingerprints were on the table. She said she only worked indoors and didn't have an opportunity to do anything with Mrs Vixen breathing down her neck."

"I can believe it. Mrs Vixen was a control freak. That reminds me. Anyone spoken to her ex-husband?"

"Yes. We had confirmation he moved to Perth after the divorce and hasn't returned to this country since," said Helen. "I arranged an early morning call. With the time difference it was already evening there, but he was accommodating. Quite forthcoming, actually." She checked her notes. "He thought she was quite sweet at first. They had a couple of good years. Then she changed. He said she was very ambitious and didn't want children. It caused a rift in their relationship. He was sad when he heard how she died." Helen sighed. "I'm glad someone gave us a different side to her. Maybe when she retired, she didn't feel the need to compete anymore. Perhaps the church would have helped her to become the person she used to be."

Mandy wasn't convinced.

"It could still be someone from her past seeking revenge."

"More than one by all accounts." Josh raised his eyebrows. Mandy thought he looked a little peaky.

"Are we sure about the geographical details from Charlie Forbes's mobile?" Mandy asked. "They don't live that far away from Cardiff. He could have taken the back gate key, made a copy and then returned one evening, leaving his phone at home as an alibi."

"Don't you think you're stretching the realms of credibility?" Lucas pointed at the board. "Look at the facts and the suspects. So many people seemed to bear a grudge but who would gain from the death?"

Mandy tapped a photo on the board. "Charlie Forbes. He inherits. And Carmichael. He gets rid of his blackmailer. Two strong suspects but no evidence. The problem is the time frame. We don't know how long the flue had been blocked. It makes things muddy, imprecise."

"You also have the access." Lucas pointed at the photograph of the house. "We are assuming access was from the back. What if it was from the front? Would that work?"

They considered it for a few minutes.

"For someone to enter the house from the front unseen would be almost impossible." Helen pointed to the aerial view of the road. "They would need to pass several houses, gain access with a key so they wouldn't be seen loitering and then go through the house to the back garden. Presumably they would return the same way. None of the neighbours reported anything." She tucked a strand of hair behind her ear. "Although, I suppose the close neighbours were away the days before Christmas."

"Could someone have gained access through Yvonne Hunter's garden to Barbara Vixen's?" asked Lucas.

"Yes, of course," said Josh. "Mary O'Rourke works for Mrs Hunter. She called Mrs Hunter by her first name – Yvonne. You don't do that unless you know them well. Especially an employer."

"They're related in some way. Second cousins. It isn't really an employee/employer relationship. She called the cafe owner Debbie. Although everyone seems to call *her* by her first name," said Mandy.

"But Debbie is quite young and informal. Older people sometimes tend to like being addressed more formally. I know my mum doesn't like just anyone calling her by her first name. She hates it at the doctor's when the receptionist calls her Gwen instead of Mrs Jones."

Mandy conceded.

"Okay. Another reason to speak to Mary O'Rourke again. Helen and Olivia can you do the tracking of phones, please? See where Charlie was – from the beginning of December until that registered visit, the one we already know about. Do the same for Carmichael. I know," she waved her arms, "We've done it all before, but double checking doesn't do any harm."

Mandy glanced at the clock. "I expect Mary O'Rourke will be at the cafe. We can start there."

Josh's face lit up, no doubt thinking they could indulge themselves with cake while in situ. He was disappointed when they found that Mrs O'Rourke wasn't there. The smell of toasted tea cakes was enticing, but Mandy was on a mission. She went straight to Debbie, the manager, who was at the counter and asked to speak to Mrs O'Rourke.

"You might find her at Mrs Hunter's house. It's her morning for working there. She comes up here at noon to do the afternoon shift." Debbie was busy, as usual, taking orders.

"Were you aware that Mrs O'Rourke had bad feelings towards Barbara Vixen after Mrs Vixen accused her of stealing?"

Debbie laughed. "Half the village was aware of that little fracas."

"Were you not wary of employing someone

accused of theft?" Mandy studied Debbie's face as she answered.

"Mary told me herself what had happened. I knew already. As I said, half the village knew. Instead of doing things quietly, Mrs Vixen called Mary a thief in the middle of the local shop. Created quite a scene. When Mary applied for the job here, it was the first thing she told me. Honestly, two apples, rotting on the ground. Maybe she should have asked before taking them," she shrugged, "but Barbara Vixen shouldn't have watched her as if approving and then bawled her out in public. Not the way to behave in my opinion. Bad form."

"Mary is an honest employee?"

"Oh yes. I trust her. That woman treated her badly. And she didn't let up either. Even months later."

"Sorry. Was there something else?" Had they missed something significant? Mandy was anxious to find out.

"The week before Christmas, Mrs Vixen was in here with a man. Usually, Mary was in the kitchen doing the food preparation, sandwiches and rolls and stuff. But I was short staffed, so I asked her to help wait on the tables. When Mrs Vixen saw her, she said to her companion in a voice that boomed across the room, 'Well, this place is going to the dogs when they employ thieves to deal with their valuable customers.' It stopped Mary in her tracks."

"What do you mean? How did she respond?"

"Poor woman. She went red and dashed to the

kitchen. She was really upset." Debbie shook her head as she remembered the incident. "Mrs Hunter witnessed it all and very kindly took Mary down to her house to calm her down. I was furious as we were run off our feet as it was."

"Was Mrs Vixen aware of the impact of her words?"

"I expect so. Her companion looked embarrassed, and they left not long after. It caused quite a stir in the cafe. People gossiping, as they do."

Josh had his phone out and showed Debbie the screen. "Is this the man who was with Mrs Vixen that day?"

Debbie pulled a pair of cheap spectacles out of her pocket and peered at the screen. "Yes. That's him. He was very polite and charming. Left a big tip too. I think it was by way of an apology."

"It was her brother," said Josh.

"Well, I never. Completely different character." She shook her head in disbelief. "I spilt a bit of his coffee in the saucer. He wasn't at all bothered. Mrs Vixen, on the other hand, tutted about it. And her face. She looked as though she'd been sucking lemons. I had to get a napkin and fresh saucer before she stopped complaining. I don't think you'll find many tears shed at her funeral – if anyone goes."

They let Debbie get on with serving a waiting customer while they discussed this new information.

"I'm surprised Charlie Forbes didn't tell us about that incident. It must have been the day he took his sister out. Do you think it's a motive for Mary to kill

Barbara Vixen?" asked Josh.

"I'm going to give him a ring and see if he can corroborate Debbie's story," said Mandy. "From what we've seen of Mary O'Rourke, I'm not sure. She's got a bit of a temper, hasn't she? I'm thinking about the first time we spoke to her. She made no bones about her dislike. Volatile. Stuffing the flue seems more planned than a spur of the moment thing."

"But we know she had the means and motive."

"True. Let's see what she has to say for herself."

Josh gazed at the cakes with longing. Mandy spotted the look. "You stuff your face while I hop over to the herb garden and ring Charlie Forbes. Ten minutes. No longer."

Josh was already ordering before she had left the cafe.

CHAPTER FORTY-EIGHT

As Mandy walked around the herb garden trying to find a relatively sheltered spot, she took a deep breath. The air was as fresh as any in the city despite the fumes from Western Avenue. She recalled the last time she'd been there, talking to the postal worker who had found the body. Barbara Vixen had spread her poison wide and far. It seemed everything she touched turned to crap. Although Mandy thought whoever had caused her death had done the world a service, she kept those thoughts locked away. Her job was to find the truth. Justice for the victim.

Charlie Forbes answered his phone on the second ring. He sounded cautious at first when he realised who his caller was.

"Mr Forbes. I wonder if you can help? We've just been to the cafe and heard about an incident we were unaware of before. Something you were witness to. When you took your sister out just before Christmas do you remember her saying anything which could have caused offence or distress?"

"Inspector Wilde, my sister spent her whole life causing offence or distress. She revelled in it. I think she thought she was being assertive but really, she was simply an aggressive bully." He paused and sighed, long and deep. "She channelled all her energies into the wrong path. I suspect that's why she joined that church. She eventually realised, after retiring, she had nothing. No husband, no children, no friends and no status. A forgotten soul."

"Do you remember her calling someone a thief?"

"Oh God, yes. It was embarrassing. I couldn't wait to leave there afterwards. That poor woman. Barbara seemed pleased, as if she'd scored a point or something. As if it was a game."

"How did Mrs O'Rourke react?"

"The same way anyone would react to being called a thief in front of a room full of people. Barbara said it so loudly. All eyes turned towards the waitress. She was mortified and dashed to the kitchen. Everyone was staring at us and whispering. I got Barbara out of the cafe as soon as possible."

"And your sister? How did she react?"

"Jubilant. Full of herself. Talking about how people shouldn't be employed if they had proven themselves untrustworthy. Apparently, the poor woman had taken two windfalls from the apple tree. Hardly a hanging offence, is it?"

"According to Mrs O'Rourke your sister watched her taking the apples and then waved goodbye, as if giving permission. Then, the following week, she gave Mrs O'Rourke the sack in the middle of the village shop."

There was no mistaking the groan at the other end of the line. "That is exactly the sort of thing Barbara would do. Underhand. Deceitful. I'm ashamed of her actions and I'm ashamed I didn't stand up to her in the cafe."

"You have no need to be, sir. They weren't your

actions."

It seemed as soon as the call finished her phone buzzed again. Helen. "Charlie Forbes is in the clear. Unless he travelled to Cardiff overnight his movements are all accounted for. He had a busy few weeks. Even a week in Scotland. The only time he was in the area was on the date he told us. It all fits. We can knock him off the list."

"That's a coincidence. I've just spoken to him about an incident in the cafe the day he was here with his sister. Something we had no bloody clue about. She had a bitch attack on Mary O'Rourke in front of everyone in the place. We're going to talk to Mary now."

"We've only got circumstantial evidence." Helen reminded Mandy.

"I know. That's been the problem all along. Nothing solid. All smoke and bloody shadows. Maybe she'll confess."

Josh was waiting by the car, still chewing and with a paper cup in his hand. She grinned. He'd be happy, for a while at least.

CHAPTER FORTY-NINE

As they approached Yvonne Hunter's house they could hear a vacuum cleaner droning. The door chime must have filtered through as Mrs Hunter came to answer it quite quickly. She seemed a little taken aback.

"Oh. Detective Inspector Wilde and Detective Sergeant Jones. I wasn't expecting to see you both again. Do come in. Mary's just cleaning upstairs." She gestured for them to enter and smiled in approval as they wiped their feet on the doormat. The house smelled of jasmine and bleach.

"It's actually Mary we came to see. We went to the cafe first. Debbie told us we'd likely find her here," said Mandy.

"I see. Nothing too important, I trust. She's already had a bad start with Emily. The poor woman is exhausted but insisted on doing the cleaning." She dropped her voice even though Mary wouldn't have been able to hear anything. "It's my little luxury to have a cleaner and besides, I think she needs the money."

Neither Mandy nor Josh commented.

"I'll just go and tell her you're here. Do sit down. I'll put the kettle on, shall I?"

"We're fine thank you." Mandy turned her head towards the stairs.

"Of course. I'll just–" Yvonne hurried out of the

room.

They heard her footsteps on the stairs and then the vacuum stopped. There was a bit of mumbling before two sets of footsteps descended. Mrs O'Rourke had a grey pallor with deep bags under her eyes. Either she wasn't getting any sleep due to a guilty conscience, or Emily was being a total demon in the night. She looked from one face to the other with a puzzled expression.

"What's this about?"

"We need to ask you a few more questions in connection with our investigation into the death of Mrs Barbara Vixen." Mandy watched her face for any change of expression. Nothing.

"I heard you'd arrested that false priest. What can Mary know about that?" Yvonne Hunter intervened.

"With respect, we wish to speak to Mrs O'Rourke." Turning to Mary, Mandy said, "Perhaps you'd prefer to talk to us at the station."

"What? Are you arresting me?"

"No. However, we do need to ask you some questions and maybe you would prefer to do that without an audience."

Mrs Hunter drew herself up to her full height. "I'll make myself scarce and you can question Mary here, in comfort." She made for the hallway.

"I don't mind Yvonne being here. I haven't done anything wrong."

Josh raised an eyebrow at Mandy. She flicked her eyes towards the sofa.

"Very well. There is something you can clear up for us."

Sometimes people said more when they were relaxed. Dragging Mary O'Rourke down to the station could be counterproductive. They all sat, except for Josh who lounged against the wall, notebook at the ready.

Yvonne patted Mary's knee and gave her a smile to reassure her there was nothing to worry about. It was a gesture friends would make, and a reminder the pair were related as well as employer and employee.

"Do either of you recall an event, in the week leading up to Christmas, where Mrs Vixen made disparaging remarks in the cafe."

"She was doing her usual showing off. Had a man with her too. Called me a thief in front of everyone in the cafe. It was full too. I was mortified." Mary sniffed. "I told you she was a nasty mean bitch."

"And you witnessed this, Mrs Hunter?"

"Yes. Totally uncalled for remarks, especially in such a crowded place. Unforgivable." Yvonne had pursed lips, reminding Mandy of Withers and his 'eating cat shit' face. She had her hands clasped on her knee now, pressing them so close together her knuckles showed white.

"I believe you had to take Mrs O'Rourke home with you as she was distraught. Is that correct?"

"Yes," said Yvonne. "I didn't want her to go home in such a distressed state."

Mandy decided to change tactics.

"You said, Mrs O'Rourke, you didn't move the

patio table in the garden next door? Is that correct?" Mandy glanced towards Josh for confirmation. He nodded.

"I don't remember moving the table. She usually got me to do indoors. Three hours to clean from top to bottom with her breathing down my neck. Not so much as a glass of water offered either."

"Perhaps you can explain then how your fingerprints were found on the underside of the table?"

Mary's frown seemed genuine. "Under the patio table? Under it? I don't get it."

"As if you gripped it to move it." Mandy didn't mention that Cassian's fingerprints were also found on the underside.

She shook her head. "Honestly, I don't remem–" she stopped, gazing into the distance, eyes narrowed. "Cass was doing something in the garden and needed the table shifted. It was as I was leaving. I gave him a hand. It was one of those aluminium ones with the glass top. Lightweight. He could have done it himself, I suppose. Sorry. It slipped my mind."

"Did it?"

"Now wait a minute, Inspector. Everyone forgets things. It's not significant, is it?" Yvonne Hunter intervened.

"It could be very significant. We believe Mrs Vixen was poisoned deliberately. The flue was partially blocked with newspaper. It would take a step ladder to reach the flue or," Mandy paused, "someone could access it by standing on the patio table. The top had been wiped clean but your fingerprints, Mrs O'Rourke, were underneath."

Mary gripped Yvonne's hand and took a few gasping breaths.

"Perhaps you'd like to join us at the station for further questioning." Framed as a question it was more a command.

As Mary O'Rourke got to her feet she swayed. "Emily?" Her voice was a whisper.

"We'll send someone to look after your daughter. Someone she's familiar with if possible. With luck we can sort this out quickly. You are, of course, entitled to have a solicitor present."

Both Mandy and Josh could see she was in shock. Why hadn't she, or Yvonne for that matter, told them about the incident in the cafe? Why hadn't Charlie? They just hadn't asked the right questions. Josh supported Mary by putting his hand under her elbow as she stood and then stumbled towards the front door.

As they reached the door, Yvonne Hunter, who had been watching, horrified, shouted, "Stop!"

They turned to look at her. The woman was shaking, her eyes filling with tears. Now she had their attention Yvonne seemed to gather herself, pulled her shoulders back and took a deep breath.

"Mary didn't do it. I did."

CHAPTER FIFTY

A shocked silence followed. Mandy and Josh exchanged glances. Mary O'Rourke opened and closed her mouth a couple of times as if she was practising being a guppy.

"I'll come with you," said Yvonne. "You can let Mary go."

As soon as Josh released the hold on Mary's arm she dashed over to Yvonne. "I don't believe you. They'll think you're doing this to protect me, but I've done nothing wrong. I swear to God, I didn't kill her. No way can they put me away for something I didn't do."

Yvonne patted her on the arm. "I'm not trying to protect you. I know you're innocent. I can't carry on with this charade. Somebody else could get the blame for something I did. I couldn't live with myself if that happened."

* * *

Yvonne Hunter was subdued on the way to the station. They settled her in an interview room, informed her of her rights and gave her a glass of water. She lifted it with trembling hands, touched it to her lips.

"I don't know where to start."

"Wherever you wish, Mrs Hunter." Mandy switched on the recorder and after a deep breath,

Yvonne began her story.

"Barbara Forbes, as she was then, was always a bully. Even in primary school, as I told you." She gave Josh a weak smile. "I had long hair in plaits, and she spent playtimes pulling them and saying, 'gee up horsey.' She was a big girl. I was a tiny little thing. I can't tell you how relieved I was when the family moved. I thought I'd never see her again."

"But you did come across her again, didn't you?" Mandy prompted her to continue her story.

"Yes. I sailed through secondary school and university. I got a job as a legal secretary in a small firm. They merged and I found myself in the same office as Barbara. She was Mrs Vixen by then. The marriage was already on the rocks, so she was fractious to say the least. As the numbers in the secretarial pool increased the rumour was that a new post, someone overseeing our work, was going to be created. I'd arrived with a degree and excellent references, so I suppose she saw me as a threat. She wanted the job." Yvonne gave a low laugh. "This was all so long ago. I suppose you think it isn't relevant."

"On the contrary, it's important for us to know the context. I take it she made life difficult?"

"Right from the start. She started picking holes in my work. Never in front of others, you understand. Sarcastic comments at first. She'd follow me to the kitchen and complain I hadn't washed my cup properly. She told the other girls I was trouble, accused me of talking behind her back. She'd ask why I was so long in the toilet. If I was a second late,

I was lazy. If early I was trying to toady favour. That coming from the most sycophantic person I'd ever met. It was pathetic really."

"How did that make you feel?"

Yvonne swallowed. Her voice was almost a whisper. "It went on for a year. Constant criticism until I believed I was useless. I lost weight. I couldn't sleep. I was a wreck. I had pains everywhere. I was off for a month because I lost my voice. And do you know what happened when I went back in?" Her tone had changed, almost a touch of hysteria evident now. "The first thing she did was corner me to tell me how much better things were when I wasn't there."

"Did you report this?"

"I did. Several times. Sympathetic noises but no action from the partners. I was in despair. I used to drive home fantasising about steering into a wall or a tree, so I wouldn't have to go to work. In the end I faced Barbara myself. I told her how her behaviour was impacting my health, and I wanted her to stop." Yvonne paused. "She laughed in my face. Told me she'd do it all again."

Yvonne gave her a weak smile before continuing. "I had no choice. I resigned and wrote a letter to the partners explaining what had happened and why I was leaving. They gave me a brilliant reference and a golden handshake, I suppose you'd call it. I had to sign an NDA. The last thing they wanted was any fuss. I was very ill for months after that."

She coughed, sipped the water as they waited for

her to regain her composure.

"It was a traumatic time for you. You were brave to face her." Mandy wanted the rest of the story.

Yvonne just nodded. "Stupid, more like. It was all so very long ago. During my recovery I went to a yoga retreat and that's where I met John, my husband. He was teaching yoga and meditation. It's all so trendy now. Then it was a bit hippyish." She almost giggled. "He had long hair in a ponytail and was such a gentle soul. He helped me to heal and achieve some inner peace. I fell head over heels in love with him. And the rest is history, as they say."

"And Barbara Vixen?"

"I trained as a yoga teacher and started a new life. As the years passed, I almost forgot about her. I had a loving husband, two children and, in time, their partners and grandchildren. They filled my life. Barbara Vixen became a bad memory."

"Until she moved next door." Mandy prompted her. The background story was interesting, but something had triggered Yvonne to kill her neighbour, and that information was vital to their investigation.

"I didn't recognise her at first. She hadn't aged well, and she'd put on a lot of weight. It was her voice I remembered. And that superior manner. She didn't recognise me, and I didn't remind her who I was. But I found it disturbing. I started having anxiety attacks in the night. Waking up in a panic. I knew what it was, of course. Seeing Barbara and having her living next door brought back all those awful times and I didn't have John to comfort me."

She took a sip of water and licked her lips. "She wasn't a bad neighbour apart from complaining about Sukey soiling in her garden. As if anyone can stop a cat from doing what cats do." A little shake of the head. "Barbara and I ignored each other most of the time. I didn't hate her anymore. Too many years had passed. In fact, I was sorry for her. She was lonely. I think that's why she joined The Church of the Forgotten Souls."

"You experienced no enmity towards her?" Mandy asked.

"No. Well I tried not to, but I was still a little scared of her, I think."

"Then why did you kill her?"

CHAPTER FIFTY-ONE

Yvonne looked Mandy in the eyes. She blinked away tears.

"I swear I never meant her to die. When I came back after Christmas and discovered she was dead I just thought she'd had a heart attack or a stroke. I really hoped that's what had happened."

"But you stuffed the flue with newspaper? Why? You must have known what that would do to her? The danger? Your gas engineer, Alan Jordan, must have warned you. You don't expect us to believe that wasn't intended to kill her, do you?" Mandy maintained eye contact and her tone was more perplexed than accusatory.

Despite Yvonne's past encounters with Barbara Vixen there was a difference between bullying someone and committing murder. They had some inkling of motivation, but it still wasn't clear. What had been the trigger?

"Alan warned me to make sure the flue outside didn't get blocked up. Sometimes leaves gather in the vents apparently. He said I could become quite sick if that happened. He fitted an alarm for me and said to make sure I kept the boiler free from any obstruction. I… I thought if I put a bit of paper in her flue it would just make her sick. She deserved to be sick after what she did."

"What did she do? What, after forty years,

prompted you to kill your neighbour?"

Yvonne shuddered at the word 'kill'. She stared at her hands, twisting them together.

"Mary is more than my cleaning lady. She's my cousin, my friend, my confidante. I could see it all happening again. To her. First the public sacking in the shop and then the humiliation in front of everyone in the cafe. It was excruciating. It brought it all back. I wanted to slap Barbara. Even the man with her looked embarrassed." She became more animated.

"As you know, I took Mary home that day. She was distraught. Mary told me of several other incidents, designed to make her feel uncomfortable when she went to the village. The cafe debacle was the final straw. It made me furious. I went next door as soon as Mary left." She took a shuddering breath. "It took some doing to face up to Barbara again. I was shaking with fear. Ridiculous after I'd put things behind me for so long. But I knew I couldn't let her destroy someone else's life the way she'd tried to destroy mine. I had to stop her."

"How did she react?"

"She laughed. Laughed." Her voice rose in indignation. "Just as she'd done all those years ago when I was her junior. I told her who I was. Reminded her what she'd done to me. She said she didn't remember me. I must have been pathetic if I'd run away. It made me so angry. I wanted to punish her. Something inside snapped. She deserved to be punished for what she did to me. What she probably did to countless others over the years. I wanted revenge, for myself and for Mary. I… I never thought she'd die."

She hung her head. They waited.

"That evening, when she went to the church, I opened the connecting gate and took my step ladder next door. I pulled off the protective mesh grid and pushed a bit of paper in the flue. Not a lot. I made sure of that. I just wanted her to feel sick."

Mandy looked at Josh. Did he believe her? Would a jury?

"It didn't seem to have any effect. I saw her coming and going and the argument with that priest. It was such a busy time. I went away for Christmas and just forgot. When I heard she was dead I was relieved. I didn't think about what I'd done until–"

"Until you knew she'd died of carbon monoxide poisoning. Then you removed the evidence." Mandy let that sink in for a moment. "Unfortunately for you, a sliver of newspaper was still in place. It led us to believe this was not an accidental death. Why didn't you come clean before? You delayed the investigation, wasting police time. Did you think you'd get away with it?"

Yvonne shook her head. "It was an accident. She wasn't supposed to die. Was it really all my fault? When I went to remove the newspaper after… after I heard the news, the mesh cover had come off. The paper was still there but leaves and cobwebs were in the flue as well. It was only a small bit of paper. I didn't want to kill her."

* * *

There was little jubilation in the station when they had finished booking her. The case was solved but it had been a sad tale. Helen and Olivia were dumbfounded.

"Imagine that then. Still being pissed off with someone who bullied you in school enough to knock them off, like."

"It's a bit more complicated than that, Olivia. Mrs Hunter thought she was defending her friend. Somehow, I think the two scenarios had combined in her mind. The unfairness of her treatment as an office junior must have been festering subconsciously all these years. I suppose If Mrs Vixen had more friends perhaps someone would have noticed her illness and absence earlier. Maybe her nasty streak was honed by loneliness. On the other hand, a bully is always a bully. Who the hell knows?" Mandy shrugged.

Lucas joined the deliberations. "The duty solicitor is there now. I doubt if the CPS will prosecute. We have no evidence except her confession. No DNA. No witnesses. We'd be skating on thin ice in a courtroom. Besides, it seems Mrs Hunter has liver disease with a few months to live. She'd not make it to court."

"Karma," said Olivia. "She got her revenge, 'suppose.'

Mandy sighed. The case had been impossible from the start although they had the satisfaction of knowing who had killed Barbara. Plus, busting

Carmichael. As if reading her mind, Lucas reported on the case against the bogus priest.

"There have been interesting developments at The Church of the Forgotten Souls," he said. "It seems Carmichael was using former colleagues to sell the porn he was generating. He'd skipped out of the States owing a substantial amount to some very dodgy characters. They threatened him so he was forced to find a way to repay his debts. Then he started an account called the Relief Fund. They think it was for his own use, in case he needed to skip the country in a hurry. He seems to have a knack of annoying the wrong people."

"And Barbara Vixen found out something and was blackmailing him. It must have pissed him off big time. It's a wonder he didn't knock her off the perch." Mandy grimaced. They'd been right to suspect him.

"He was forced to use the Relief Fund for various church activities, but he also confessed to hiding cash in the building," said Josh. "It's been recovered from his hiding place and, in time, will be given to build a proper community project."

"So, it will do some good after all. Bloody weird way of doing things. I mean, using porn to help the church. It doesn't fit together too well, does it?" Mandy shook her head.

Olivia was angry. What she had witnessed first-hand didn't sit well with her moral code. "Exploiting those kids wasn't good. I wish now I'd confronted him. Kicked him in–"

"He's going down for a long stretch. I don't think

he'll have much fun in prison when word gets out about his little exploits." Lucas smiled at her as if amused by her little outburst.

Somehow, the Barbara Vixen case had helped to make him a part of the team. They accepted him now. With her secret knowledge about Lucas and her niece, Mandy seemed to be the only one uneasy about the future. Would Muriel keep the secret? Should she? And, another six months working with him as her line manager. Mandy wondered if Lucas would be a bolster between her and Withers or a thorn in her side.

ENDS

Printed and bound in the UK by CMP Books, Dorset